SANDMAN

BY

MORGAN HANNAH MACDONALD

SANDMAN

Copyright © 2012 Morgan Hannah MacDonald

Cover art and design by Owen Moody

Copy Editing by Jim Thomsen

Proofreader Trisha Wilson

Formatting by IRONHORSE Formatting

ISBN: 978-1470033309

DEDICATION

This book is dedicated in loving memory of my father.

August 27, 1930-May 4, 2010.

He supported me my entire life and always had faith in

me no matter what path I chose.

He was truly the wind beneath my wings.

I love you, Dad.

Thank you.

Your favorite daughter.

giggle

ACKNOWLEDGMENTS

First I would like to thank my mother for putting up with me through the long arduous task of getting this book published with grace, patience, love and support. Love you mom!

Next I would like to thank Trish McCallan, for if not for her this book would not have been published. Thank you, Trish, for graciously sharing your journey and insights with me and many others. You are a true inspiration.

To my friends and family. I couldn't have gotten this far without you. Thank you so much for your love and support. I love you all!

I'd like to thank my first readers:

Barbara Kenton

Kathy Wilson

Jana Murphy

Tracy Mangold

If I forgot someone I apologize.

To my critique group extraordinaire; Lethal Ladies for keeping me on my toes and making sure I didn't get lazy. You helped to shape this book and make it better. Many thanks.

To IRI. Thank you all for sharing your knowledge. You guys are the greatest group!

To Trisha Wilson. Thank you for your wonderful proofreading as well as getting the job done so fast!

And a special thank you to Owen Moody for the fantastic cover and webpage. You are an amazing talent.

Beware the SANDMAN. He'll put you to sleep...forever.

A serial killer on the loose, a woman being stalked, and a homicide detective who must find the connection between the two before she becomes the next victim.

He collects women. He imprisons them, plays with them, tortures them. Until they bore him. Then he removes a souvenir. They call him the Sandman.

Meagan McInnis is being plagued with late night calls, yet when she answers, no one is there. Then one night she makes a grisly discovery in her own backyard.

The caller is silent no more.

Homicide Detective J.J. Thomas realizes that Meagan is the key to finding the Sandman. Now, not only must he protect her, but he must find the connection between Meagan and the killer before she becomes his next victim.

ONE

The night was winding down and the moon hung low on the horizon. It wouldn't be long before the sun's first rays kissed the sky. Sean O'Brien parked his Ford Explorer along Christianitos Road at the top of the trail that led to Trestles Beach.

He opened the door while raising his mug to swallow the last bit of coffee. He only had time for one cup today, he was in a hurry. He wanted to hit the water before sunrise. Exiting the SUV he cupped the keys, grabbed his backpack, then slammed the door shut with his foot. He proceeded to the back of the truck, where he pulled his surfboard out through the tailgate.

The half-mile descent to the beach stretched before him. The crickets' familiar melody kept him company. There was a rustle of leaves close by as an animal scampered through the dense foliage. His anticipation grew at the sound of the waves crashing below. Two long months had passed since he'd been surfing. He wasn't a kid any more. His work and family kept him busy.

Sean had been born here in San Clemente, a quaint little beach town in Southern California, just north of the San Diego County line. The town gained infamy back when President Nixon owned a home on the cliffs above Trestles that was commonly known as the Western Whitehouse.

Although the calendar said it was winter, the outside temperature was a warm sixty-five degrees due to the storm brewing off the coast of Baja. The latest surf report promised six to eight-foot swells and the water temp hung at around fifty-eight. He couldn't pass up this opportunity.

He'd shimmied into the bottom half of his spring wetsuit at home and let the top dangle loosely down his back. A fisherman knit sweater covered his naked chest. He carelessly pulled his long sandy-blond hair back and tied it with an elastic band at the nape of his neck.

Once he reached the end of the trail, Sean turned left and headed down the beach to his favorite spot. His rubber thongs slapped sand against the back of his legs. He walked a couple hundred yards further before he threw his backpack on a mound of seaweed against the base of the cliff, far out of reach of the incoming tide. He needed dry shorts for the ride home.

He stepped out of his flip-flops and carelessly threw his sweater in the general vicinity of the backpack. Then pulled on the rest of his wet suit, grabbed his board and ran toward the waves. When he hit the water he dove in, immersing himself completely. Once he surfaced, he drew in a quick breath. The cold water shocked his system, but swept away the last remaining cobwebs in his brain and made him feel alive.

Sean paddled out past the break and turned around to face east. Bobbing up and down, he watched the sun's rays break through the clouds, reaching their long arms down from the heavens. The sky, once purple, turned pink, then orange as the lazy sun crept above the surrounding cliffs.

God it was beautiful. This was his church, his religion.

When the show was over, he lay back down on the board and paddled toward the shore to catch his first wave of the day. After two hours of near-perfect sets, it was time to join the real world. Life was good.

Sean climbed out of the water with his board under his arm. He dragged his hand down his face to brush the salt water away from his eyes. His breathing was labored; he'd gotten in a good workout today. He walked up the beach a ways before he detected a strange odor. As he neared his destination, the stench invading his nostrils became more pungent. I hope there wasn't another damn sewage spill.

Soon he heard a strange buzzing sound. He stopped, brows furrowed, and concentrated on zeroing in on the exact location of the noise. Failing at this, he shrugged, and then continued up the strand. But with each step his uncertainty grew. The irritating cacophony had increased in volume.

Within seconds he found himself about fifty feet from where he'd left his gear. Before him lay a blanket of black that appeared to be moving. "What the fuck?" He hesitated, waiting for the synapses in his brain to start firing, before taking another step.

When he found no logical explanation, he gently rested his board on the sand and made his way closer until he stood directly in front of the sight. His hand cupped his nose. The stench reminded him of hard-boiled eggs gone bad. Very very bad.

Okay, strike the moving blanket crack. It was more like a black cloud hovering over his belongings. Flies. He had an inkling that it was not the seaweed they found interesting. Something dead had washed up on shore and he was less than eager to find out what it was. His mind conjured up a few possibilities; a seagull, a fish, a seal? Whatever it was, it would not be pretty no matter how long it had been dead.

Slowly, he reached down to pick up his sweater with one hand, while the other reached for the strap on his backpack. His actions were no more cautious than if he were lifting a bomb.

The flies swarmed up for a brief moment, just long enough to reveal their prey, before settling back down into a dark writhing carpet.

An unintelligible sound escaped his lips. He gasped for air while instinctively taking a step back. He'd seen some hairy things in his life, but nothing even close to this. Icy fingers of fear raced up his spine, his heartbeat hammering in his chest.

4

Sean couldn't look away even if he had wanted to. Some strange fascination took hold of his brain and wouldn't let go. Systematically his mind dissected the grisly scene before him.

Sticking out of the rolling mound of seaweed was a woman's arm, stiff as a mannequin's, extending skyward as if reaching to him for help. The mottled blue hand wore long red fingernails, two of which had been broken down to the quick. Seaweed was wrapped around her arm like a feather boa.

Sean's gaze then locked onto another object protruding from the sandy grave. A leg severed mid-thigh, but closer inspection revealed it was really half-buried. It too appeared tangled in the bubbly brown vegetation.

The foot, like the hand, wore a shock of bright red polish on its perfectly manicured toes, clashing with the bluish pallor of the flesh. His eyes grew wide at the sight of flies and sand crabs greedily devouring the soft tissue. He choked back bile.

The spell was broken.

Sean stepped backward so fast he tripped over his own feet and landed on his butt. He scrambled up and raced toward the shore. He couldn't get away fast enough. He reached the water's edge before collapsing to his hands and knees. His insides lurched so hard that he thought he would spew his stomach lining. Dry heaves continued long after his stomach had emptied. He collapsed on the sand, exhausted. A wave washed over him, but he hardly noticed.

TWO

Homicide Detective J.J. Thomas woke from his coma-like-sleep to mass confusion. The ringing phone dueled with the incessant shrilling of his alarm, and the combination hit his head like a ton of bricks. He glanced at the clock a mere second before swatting it off the nightstand in an effort to quell the infernal noise. No such luck. At least he could quiet one of the offending devices without actually having to get out of bed.

He snatched the receiver. "What!"

"You think you're on vacation or something?" the captain bellowed in his ear. Thomas winced. He wished he would lower his voice to a dull roar. "Jesus Christ, Thomas, Carla's been trying to reach you for the last fifteen minutes since dispatch failed. You know how hysterical she gets, she was ready to call in the National Guard. Now get your lazy ass down to Trestles Beach. I trust you know where that is?"

"Yeah, be there in twenty," Thomas grunted.

"Make it ten!" The line went dead.

Why the fuck does the captain always feel compelled to bust my balls? Does he think the corpse is going to just get up and walk away?

Thomas rarely had the luxury of an entire night's sleep, so, given that he had made it until seven-twenty, he considered himself lucky. Throwing back the covers, he swung his legs off the side of the bed, and sat up quickly. Too quickly. Instantly his hands flew up to his temples in an attempt at keeping his head from exploding all together.

Stumbling into the bathroom, Thomas leaned against the wall as he relieved himself, then sidestepped to the sink to splash his face with cold water. Bracing himself on the sides, he leaned into his reflection in the mirror. He felt like shit and looked even worse.

He opened the medicine cabinet and after careful deliberation, grabbed the mouthwash to take a swig. He swirled it around in his mouth a few times before spitting it into the sink. He walked back into his room with a much sturdier gait and pulled on the pants that hung over a nearby chair.

All but stumbling down the stairs, he glanced into the living room and noticed the empty bottle of Chivas Regal lying on its side next to his favorite chair. His step quickened as the aroma of fresh-brewed coffee pulled him to the kitchen as if under a spell. He silently thanked the Gods for inventing coffee makers with automated timers.

Minutes later, Thomas was speeding south down Pacific Coast Highway away from Laguna Beach, his black BMW

330i cutting in and out of commuter traffic. Head still pounding, he opened the glove box, found the aspirin, and shook out four. He tossed them into his mouth and washed them down with the steaming hot liquid, feeling the burn down the back of his throat.

Thomas arrived at the top of the trail about the same time as the medical examiner. The sun was well into the sky, but the dark clouds moving in looked threatening.

The coroner was Cheryl Gardner, a fifty-five-year old veteran in the trade. She stood an even six feet tall, five inches shorter than Thomas. Her spiky blonde hair went well with the numerous punk-rock t-shirts she owned. Today she wore a Talking Heads one in bright orange, with "Psycho Killer" emblazoned across the front in lime green. Her crystal blue eyes always twinkled like she knew a secret.

Her age showed on her face. It was obvious that at one time she was a serious sun worshiper. Her gruff demeanor intimidated most rookies, but Thomas knew she was just blowing smoke up their asses. Inside she was mush, if you knew where to look.

"And how are you doing this fine morning, Ms. Gardner?" Thomas walked over to greet her.

A set of keys dropped to the ground. "Son of a bitch!" She slid out of the van to retrieve them. Looking up as if noticing Thomas for the first time she said, in her gravelly smoker's voice, "Hey, ugly. How they hangin'? When are you going to marry me and take me away from all this shit?"

"Soon, Cheryl, very soon." Thomas smiled and delivered a

peck to her cheek.

"Well, it ain't soon enough for me." She pocketed her keys.

Overdramatic as usual, Cheryl's complaints spewed forth like Old Faithful. But Thomas knew that she'd probably be slicing and dicing cadavers until her last breath. She was married to her work and no one had a happier marriage.

"You been down there yet?" She reached into the van to retrieve her kit.

"Just getting here same as you." Thomas leaned over and took the bag from her.

"Then I guess we're both in for a treat." She headed toward the trail.

"Looks like that storm's moving in pretty quickly. Won't have much time before we're working in water." He talked to her back as he followed close behind.

"It wouldn't be the first time, and it sure as shit won't be the last."

Once they hit the beach, they headed down toward the crew. Trudging through the sand, Cheryl screwed up her face in disgust. "Fuck me, I *hate* getting sand in my shoes. Why couldn't the killer have been thoughtful enough to leave the vic up there by the road?" She hooked her thumb like a hitchhiker in the direction they had just come.

Thomas just smiled.

When they reached the others, Thomas handed Cheryl her kit. The CSU was unpacking its gear. He greeted the uniformed officer walking toward him.

"Morning, Cooper, you first on the scene?"

"Yes, sir, the body was discovered by that guy over there." He pointed to a man sitting on a rock about a hundred yards down the beach, hands covering his face. "He came down here to surf early this morning. It was still dark when he arrived.

"Dropped his gear right on top of what he thought was a pile of seaweed, but by the light of day was actually the vic. Boy, did he get the surprise of his life. By the time he came back to retrieve his goods, the sun had been up awhile. Claimed he smelled her first."

"I bet he did. The temp rose with the sun. The reading on my dashboard said it was already seventy-five. Good old El Niño at its best."

"Yeah, I hate this damn humidity. Anyway, he picked up his backpack and found the stiff underneath."

"I'll get to him in a minute. Go move the crime scene tape a few hundred more yards. I don't want anyone near this crime scene."

"Yes, sir." Cooper hitched his belt.

"When you're done with that, get another uniform to stand post with you. The cliffs will keep the rest of the scene private from the gawking eyes of the public."

Thomas walked over to another uniformed officer, "Hey, James. I want you up at the top of the trail. Don't let anyone down. Tell them the beach is closed due to a sewage leak. Get the city on the horn and have them bring down some of those signs to set up. We're going to be here awhile."

"Yes, sir." James turned on his heels.

Thomas moved on to inspect the scene. Matt was busy taking photographs. He stood just out of the way. He watched as Sue brushed sand crabs from an arm, then a leg that had been exposed by the angry sea. She kept waving at the flies in an effort to keep them airborne. Flesh dangled from the appendages making the site pretty gruesome. He felt for the poor guy who found her. Civilians weren't privy to the kind of carnage he had gotten used to over the years.

It took a while for the corpse to be fully uncovered.

Thomas was shooting the shit with Cheryl when they were summoned to review the grisly site in its entirety. Lying on her back was a woman who appeared to be in her early- to mid-thirties. Rigor had come and gone. It was difficult to tell the color of her hair, because it was wet and matted with sand.

Her eyes and lips had been sewn shut with thick black thread. The breasts had been removed and were nowhere in the near vicinity. *At least there aren't any maggots. Yet. If there's one thing I can't stand it's maggots,* Thomas thought. Matt was busy snapping photographs again. Thomas took out his cell phone and walked down the beach for some privacy before he dialed Captain Harris.

"Looks like we have a serial on our hands," he said without identifying himself.

"Fuck that. You know damn well we have to have at least *three* bodies in order to call it a serial killing."

"There may be only two stiffs we know about, but I wouldn't be surprised to find he's been at it awhile. The eyes and lips are sewn shut and the breasts are missing. I bet money we find she was tortured for some time before killed like the last girl.

"There's bruising around the neck and ligature marks around the wrists and ankles. We won't know anything else for certain until she's cleaned up. The sand is moist and clinging pretty heavily. There's no sign of blood. This is a dump site. So what would *you* call this, Boss, coincidence?"

"Shit. Look, if I hear one word about a serial killer loose in Orange County, it'll be your ass. You hear me?"

Then Thomas heard a dial tone.

THREE

Meagan McInnis and Godzilla, her Labrador-Newfoundland mix, were also on a beach in San Clemente, this one further north of Trestles. She began this morning as she did each morning, with a quick jog along the shore below her apartment. Her long sleek legs carried her along the water's edge toward the pier; once there she'd turn around and head home.

Godzilla streaked ahead, his giant paws kicking up sand in his wake. He weaved his way up the beach visiting people or other dogs, or chasing the squirrels that lived in the rocks. Anything to pass the time while he waited for Meagan. Once she passed him, he'd lose interest in his current activity only to find another more promising one up the beach. They played this game of tag every morning without fail.

Meagan had adopted Godzilla from the pound when he'd been just three months old. She'd named him for the tremendous paws that were way out of proportion with his tiny body and the irony of his disposition. He was anything but a monster, but someone knocking on her door late at night wouldn't know that when she called his name or heard him bark.

She knew he would mature into an enormous dog one day, but she just didn't know it would be so soon. Godzilla weighed somewhere around a hundred pounds, stood almost to her waist, yet was still shy of his first birthday. He could bowl her over easily, and often did.

Originally she'd wanted a dog not only for the company, but because it was a good idea for a woman living alone to have a watchdog. He had proven to be a great companion, but unless he licked someone to death, she had to shelve the watchdog idea. Also, he rarely barked. Which was a plus when your neighbors lived as close as hers.

Sweat permeated Meagan's body. Her tank top clung to her skin. She stopped, removed her sweatshirt, wiped her face, and tied the sleeves around her waist before continuing on. Her naturally red curls were clipped high on her head. Fallen wisps glued themselves to her face and neck. Ladies don't sweat, they glisten, Meagan's grandmother always said. Well, right now she was glistening up a storm. And it felt good.

As she ran along the shoreline, her thoughts were on her birthday. Tomorrow she would turn thirty-five. How did she get to be so old without a husband or family to show for it? Unfortunately, her luck with men sucked. She still felt the burn from her last relationship debacle. She had been seeing

Brad Landis for five months, but had known him professionally for over a year.

Being a hairdresser in the Ocean Ranch area of Dana Point, Meagan's salon catered to a very affluent clientele. Brad had been one of her clients. He was forty-five, the vice president of sales for a Fortune 500 company, and he traveled a lot for dealings with clients. He had given her a card with all his possible phone numbers, or so she'd thought.

He'd confessed his love for Meagan on the first date and that had freaked her out. She'd never trusted a man who fell so hard so fast, but she'd been having too much fun to heed the uncomfortable feeling that needled her. Then, just when Megan thought she might have fallen for him, it happened.

Brad met with the president of the company at their main office in downtown Los Angeles. The meeting should have ended around noon. He promised to call Meagan the minute his meeting had finished so they could make dinner plans. The afternoon soon turned to evening.

There had been no call.

The rain came down in sheets that day. The drive from L.A. to Dana Point was around two hours on a good day. With Friday traffic, slick roads, and dense visibility, the drive was difficult at best.

Frantically, she left several messages at all of Brad's numbers, but her calls were not returned. She contacted the highway patrol and all the hospitals. She scarcely ate or slept the entire weekend. She wouldn't allow herself to leave the house. Even with her cell phone, she feared that she might somehow miss him.

By Sunday afternoon, consumed with exhaustion, Meagan figured that Brad was dead. Still she kept up her vigil. After a third straight sleepless night, she gave in and called his cell phone one last time Monday morning. He answered.

"Oh, thank God. Where are you? Are you okay?" Meagan choked back a sob.

"Fine. Playing golf with a client." His manner was distant, detached. Nothing like the man she had come to know.

"What!" She wiped the tears from her face.

"Look, I'm going to have to call you back. I can't talk right now." The line went dead.

Meagan stared at the phone. Brad actually called her back a couple of hours later, but by then she was already over it.

And him.

He said that he had moved back in with his estranged wife, but they slept in separate rooms. His wife was having a hard time accepting the divorce, he said. She was fifteen years his senior and he worried about her health, as well as her mental state. But that didn't mean that he and Meagan had to stop seeing one another, he rushed to add.

Meagan was silent while she processed this bit of information. He hadn't acknowledged who she was on the phone in front of his "client." She'd never seen his apartment; he'd told her that he lived with a roommate who was a slob and that he preferred her place because of the privacy. There'd been a lot of weekends he'd spent "out of town" on

16

business. Brad never answered Meagan's calls directly; instead he'd called her back after she'd left a voicemail.

The bastard had been married all along!

Calmly she replied, "Thank you for clearing that up." She hung up before she fell apart.

Furious. Disgusted. Shattered. Meagan had been all of the above. In the end, she realized she was angrier with herself than with him. How could she have been so stupid? Why hadn't she put the pieces together sooner?

That's when she decided she was through with men. Godzilla would be the only male in her life from then on.

Unfortunately, it wasn't that easy. Brad wouldn't give up. He wasn't the type of man who was used to hearing the word no. He sent cards, flowers and gifts, and she returned them all. Many times she'd come home to an answering machine full of messages from him.

At first, he pleaded with her. He would move out of the house. Buy a home on the beach for Meagan. They could get married. So on and so forth. The bullshit never let up.

One evening, while Meagan locked up the salon, she spotted him sitting in his car watching her. It was then that she realized that the salon was like a fish bowl once it became dark outside. She wondered how many evenings he had done that. It had given her an eerie feeling.

Then Meagan spotted Brad's car parked on her street. His bright red Corvette didn't exactly blend in with her neighborhood.

He was stalking her. Just how far would he go?

That's when Meagan decided to get a dog. She added dead bolts to her doors. She kept her curtains closed at all times. She spent every evening huddled in her cocoon, wondering when he would come in after her.

Afraid of becoming a star in her own Lifetime movie, Meagan asked a client of hers who was a sheriff's deputy about what she should do. He told her that legally there was nothing unless Brad threatened bodily harm. But, off the record, he could scare the living shit out of the guy if she wanted, he told her. Meagan laughed and thanked him, but declined.

Then one evening while she sat in her living room reading, the phone rang. Meagan had become accustomed to letting the machine screen all her calls. This time she became unnerved. Brad was leaving another of his endless messages, but this time his rant edged on insanity.

"Who the hell do you have in there, Meagan? I know you're entertaining some man, there's a strange car parked in front of your apartment. Who is he?" His amplified voice echoed throughout the room.

She stared at the machine in disbelief. Her fear quickly turned to rage. "Is he totally nuts? The entire street is lined with apartments. Who the hell would know if there was a strange car parked out there?" she screamed back at the machine.

Without thinking, Meagan jumped off the couch and ran to the phone. Anger seethed from every pore. She snatched up the handset and yelled, "Leave me alone, you lunatic, or I'm calling your wife!" She slammed the receiver and stared at the phone.

Silence.

Meagan turned off the lights, peeked out the window. His car was still out there. She spent the rest of the night cowering under a blanket on her couch with a knife in her hand. That had been three months ago, and she had heard no more from Brad. It couldn't have been that easy. Could it?

FOUR

Thomas slipped his phone into his jacket pocket and walked to where Cheryl was busy bagging the hands on the corpse.

"Got TOD yet?"

"My best guesstimate would be between five and midnight," Cheryl told him. "I'll be able to narrow it down after I get her back to the morgue."

"COD?"

"I can't give you cause of death definitively, but she's been strangled. You can tell by the bruising around her neck. Can't exactly check the eyes here, but if she's anything like the last victim, there will be petechial hemorrhaging. You know I hate to speculate, but if he's keeping true to form, it will be exsanguination. The sick fuck." Finished with the hands, Cheryl glanced up.

"That he is." Thomas stared out at the ocean.

"Who knows," Cheryl's voice softened. "Maybe he got so carried away this time he ended up strangling her to death and had to remove her breasts postmortem." Cheryl stood, slipped off her latex gloves, and brushed the sand from her pants.

"That would be some consolation, better than being alive while some psycho slices off your body parts then watches as you bleed to death." He kept his gaze on the tumultuous sea. The sky, now blanketed with heavy dark clouds, looked as if it would open up at any moment.

"Okay, she's ready to be bagged," Cheryl said before she joined Thomas. He felt her hand on his arm and turned his attention to her.

"Look, maybe he fucked up this time and left some evidence." She shrugged. "It could happen."

A sarcastic laugh escaped. "Yeah, right, and monkeys could fly out of my ass."

Cheryl chuckled. "I'd pay good money to see that."

He heard a commotion up the beach and turned his head.

"Shit, looks like we've got company." He nodded toward the TV crew heading down the beach.

Cheryl followed his gaze. "Goddamned piranhas," she grumbled.

Thomas ignored them and headed in the opposite direction toward the witness. After listening to the guy's story, he asked the surfer to stop by the station sometime that afternoon to make a formal statement. Thomas gave the guy his card and asked him to call if he remembered anything else.

The poor guy was in shock, Thomas could tell. His nightmares were going to be a bitch. He would be a good candidate for post-traumatic stress disorder. As an afterthought, Thomas reached into his wallet and got out the card of a friend whose expertise was PTSD. He hoped he wouldn't need it, but it was better to be safe than sorry.

The victim was ready for transport by the time he caught up to Cheryl. "Hey, I'm heading out. Give me a heads-up when you're ready to start the autopsy."

"Will do. Oh, and be careful." She crooked her head toward the camera crew blocking the path.

"Damn straight. I don't want to see *my* ugly mug on the eleven o'clock news."

Cheryl laughed. "Better you than me." She turned back to the gurney and checked the straps.

Thomas trudged up the beach to meet the trail. He hoped to sneak by while the reporter interviewed some poor sucker who'd happened by. No such luck. The petite blonde with big hair intercepted him; her name was something like Misty Waters, or Stormy Weather, some asinine name like that. Thomas couldn't remember and really didn't give a shit.

She planted herself right in his path. "Detective, is it true you found another woman's body in the same condition as the victim found in Huntington Beach?" Her high-pitched voice sounded like she'd been sucking helium.

The microphone thrust in front of Thomas's face. *Where the hell do these people get their information?* His jaw clenched. He had a strong urge to shove it down her throat, but thought better of it. He liked walking around as a free man. He gave her his best death stare.

"No comment," he grumbled in a voice that made the toughest men tremble, then sidestepped her.

She jumped in front of him again. "Do you think it's the same man who brutalized young Jennifer Hooper?" There was that damn microphone again. This woman could not take a hint.

"What part of 'No comment' don't you understand?" She reminded him of a little dog running around in circles, barking, and jumping up and down. He wouldn't be surprised if she didn't piddle in the sand while she was at it.

"Was today's victim a young collegiate like poor Jennifer Hooper? Should college girls be alarmed? Do you think—"

"Look, lady—" Thomas's hands shot out, grabbed her on either side of her arms, then lifted all ninety-eight pounds of her and set her out of his way. She gasped. Good, he had her attention.

"Sissy," she interrupted. My God, she had the IQ of a gnat!

"Get out of my way," he finished through clenched teeth.

The news crew silently backed up. Sissy, the blond-haired Pekinese, simply stared at him.

He stomped up the trail toward the road, steamed about the encounter. He shouldn't have lost his temper. He would hear about it for sure, but it always amazed him why anyone would choose to be a bottom-dwelling, scum-sucking "broadcast journalist" as they liked to call themselves.

By the time he reached the top, it had started to sprinkle. He noted the *Beach Closed* signs and Officer James guarding the head of the path.

"James, after they clear out down there, I want you and Cooper to start canvassing the homes along the cliff."

"Yes, sir."

***

Driving up Interstate 5, Thomas' windshield wipers kept time with an old blues tune by Jimi Hendrix. One of the best things about his new car, he thought, was the stereo.

Once he hit the station, he went directly to the office he shared with Malone and Campanelli, two other detectives in homicide. He was glad to find he had the office to himself and started thumbing through the active files piled high on his desk.

Finding what he had been searching for, Thomas sat back in his chair and put his feet up. File in his lap, he began reading the case he'd been working before hitting a brick wall.

Jennifer Hooper, was a twenty-two-year-old senior at Cal State-Berkeley majoring in marine biology. In life, she stood five-foot-five and weighed one hundred and fifteen pounds. She had blue eyes and long blonde hair.

Jennifer was last seen by her roommate on a Friday afternoon. She was driving home for the weekend to see her parents in San José. When she hadn't shown up by midnight, her worried parents called all her friends. The police weren't able to file an immediate report because she was a legal adult.

By Monday morning, she hadn't shown up for classes, so the San José Sheriff's Department filed the missing persons report. Jennifer's body was found ten days later in Huntington Beach, more than three hundred miles south from where she went missing.

Her eyes and lips had been sewn shut and her breasts had been removed. She had been brutally raped and repeatedly sodomized. Because of the overlapping bruises around her neck, it was obvious the perp had tortured her over the course of several days, strangling her to the point of passing out, but not enough to end her suffering.

Her body was covered with shallow cuts. Some, probably the first wounds, had become infected and gangrene set in. In the end she bled to death from the removal of both breasts.

She was alive, although just barely, when the sick bastard performed the operation. Cheryl informed Thomas that by the time she died, her body was more than likely emitting the odor of decaying flesh. That was why the guy decided to get rid of her, Thomas concluded.

Lividity proved she'd been lying in a prone position after death. A strange waffle-like pattern appeared on her upper torso, buttocks and the backs of her legs.

Semen was found in the vagina as well as the rectum, but the perp was not a secretor, meaning that he was part of the twenty percent of the populace that did not leave DNA in their saliva or other bodily fluids. Therefore Thomas couldn't get any hits off CODIS, the Criminal Offense DNA Indexing

System.

He wondered if the perp knew this. How else could one explain why the guy didn't care that he'd left sperm in the victim's body when everything else he had done proved he was nothing less than a pro? The body had been thoroughly washed with bleach from head to toe. No fibers, skin cells or hair for them to find. Thomas sensed this guy was too good to be an amateur; now he was certain the perp had killed before. But where? And how many times?

It took Thomas over a week to find Jennifer's 2001 red Toyota Corolla. After he came up empty from the APB on her car, he had to resort to calling all the towing companies between Huntington Beach and San Francisco. He finally found the vehicle in an impound lot in Fremont.

It had been abandoned on I-5 with a flat tire not fifty feet from a highway call box. A clean cut was found in between the tread. It was deliberate. Most likely the guy put it there himself, then followed the girl until the flat made her pull over. If it were night, there would be no way for her to know she was being followed on the busy interstate.

Thomas checked the records; no calls had been made from the callbox since the Tuesday before, then not again until another four days after Jennifer's car had been discovered. The perp was probably on her before she knew what was happening, pretending to be a Good Samaritan.

No evidence was found in the car, no sign of a struggle. Her overnight bag and purse were found in the trunk. Her wallet lay in the glove box; it still held fifty dollars. So robbery was not a motive. With no fingerprints or evidence to go on, Thomas was forced to move on to other cases.

But the image of Jennifer's mutilated body haunted him. It crept into his thoughts when he least expected it, taking a shower or simply driving his car. But nights were the worst, and sleep proved elusive. It was the most disturbing case he had worked so far. Of course he'd seen plenty of dead bodies in his career, but this particular one was especially obscene.

His ringing cell snapped him out of his thoughts.

"Thomas, here."

"Where the hell are you?" came the familiar bark of Captain Harris. "I expected you back at the station an hour ago. When you get here, I want you to come straight to my office. You got that?"

"Yes, sir, I'll be right there."

The line went dead.

Thomas reached into the top left drawer of his desk and pulled out his electric shaver. He ran it across his face haphazardly, then dropped it back in the drawer and stood.

He walked out of his office and strolled across the bullpen as if he didn't have a care in the world. As he opened the door, the captain looked up in astonishment.

"What the—"

"I got here as soon as I could, sir," he said with a smile before the captain could finish his sentence.

"Sit down, smartass."

The captain reminded Thomas of a bulldog: short, bald, and stocky.

Captain Harris took a deep breath and looked at him seriously. "Thomas, I want you to start seeing the department psychiatrist."

"What the fuck!" That was the last thing he expected him to say. "I don't need the services of a shrink, thank you very much."

"Really." His voice dripped with sarcasm. "Well, you look like shit warmed over. Your suits are always wrinkled, your eyes are bloodshot, and it looks like you've been shaving with a weed whacker. Most importantly, I don't feel I can count on you anymore. You're like a loaded gun ready to go off at any minute." The captain stood and began pacing.

Look who's talking, Thomas thought.

"You walk around with a permanent hangover, and it's evident you're not sleeping."

"Show me one detective in the department that *does* get a full night's sleep, and I'll show you one that's not doing his job. It's not a luxury I can afford. It happens to go with the territory."

"Oh, bullshit. You know damned well what I'm talking about. You've got to get it together. I need you sharp. You're no good to anyone like this, least of all the department." The captain came around and sat on the edge of the desk in front of him, his voice softened. "Look, I've given you a lot of slack, but it's been almost two years. You need to get it together."

"But Captain, I—"

"This is *not* a discussion." The captain returned to his chair and sat down. "I'll put you on a desk so fast your head will spin if you don't get your head out of your ass and I'll make you ride that desk until I see a complete one-eighty. Got it?"

"Fine, whatever, but I need to talk to you about this case. You know we may have a serial killer on our hands. The MO is too close to the Hooper case to be ignored. I'll know more after the autopsy, but I'm certain the rest will follow suit. And I don't think these women are the first. Everything is too clean, too precise."

"Shut the fuck up." He looked down, drew his hands through his buzz cut, then looked back at Thomas. "I do *not* want to hear this shit right now. Not now, not ever." Then after a short hesitation, he leaned on his desk. "Fine. See what you can dig up. But keep it on the QT. I'm serious as a heart attack. I don't want the media in on this. You got that?"

"I'm afraid it's too late for that, sir. That lady from Channel Five caught me as I was leaving the scene. She's already asking if there's a connection between the two cases."

"Shit. I'd better call the chief and get it over with. Dammit!" He hit the desk with his palm. "Thanks for the heads-up."

Thomas nodded, then stood. He'd made it as far as the door before he heard the captain yell behind him.

"Wait!"

He turned back, Harris was rifling through his desk drawer. His hand came out with a business card and handed it to him.

"You're going to need this."

Thomas took the card and read it. "Oh, joy."

"Make that appointment ASAP."

Thomas shoved the card into his jacket pocket, and left without another word.

FIVE

The little boy was on a beach with his mother, giggling as they played tag. He ran toward the water, then as soon as a wave approached, he'd run back and his mother would chase him.

He wished the day would never end.

She caught him around the waist, pulled him down in the sand, and tickled him until he thought he would pee his pants.

His mother was the most beautiful woman in the whole wide world. Her yellow hair was long and when the breeze picked it up, she looked just like the angel in the picture above his bed.

Suddenly the tickling stopped, her laughter died. The boy followed her gaze; a dark figure loomed above. The sun was so bright that the boy saw nothing but a large shadow. The ominous figure growled.

The boy screamed.

His mother stood quickly. A large hand appeared out of thin air and slapped her across the face. She snatched the boy up into her arms and ran. Her tears soaked the top of his head.

The man awoke with a start, drenched in sweat. His heart beat out a quick staccato. He got up to take a leak, the nightmare a tangle of confusion. On his way back to bed, he noticed a shock of light that crept around the edges of the well-worn curtains.

He sat on the edge of the bed, picked up a roach and lit the end. Drawing the smoke deeply into his lungs, he held it until he began to cough. He took another hit, then dropped it back in the ashtray when it burned the ends of his thumb and finger. He lay back down and covered his head with a pillow while he waited for the pot to take effect. Soon his brain was numb, the fear gone, and hopefully sleep would not be far behind.

Six

Returning home, Meagan pulled out the key that hung on a shoestring around her neck. The second she got the door open, Godzilla pushed her aside, almost knocking her down. While she locked the door, she could hear him behind her slopping up water from his industrial-sized bowl.

Meagan followed him into the kitchen and pushed the button on the coffeepot, then opened the fridge and grabbed a bottle of water. As she drank, she looked out at her garden through the window above the sink and inspected her camellia bushes, which were pregnant with blooms.

Her garden was more than just a hobby. Everything in it she'd planted herself. It had all her favorites; giant bird of paradise, hibiscus, jasmine, gardenia, hydrangeas, ferns, and of course the two camellia bushes. It was her own little rain forest. She loved sitting out there with a glass of wine and a good book. It was her idea of Zen.

Meagan lived in a duplex with only one adjoining wall, no one above or below, so it was more like a house than an apartment. She loved to keep all the windows open so she could enjoy the cool ocean breeze. That was something she had dared to do only recently, thanks to Brad.

Her home was filled with plants and dark wood furnishings. Her couch and the overstuffed chair with ottoman were covered in a retro tropical design featuring bird of paradise. Candles of all shapes and sizes surrounded the room in lieu of a fireplace. Her china cabinet was filled with photos of loved ones.

She loved her little beach cottage in San Clemente; she couldn't imagine living anywhere else. She moved here after her divorce and loved the fact that she got to make all the major decisions. Godzilla was a great roommate, too. He never complained about her music; he also liked Joni Mitchell. He didn't care about her scented candles, incense, or whether or not there were dirty dishes in the sink.

Meagan glanced at the clock and kicked it into high gear. After her shower, she chose a brightly colored skirt, simple black top, and her silver hoop earrings. Her red curls were nearly dry, so she decided to wear her hair down today.

She ran into the kitchen, poured a cup of coffee and grabbed one of the fat-free bran muffins to eat in the car. While juggling her purse, keys and coffee, she stuck the muffin in her mouth so she could get the door.

Suddenly the phone rang and she stopped to stare at it. She turned her hand to look at her watch and spilled her coffee on the floor in the process. "Shit!" Godzilla ran over and lapped it up.

"Thanks, Godzilla, I knew I could count on you." He always had her back. She glanced once again at the ringing phone, and deliberated. In the end she continued out the door and slammed it shut behind her. She ran to her frosty mint-green Honda CRV and jumped in. Soon she was speeding up Interstate 5.

Meagan's license plate holder read; *Get in, Sit down, Hold on and Shut up!* She liked to drive fast. It wasn't because she was always late, although she usually was. She just loved the rush, the feeling of power it gave her.

She looked at the ocean on her left and sighed. Her life's motto was *Life's a Beach, and Then You Die.* That's why she chose San Clemente; the Pacific Ocean was so readily accessible. It was visible from the freeway all the way to work.

Meagan zipped into a parking space behind the salon and jumped out. She was ten minutes late and knew she was going to hear about it. Dropping her stuff off in the back room, she rushed onto the floor. The minute she cleared the back door, Jerome's voice came bellowing across the room, "You're late, Red!"

"I know, sorry." She walked into the reception area and called her first client.

It was a mystery to her, but none of her clients seemed annoyed at waiting for Meagan. They forever complimented her on her talent and many appreciated her humor. Above her station hung a sign that read: *For your own safety, please remain seated at all times.* She got it from a friend who used to work at Disneyland.

After she put her first client under the dryer, she went up to the front of the salon to say hello to her friend Lilah, the receptionist.

Lilah was a college student putting herself through school. She stood five feet, five inches, wore her blonde hair in a chin-length bob, had blue eyes, and looked like a model of innocence. The only thing keeping this angel from getting her wings was the nose ring.

"Jerome's been chomping at the bit," Lilah said as Meagen slid beside her. "I swear he watches the clock and the minute you're late, he comes to me and starts bitching about it."

"I'm so sorry, I'll try to do better in the future." Meagan flipped through the scheduling book's pages as she checked out her appointments for the week.

"I don't know what his problem is with you, but he doesn't have me call any of the other stylists when they're late."

***

Meagan started back to work five years before after going through a bitter divorce. Her ex-husband made her quit her job. He was a bit old-fashioned that way, and she was too young and too in love to know any better. Now she did.

After a few short years in the business, her creativity was stifled by that fateful trip to the altar. So when she started at this salon, she had to build her clientele from scratch. She advertised like hell, practically giving her services away, and before long was able to support herself. Not a good way to win friends and influence people in her highly competitive field.

However, that wasn't Jerome's problem. It just made him one more person to jump on the I Hate Meagan bandwagon. No, Jerome's problem with her was personal, and for Lilah's sake, Meagan had decided to keep it that way. It was better not to put her in the middle. She was a faithful friend, and Meagan didn't want to be the cause of any problems for her at the salon. She needed this job just as much as Meagan did.

***

The problem with Jerome started back when Meagan was new to the salon. Sandy, the owner, had asked her to work one evening at her other salon on the lake in Mission Viejo. They had three girls out sick and only one hairdresser trying to cope with a scheduling nightmare. Meagan was more than happy to oblige, so she packed up her tools and made the thirty-minute drive.

The minute she entered the salon, she observed the waiting area and it was not pretty. Lots of angry faces. The receptionist looked like she was ready to quit. Her stress was almost palpable. The phone rang incessantly. She juggled answering it, with calling clients to tell them not to come in and rescheduling them.

Meagan listened as she patiently waited to get the girl's attention. Finally she disconnected the phone and Meagan jumped in to introduce herself. The girl was noticeably relieved. She pointed out the station Meagan was to use.

She was bent over trying to feel underneath the counter to plug in her blow dryer when she carelessly looked up into the mirror and stopped. Three chairs down stood the ebony version of Adonis, with chiseled features and a bald pate. Meagan held her breath, eyes riveted. He was well over six feet, more like six-two.

He definitely lifted weights. The bulk of his chest strained against the buttons of his white dress shirt. He wore a paisley print brown tie, pleated brown slacks and expensive-looking alligator shoes with a belt to match. He could have been a lawyer in that getup. He looked ridiculously out of place in a hair salon.

Meagan watched as he shamelessly flirted with the elderly woman in his chair. She giggled and covered her mouth like a schoolgirl. The corner of his mouth went up in a kind of half-smile; the glint in his eye was mischievous.

Damn, he was sexy as all get out. Something stirred between her legs as she imagined him slamming her up against the wall, her legs wrapped around his waist and her holding on tight for the ride of her life. Yah Whoo! *Down girl, he's probably gay.* Her eyes roamed down to his left hand where she spied a gold band glittering with tiny diamonds.

Oh, well, it never would have worked out anyway. Men

like that usually had an ego the size of Texas. But I bet the sex would have been great.

The fantasy slipped quickly from her mind and reality reared its ugly head when her eyes slid up his arm and looked at his face. He was staring right at her. A slow smile came to his lips. Meagan felt her cheeks flush, she stood up abruptly.

In an effort at recovery, she quickly blurted out, "Hi, I'm Meagan. The relief crew that was sent in."

The man's deep baritone filled the room, "I'm Jerome, glad you could come. I've been working as fast as I can, but I was already booked with my own appointments. It's just too much for one person to handle."

His voice made her quiver. *Stay focused.* Meagan turned away and called her first client.

The evening flew by and Meagan enjoyed every minute of it. She and Jerome joked and laughed, and even sang to the Motown hits that rang through the salon speakers. That's why she didn't flinch when he asked her to go for a drink after work. By then her jets had cooled. The man was obviously spoken for, so she figured the invitation was innocent enough.

SEVEN

Meagan followed Jerome to a nearby sports bar where everyone greeted him by name. He led her to an open table.

Once seated, he took her drink order and headed for the bar. She passed the time watching the big screen TV, feigning interest in the football game.

Jerome returned with a pitcher of beer and two glasses. They sat and talked for a couple of hours. Meagan told him about her divorce and moving from her four-bedroom home in Dana Point to the one-bedroom duplex in San Clemente. How she didn't have any children, but would like to one day. She told him of her return to the hair business and how much she enjoyed the ocean and boogey-boarding.

He told her he had two children, each with different women. He hadn't married either one of them. But he did pay child support, which took a good chunk of his pay. He told her he had been married for nine years, but he and his wife now slept in separate rooms. They wanted to divorce, but couldn't afford it. So they co-existed under the same roof. He lived his life and she hers.

Gee, like I've never heard that one before.

All at once she put two and two together.

It was in the way his arm rested on the back of her chair, the way he leaned in close and spoke intimately into her ear. It actually wasn't that loud in there. She turned her head from the TV and looked at him, really looked at him. His expression was not that of a fellow co-worker, but of a man in the midst of seduction.

That explained the uneasy feeling in the pit of her stomach and her increased anxiety that had her leaning as far away from him as she could. It wasn't her imagination.

Jerome hit her with an invitation to a Chargers game that Sunday. Keeping it light, Meagan told him she wasn't much of a sports fan.

Glancing quickly at her watch, she stood up so fast she nearly knocked the table over. She caught her glass before it toppled to the floor. "I should be going," she told him. "I've got an early client."

"I'll walk you to your car." Jerome stood alongside her.

Damn. "That isn't necessary. You should stay and finish your beer." She feigned a smile.

"Don't worry about it." He put his arm around her waist and hugged her snug against his side.

Meagan decided to keep her mouth shut as she made her way across the parking lot. A few minutes from now she would be out of there and never have to see the guy again. As she unlocked the car door, she felt Jerome's hot breath on her neck. *Can you say awkward?*

She pretended not to notice and swung the door wide, pushing him back with her butt. "Well, have a good night. Maybe we'll work together again sometime," she said, the words flying out of her mouth as she readied herself to slide into the driver's seat.

Jerome grabbed Meagan's arm, spun her around and planted a big fat kiss on her mouth. She tried to hold her lips together, but his tongue was insistent. He clamped one hand on her butt, while the other grabbed onto a breast like it was a door handle.

She flashed on her earlier fantasy and cringed. What the hell had she been thinking? Her hands pushed firmly on his chest until she was finally able to end the kiss, if that's what you wanted to call it, and pried herself from his grasp.

"Look, I'm really sorry if I gave you the wrong impression, but I don't date married men." *On purpose, that is.*

"Oh, playing hard to get, are we?" He dislodged her hands, grabbed her butt with both hands and pulled her tight against his large erection. She was going to have to get serious on this guy's ass.

"Nope, not playing here." She reached around and started prying his fingers from her derrière one by one.

"Come on, I saw you undressing me with your eyes."

"My mistake." She pulled back on his pinky. He yelped and grabbed his hand.

"What the fuck, bitch!"

Meagan jumped in her car, locked the doors and hightailed it out of there. Her tires screeched as she made her escape. He was right, and she knew it. The entire mess was her fault. She had been openly drooling over the guy. *Restless hormones can be dangerous things. Chalk it up to stupidity and just move on.*

Luckily for her, they didn't cross paths again for another two years. Then one morning she noticed Jerome shampooing some woman in *her* salon. His gaze locked on hers, a wicked smile curved his lips. *Dammit!* Suddenly she couldn't catch her breath.

Running to the front of the salon, she found Lilah cashing out a customer. When she was through, Meagan pulled her aside. "What's *he* doing here?" she said in a mock whisper.

"Who, Jerome?" Lilah looked to the back of the salon, where he was drying his client's hair with a towel, his eyes glued to them as they talked. His smile never faltered. Lilah's voice dropped to a whisper. "Isn't he a hunk?" Then she finished in a normal tone. "He's going to be working here every Tuesday from now on. Sandy asked if he would help out since we're short-handed. Are you all right? You look white as a sheet!"

"Yeah, yeah, I'm fine," she answered distractedly.

As the day wore on, Meagan found him hard to ignore. His station was directly behind hers. She could see his reflection in her mirror. The more she tried, the harder it became because every time she looked up, he was staring right at her with that shit-eating grin. She prayed people didn't think they had slept together.

It unnerved her, made it difficult to concentrate on anything else. If she cut herself one more time, she was going to need a blood transfusion.

Meagan called her last client of the night, Stan. As they headed to the back of the salon, she felt someone brush a hand across her butt. She flicked her head back with the dirtiest look she could muster. Stan stared at her in shock, shook his head and put his hands out in front of him in surrender. Then nodded his head to her right. She turned in time to see Jerome pass by with a wink. *Oh, no, he did not just do that.*

They reached the shampoo bowls and Stan lay down in the chair. She wet his head and began the shampoo process. She was leaning over him, rinsing his hair, his head cradled in her hand when Jerome walked out on the floor from the back. He leaned in and whispered, "That's my favorite position."

Stan's eyes shot open, noticed Meagan's breasts only inches from his face, then quickly shut them. Obviously embarrassed.

"I'm so sorry about that," Meagan said through clenched teeth. She felt bad for the poor guy to be stuck in the middle of this ...*thing.* Whatever this *thing* was. She would put a stop to it the moment she got him alone.

"You shouldn't have to apologize for the asshole. You've done nothing wrong. Hasn't he ever heard of sexual harassment?" Stan shook his head.

Meagan led him back to her chair. "You read my mind."

They had been quiet through most of his haircut. Her mind reeled. She didn't know she had been projecting her anger until Stan's voice broke into her thoughts.

"Would you like me to punch him in the nose for you?"

Meagan laughed, her shoulders relaxed. "And deprive me of the privilege?" She schooled her temper after that and kept things light.

She hadn't seen the manager all day. She didn't think Jerome would have the balls to carry on this way if the manager were around. After she had finished cashing out Stan, she said goodbye and turned to Lilah. "Where's Vicki?"

"Oh," Lilah had been writing something, stopped, then looked up. "I thought I told you, Jerome is acting manager on Tuesdays from now on. Vicki can't get a babysitter to cover that day so she's asked for it off."

The day from hell just keeps getting better and better.

At the end of her shift, Meagan was in the back retrieving the broom and dustpan when Jerome came in through the back door, reeking of cigarette smoke. "Hey, hot stuff." He leered at her.

Meagan grabbed his arm and pulled him into the dispensary and she shut the door. "What the hell is wrong with you?"

"Oooh, you're sexy when you get angry, Red. You give me a hard-on just looking at you." He reached out and touched her cheek. "Stop it." She slapped his hand away. "And don't call me Red, I hate that!"

"Sure, Red, whatever you say."

"Haven't you ever heard of sexual harassment? My, God, you've broken about a million laws today. Sandy won't put up with this. She'll fire you the moment I tell her."

Suddenly he snatched her by the arms and pulled her to within an inch from his face. "No, she won't. I already told her how you came onto me one night when I was too drunk to say no, and I fucked your brains out. Obviously I was the best you ever had, because you wouldn't take no for an answer after that. Kept hounding me, waiting for me outside the salon. She thinks you're pathetic, a real sore loser." He ground the words out through his teeth.

"But—" Meagan's arms were starting to hurt.

"She said she'd rather fire *your* ass, than *miss* mine." His grin was lecherous.

Meagan was struck dumb. This couldn't be happening. He let go of her and she stumbled back a couple of feet, her hands rubbed her sore arms. "So, you can cry sexual harassment all you want, doll. But Sandy already has the paperwork filled out, dated and signed by yours truly. No one is going to believe a word you say."

Meagan backed away, turned and fled. She cleaned her station as quickly as she could and raced home. After her second glass of wine, and an hour on the phone with her best friend, Katy, she'd decided to take Tuesdays off from then on. It would hurt her paycheck, but at that point she didn't care.

***

A year and a half later, Sandy called a staff meeting. Meagan couldn't help but notice Jerome. If he stood any closer to Sandy, he would be in her lap. She tried to ignore him, and look only at her boss, but it was hard. His eyes never left Meagan's face, and his smile unusually wide and toothy.

She tried to focus on Sandy's words. "As you all know, Vicki has left to have her baby. What you may not know is that she has decided to quit and become a stay-at-home mom." A round of groans went around and people looked expectantly at each other to see who would take her position. "Fortunately for us, Jerome has graciously agreed to move to this location and take Vicki's place as manager full-time. He might lose some clients—"

Some, make that at least half. Meagan realized her mouth had become unhinged, and quickly shut it.

"—but he's willing to make that sacrifice to do me this huge favor. So let's all give Jerome a nice warm welcome—" Applause filled the room.

Double crap! Meagan began to sweat, her mind raced. Sandy must be paying him awfully well because a move that far is career suicide in this business. She felt his eyes boring a hole through her and looked at him pointedly. He greeted her with a big ugly smirk.

She returned the favor with the hardest look she could muster. Clint Eastwood would be envious. When she tore her gaze away, she looked around and noticed the other girls following the exchange between them. They glanced at each other, shock registering on some faces. The faces of others gave knowing looks, with giggles and whispers.

Triple crap. Meagan felt the heat in her face. This was a nightmare. She had spent too much time building her clientele. She couldn't just leave. Odds were no matter *how* good you were, or how close the other salon was, you were sure to lose up to fifty percent of your clientele. And there was no way Meagan could afford to start over. When she'd moved there years earlier, right after the divorce, she had the money from the sale of the house. That money was long gone, spent on furniture, moving expenses and simply living, until she'd built her clientele. She no longer had that cushion.

That night she barely slept. The next day she dragged herself into work, arriving ten minutes late. Jerome's voice bellowed across the salon, "Red, you're late!" He threw his comb and shears down then pointed, "Get in my office. Now!" Spittle flew from his mouth, the veins in his neck stuck out.

Reluctantly she obliged. Once in the office Meagan turned to Jerome, "You know I have a client waiting out there."

"Let them wait! From what I hear, your clients are used to that."

"Well, if that's all, I have to go." Meagan turned toward the door.

Jerome grabbed Meagan's wrist, yanking her back into the office. With his foot, he slammed the door.

"I'm not through with you yet," he growled and pulled her closer. Meagan's heart raced. His pupils were the size of dimes. He kept sniffling, and rubbing his nose. He had to be high on something. Her wrist ached from his grasp, but she kept her mouth shut. He wasn't in his right mind, she knew better than to try to reason with someone under the influence. Her alcoholic husband had taught her that.

Meagan swallowed hard, her breathing quickened.

"Just remember this, Red. I'm watching you. You do *anything* wrong, I'll be on you like flies on shit. I'm going to make your life a living hell if you don't follow my rules. That means not one fucking minute late. You got that?"

Meagan nodded. He pushed her away as he released her arm, and stormed out of the office. Stunned, she sat down and rubbed her wrist.

From that day forward, Jerome kept his word. His harassment of her continued on the sly. He found any excuse to berate her. He blamed her for anything that went wrong in the salon. His drug use was now a constant. All she could do was pray that he screwed up a client's hair bad enough that they sued the salon. Surely Sandy would be forced to fire him then.

Meagan knew the other hairdressers. They reveled in his treatment of her, some secretly, some less so. Waiting like a bunch of vultures for her to quit so they could pounce on her remaining customers. She wouldn't give them the satisfaction.

EIGHT

Thomas sat at his computer and scanned the last few weeks of Missing Persons reports. If this guy ran true to form, he'd kept her awhile. He'd received the crime scene photos, but it wasn't exactly like looking at a live shot of a victim.

Until he got a lead from forensics, the guys canvassing, or Cheryl called him regarding the autopsy, he might as well get a start on the photos. He had the dimensions of her face, general age, and he'd use blonde with blue eyes to narrow the field.

There was no telling what this guy's MO was at this point, so he'd go with blond and blue for now. Normally he'd pass the job off to someone else, but he didn't like sitting around with his thumb up his ass. Waiting was never Thomas's strong suit.

Orange County turned up nothing, so he broadened his search to the surrounding counties. He'd flagged a few reports to come back to later: one in San Diego, another in

Riverside and a couple in Los Angeles County.

Her prints weren't in AFIS, the automated fingerprint identification system. Not that he was holding his breath on that one. He didn't think the woman was a criminal or working girl. She was well-nourished, no track marks, and her fingernails were too nice. She could have been a high-priced call girl or in the military at some point, but again, those were long shots. In his experience victims were just that, victims.

The house-to-house search on the cliffs above the dump site yielded nothing. A few residents weren't home at the time, however, so it was still possible they'd find a witness. Again, Thomas wasn't holding his breath, but he had to admit to a tiny glimmer of hope. Cooper and James would resume their canvas around dinnertime.

One problem with the wealthier neighborhoods was that people pretty much kept to themselves. Although the general populace of San Clemente was considered more down-to-earth than, say, a neighborhood in Newport Beach, a home overlooking the Pacific still ran in the several-million-dollar bracket. Thomas knew from experience that the residences of these homes valued their privacy.

He was certain the perp did all his maneuvering in the wee hours under the cover of night. Most folks were asleep by then. *Give me an insomniac any day.* The distance from the cliffs to the sand didn't help much either, but it was possible that someone noticed a strange car or a person who seemed out of place.

He'd made his own murder board by posting the latest photos, along with those of the first victim on the window next to his desk. That way he could note the differences as well as the similarities between the two cases. Thomas rolled his shoulders, rubbed a kink out of his neck, then leaned back in his chair and stared at the photos. The ringing phone broke his concentration.

"Thomas," he answered distractedly.

"Detective, this is Joe Nguen at the morgue. Dr. Gardner wanted me to let you know she's about ready to begin the autopsy on your Jane Doe."

"Thanks, Joe, tell her I'm on my way." Thomas stood up and stretched. He was just shrugging into his jacket when the phone rang again. He picked it up and heard Kim Johnson on the other end. She was Homicide's IT specialist. She'd joined the force when she returned from Afghanistan and her stint in the Navy had ended.

"Thanks for getting back to me. I need you to run some searches for me in VICAP. I'm running out the door right now, so you'll need to jot these down."

"Okay, shoot."

"Search for women's bodies buried in sand by the ocean or other large bodies of water, raped, kidnapped and held for an indeterminate amount of time, tortured, removal of body parts, especially the breasts, and lastly his signature of the black thread through the lips and eyelids. Do it in first singularly, then as a group."

"Got it," Kim said.

"I know this is going to take some time to do it in steps like this, but I'm certain this guy didn't just wake up two months ago and decide to start mutilating women. He's too damn good. Who knows what he's added to his play list along the way." Thomas knew that the FBI's Violent Crime Apprehension Program would give him some answers, even if the answer was no.

"No sweat. Anything else?"

"On second thought, run that search backwards. Let's see how many other vics out there meet the same MO first, then go back and break it up."

"Roger that."

"Thanks, Johnson, gotta run."

***

When Thomas returned home that evening, he walked into the kitchen, deposited his keys, then immediately poured himself a scotch on the rocks. This time he reached for the Glenfiddich, having forgotten to stop at the liquor store on his way home.

In the living room, he flung his weary body into his favorite chair. He put his feet up on the ottoman, then snatched up the TV remote. He wanted—no, needed to numb his brain.

He thought a good Hitchcock movie would do the trick, so he started channel-surfing on the off chance he could find one. TV guides were for pussies. Then something caught his eye and he backed up. Yup, just as he thought, it was that ditzy reporter from this morning.

"The mutilated body of an unidentified woman was discovered this morning on Trestles Beach, a popular destination for surfers here in San Clemente. This is the second such victim found in the last two months.

"The first, you'll recall, was Jennifer Hooper, the young coed whose body was discovered in a shallow grave near the pier in Huntington Beach back in September. So far, the police have no leads, but fear this could be the work of a serial killer."

"Son of a bitch!" Thomas jumped out of his chair.

"The folks here at KBBT are issuing a warning to all the women in Orange County to be vigilant about their surroundings. Be extremely cautious after dark. Make sure you stay in groups when walking to your car after work. Let's all pray the police catch The Sandman soon so we can all rest a little easier—."

His cell phone rang.

"Yeah," he said, muting the TV, still staring at the screen although the segment was over.

"Hey, you were just on TV. Harris is not going to be too happy with you." Malone laughed. "Damn, Thomas, you've got balls of steel picking up that reporter. That was hilarious!"

"She's a major pain in the ass. I just caught the tail end of the segment. Harris is going to shit bricks about the serial killer crack."

"It's not exactly a stretch. Anyone with half a brain can connect the dots."

"Hold on, Malone, I'm getting another call." Thomas hit the send button on his phone.

"Dammit, Thomas—" *Speak of the devil.*

"Hold on, sir." He put the captain on hold and went back to his waiting buddy.

Malone chuckled. "Good luck with that."

Thomas needed more than luck after the day he'd had. He switched the line over to the captain, not at all ready to hear what he had to say.

"Sorry, sir, I had Malone on the other line."

"I just got off the phone with the chief. What the fuck were you thinking, picking that reporter up like that? We'll be lucky if we're not sued for sexual harassment or some other such bullshit like that. If Gloria Steinem hears about it, we're screwed!"

"She wouldn't take 'no comment' for an answer, just kept buzzing around me like a fly at a picnic. I snapped, I'm sorry, but I'd like to see what you would do if you had someone constantly shoving a microphone up your nose."

"We're not talking about me."

"No, and you weren't there. I didn't catch the beginning of the segment, but I'd bet they didn't show how I politely declined answering her stupid questions several times before I got fed up."

"You're right, I didn't see one iota of polite and I'm sure it was expertly edited, but that's not the point. This is exactly what I was talking about this morning. I can't afford to have you out there losing your temper. Especially when every clown and his uncle has a video app on their cell phone nowadays."

"You're right, sir, I'm sorry."

"Look, Thomas, I can't keep covering your ass. The mayor called the chief, then the chief called me, so now I'm telling you. One more outburst like that, and I'm going to have to suspend you. I already had to do quite a tap dance to keep you from getting put on permanent leave for that little stunt you pulled."

"Shit." Thomas ran his hand down his face. "I'm sorry, I guess I wasn't really thinking about the big picture."

"Exactly. That's been happening a lot lately. Now, do me and yourself a favor, and get your shit together. Call the number on that card, or find another shrink, I don't give a shit, but do something *now* before you fuck up so bad that only God can save you."

"Yes, sir." Thomas turned off his phone, downed the rest of his scotch, and poured himself another.

NINE

Meagan didn't get home until after ten that evening. She dragged herself through the door and into the paws of an overly excited Godzilla. The love fest didn't last long; he needed to go out. She filled his bowl with dinner while she waited for him to come back in. She was just topping off his water when he returned wagging his tail. She locked the door and headed to her bedroom.

A moment later, stripped down to panties and bra, she plopped on the edge of the bed. Damn, but it felt good to sit. Godzilla bounded up next to her and bowled her over, licking her face. She grabbed his head with both hands and held him at bay, "I love you too, handsome."

She began rubbing her feet and sighed. She wished she had someone to do this for her. Perhaps a scantily clad man with chiseled features who would greet her at the door with a glass of wine, then give her a full body massage with a happy ending. One could only dream. No, the way her luck was running, she'd end up with a guy greeting her at the door holding an axe and wearing a hockey mask. *Then again, if that was all he was wearing...* She chuckled.

Meagan threw on a pair of sweatpants and a tank top, then headed into the living room. The flashing red light on the answering machine blinked at her, and she hit the play button and listened as she headed back to the kitchen. There was a glass of wine in there with her name on it.

The first three calls were hang-ups. She took a satisfying sip of Merlot and was on her way to a relaxing evening when Katy's voice echoed through the room. "Meagan, call me the *minute* you get in, no matter how late."

Wow, it must be important if she's willing to risk waking the boys.

Katy O'Brien had been Meagan's best friend since high school. Now that Katy had a family, they didn't see each other as often as she would have liked, but they did keep in contact almost daily by phone.

The phone rang only once before Katy answered in a dramatic whisper, "Just a sec, I've got to go in the other room."

It was only a moment before Katy was back on the line speaking more audibly. "Sorry, Sean's asleep. You know it would normally take a cannon to wake him, but tonight I don't want to take any chances. It took three sedatives to get him calmed down enough to close his eyes."

"What happened?" Meagan perked up her ears.

"He went surfing this morning and found a woman's body at Trestles."

"Oh, no, not another person hit by the train." Meagan sat on her couch and drew her legs up beside her.

"Not this time. Have you seen the news about that serial killer?"

Stupid question. Katy knew Meagan didn't watch the news, that she found it too depressing. She relied on Katy, the news junkie, to keep her abreast of all current events. Because of her delicate heart, Katy usually stuck close to home and kept abreast with the outside world via television.

"No way, we have another serial killer?" Meagan thought back to when Richard Ramirez, The Night Stalker, terrorized the southland. He picked homes at random along Interstate 5. He'd killed in Mission Viejo, a town roughly twenty miles north of San Clemente. At the time, everyone feared that he'd hit their town next.

"Yup, they're calling him The Sandman because he buries their bodies in shallow graves on the beach. Remember the girl two months ago up in Huntington Beach?"

"Oh, God, and Sean found this girl? Was she mutilated like the last one?" Meagan took a deep swallow of her wine.

"What he saw of her was in pretty bad shape. He only saw an arm and a leg."

"She was chopped up!" Meagan downed the rest of her wine and got up to retrieve the bottle.

"No, no, no. The high tide uncovered part of her and that's all he could see protruding from the sand. He actually threw his backpack and sweater on top of her. It was still dark when he got to the beach."

"Ew, gross." Meagan sat back on the couch and got comfortable, the bottle of wine at the ready.

"Yeah. The cops confiscated them as evidence, but he says he doesn't want them back. They can burn them for all he cares."

"I don't blame him. Poor, Sean, how's he doing? He must be devastated."

"You have no idea. The minute he walked through the door, he just grabbed me and held on tight without saying a word. It scared me to death. I couldn't imagine what had happened. I'd had a pretty rough morning myself because he was so late and forgot his cell phone, again. I was scared shitless that something had happened to him, and I had no way to find out what.

"Since he had the car, I phoned Sue down the street to take the boys to school. He finally called around mid-morning, but only to let me know he was fine and would be awhile more. He arrived home in the early afternoon. He was so shook up it took him awhile to get the story out. I've got to tell you, Meagan, I've never felt more helpless in my life."

"My God, Katy, how horrible. Poor Sean."

"I know. To make matters worse, I had to drive him up to Santa Ana so he could give them a formal statement. By the time we got home, he was wiped out, but couldn't sleep. He said that ghastly image kept flashing through his brain like a horror movie he couldn't shut off."

"You know, maybe under the circumstances, we should postpone my birthday celebration tomorrow night," Meagan suggested.

"No, we can't!" Katy's outburst took Meagan by surprise. "I'll just see if his brother William can come over so he doesn't have to be alone."

"What's so important that we can't postpone?"

Katy's tone turned jovial. "No way, girlfriend, it's a surprise."

"Well, give Sean my best."

"I will. Talk to you tomorrow."

"I don't think I'll be able to get any sleep tonight after that story."

"I know, huh? I've just been lying in bed with the TV turned low watching over Sean. Every so often I catch him in the midst of a nightmare and rub his back. After a while he calms down. Call me tomorrow when you get a chance."

"You got it. Good night."

"Good night."

Meagan turned to Godzilla who lay on her feet by her side. "Good thing I have *you,* boy." She ruffled the top of his head. "You won't let that big bad psycho killer get me, will ya?"

Godzilla panted his response, his tongue lulling to the side.

She checked the locks on the windows and doors before retiring to her bedroom and searching for the weapon Sean made for her when she'd first started living alone. It was a mallet with a three-inch circumference, about four feet long, made of wood and wrapped with black electrician's tape. Sean told her that the tape was to keep the mallet from breaking when it hit the target.

Meagan cringed at the time, and thought he was being silly if not a bit overprotective. Now she silently thanked Sean for his brilliance. She found the weapon under the bed and slipped it under the covers.

Meagan threw off her clothes and slid between the flannel sheets, loving the way they felt against her naked body. Picking up her book, she began to read until she could fall asleep.

The next thing she knew the phone was ringing. The light was on, and her book lay open across her stomach. Groggily she glanced at the clock. Half past one. Who would be calling so late?

Her heart hammered in her chest as she snatched the phone on the third ring. "Hello?"

Dead air greeted her.

"Hello!"

She sensed someone on the other end, yet for the life of her couldn't figure out why no one spoke.

"Katy, is that you, is everything all right?"

Nothing.

All at once another explanation dawned on Meagan. "Brad?" Suddenly a receiver was slammed in her ear. Of course it was Brad. She should have known that it wouldn't be that easy to get rid of him. She lay back down. *Dammit.* Now that she thought about it, she'd had a lot more hang-ups than usual over the last couple of weeks. Naturally she'd assumed they were wrong numbers. Now she wasn't so sure.

She didn't recall seeing Brad's car around lately, but then again, she'd stopped looking. Maybe he was just being a little stealthier these days. She closed her eyes, took a couple of deep breaths and tried to relax. At least her heart rate had calmed to a more normal tempo, but she couldn't stop wondering: what the hell was Brad's game?

***

The little boy was having a nightmare. A faceless man was chasing him. He ran as fast as he could, but his feet went nowhere. He opened his mouth to scream, but nothing came out.

A loud crash startled the boy awake. He sat up quickly. His bedroom door was open. He stared at the large black figure looming in the doorway. He must have screamed after all. Why else would he be there? Tears stained his cheeks. He trembled as he tried to stop crying. He knew how much he hated it when he cried.

"Sniveling little bastard." The malevolent bellow sent shivers up the boy's spine. His hands flew to his ears. "Your momma ain't coming no more. Ya hear me? She left you! She got sick of all your whining. Mom-mee, Mom-mee, Mom-mee," the voice mimicked in sing-song fashion.

The figure approached. The boy tried to shrink into the wall behind his bed, but he couldn't escape. His father was so close that the boy could feel his hot breath on his face. The foul stench of cigarettes and booze stung his nostrils.

The boy tried to stop crying, but the harder he tried, the worse it got until he ended up with a bad case of hiccups.

A large hand struck the boy across the face. "Don't you ever say that word in this house again, you hear me, boy? Your mama was a whore, she done run off. You'd best be rememberin' that. She's just like all the rest of 'em. All women are dirty lying whores!"

He slapped him again. "Dammit! You stop that, you little sissy boy. Only little girls cry. Is that what you wanna be? A little sissy boy, a little faggot sissy boy? I'll give you somethin' to cry about, ya little homo."

The man bolted straight up in the bed and searched the room. He was alone. His body drenched in sweat. He was breathing as if he'd just run a marathon. His heart pounded so hard, he thought it would escape his chest. The fear was real all right.

He found himself lying in a puddle. The smell of ammonia filled the room. "Fuck me!" he yelled, jumping off the bed. He looked down at the urine-soaked sheets, ran his hands down his face.

He stripped off his shorts, leaving them right where he'd stood and grabbed another pair off the top of the pile next to the bed. He stumbled downstairs to the kitchen and headed straight to the refrigerator in search of liquid comfort. No beer. He slammed the door and listened as bottles of condiments clanked together.

Steering toward the living room, he collapsed into the cracked and worn vinyl recliner. For a moment, he stared at the TV tray next to the chair, and started shaking the beer cans. He found an inch in the bottom of one and guzzled the warm, flat liquid.

His heart rate slowed while he sat staring at the blank screen on the TV. He tried to remember the nightmare, but it was already gone. He picked up a porno mag from the floor and started thumbing through it. That usually calmed him down.

He flipped through the well-worn pages until his eyes came to rest on one particular picture. The woman in the photo had long blonde hair, wore cut off's and her breasts were bare as she leaned against a '57 Chevy. The magazine was old, the pages torn, but he couldn't bring himself to throw it away.

Something about her was familiar. The longer he gazed at her face, the angrier he got. There was only one way to stop the demons in his head.

It was time to start the hunt again.

TEN

Thomas was leaning back in his chair looking up at his makeshift murder board when Kim Johnson came in and tossed a giant folder on his desk.

"Here's the VICAP report."

Thomas quickly sat up and swiveled his chair to face his desk. He pulled the file close. "Jesus, that's thick. Anything interesting?" He opened it up and thumbed through a few pages.

"To summarize, I came up with ten bodies accompanied by sand over the last five years in California; four women, two men, three children, and a dog—"

Thomas looked up. "A dog?"

"Affirmative."

"Was it buried alone?"

Johnson stood with her feet apart, her hands clamped behind her back. "Actually, no, it was buried alongside a seven-year-old girl."

"Interesting. I wonder if that was a one-time thing?"

"Don't know. You want me to look into it?"

"Nope, just thinking aloud. It's peculiar, that's all. "

She rocked back and forth on her feet while she talked.

"Okay, continuing on. Of the women: one brunette killed by blunt force trauma to the head and buried in the Mojave Desert, no rape or torture. That leaves you with four blondes, each raped then murdered, and either found on the sand or under it near a large body of water."

"Thanks, Johnson." He dismissed her and turned his attention back to the file, eager to start reviewing it.

Thomas immediately scanned the contents of the file. Johnson had placed the blonde murder victims on the top of the stack. Organizing the cases by date, he leaned back in his chair, put his feet on his desk and began to read.

The first victim was, Cynthia Gross, twenty-four-years old, long blonde hair, blue eyes, five feet five inches. Her body was discovered almost five years before in San Francisco, on the shore under the Bay Bridge.

Her face had multiple contusions, and she had been raped and strangled, but her cause of death was repeated trauma to the back of the head. Seminal fluid found in the vagina was not conclusive for DNA. Perpetrator a non-secretor. Thomas dropped his feet from the desk, and sat up.

What were the odds?

No mention of sodomy or mutilation. Death occurred within hours of her noted disappearance. The body had lain in the elements for three days before it was discovered. Her car was found in the parking lot of a McDonald's in downtown San Francisco. She had been a resident of Alameda. *This could very well be his first kill.*

Thomas shuffled the pages and began to read about the next victim. Found approximately three years later was the body of Ruth Katzmerik: thirty-two, five-feet-two, long blonde hair, blue eyes. She was found in a shallow grave on a beach in Morro Bay, raped and sodomized, but unmutilated. Ligature marks on wrists and ankles. Strangled repeatedly over the course of several days, he noted because of the overlapping bruises in the photos. Some were fresh; others had started to heal. COD was a subjugated larynx. *Was that a mistake? Did he mean to crush her larynx, or had he just gotten carried away?* Again, the seminal fluid found was that of a non-secretor.

Shit, I'm on a roll.

Ruth had been an attorney in downtown Los Angeles and lived in Santa Monica, roughly two hundred and twenty-five miles south of Morro Bay where she was dumped. Her body had been discovered seven days from the date she was reported missing, dead five of those days. *So he kept her somewhere for two days before he killed her.*

Found one year later was Barbara Cartwright: age twenty-nine, long blonde hair, blue eyes, five-foot-even. Body recovered in a shallow grave on a beach in Santa Barbara. Reported missing by her boyfriend when she failed to show up at his house for dinner a few short blocks away. She lived in the small town of Buttonwillow, along the I-5, roughly a hundred and thirty-five miles northeast of Santa Barbara.

When her body was discovered, she had been missing twelve days, dead only two. *Shit, he had this one for ten days!*

Her face and body were covered in bruises. ME noted the contusions had been made over the course of her confinement, evident by the different stages of discoloration as some bruises began to heal and others were made. Eyelids and lips sewn shut with thick black nylon thread. Side note: bonded black nylon thread size 346, commonly known for sewing leather.

Thomas' excitement ratcheted up. He grabbed the folder on his first vic and ran a finger down the page. "Shit." Bonded nylon thread, black, size 346. Could be found on several sites on the internet. "Bingo!"

He went back to the report and read. Neck contusions consistent with strangulation, overlapping thumb and finger marks along with discoloration of the skin indicate she was choked several times over the course of as many days.

Ligature marks found around the wrists and ankles implied that she'd been restrained. White fibers found in the grooves proved to come from a cotton cord commonly found in any hardware store across the country. Breasts removed; sliced with a serrated instrument, probably a hunting knife. Not found in vicinity of body. Cause of death, exsanguination.

Thomas wrote a note about the white fibers. His vic had no such evidence on her. She had been thoroughly scrubbed clean with bleach.

The last woman was found five months later. Thomas stopped reading and checked the date on his first vic, then at his calendar. "Fuck me." He waited three months before he killed Jennifer, and only two months before Jane Doe. *He's escalating.*

Thomas scrubbed a hand down his face and went back to the report. Mary Anne Wilson: age thirty, long blonde hair, blue eyes, five-foot-five. Missing two weeks before her mutilated body was found floating along the shore of Clam Beach, up in Eureka.

Mary Anne lived with her mother in Stockton, roughly three hundred and thirty-five miles southeast from Clam Beach. Her car was found with a flat tire along the southbound Interstate 5. The ME could not place time or manner of death due to the condition of the body. Her flesh had been eaten away in many places by the marine life.

Between that and the bloating of the remaining flesh, it was nearly impossible to ID the body; they had to resort to DNA and dental records. The ME noted that most trace evidence had likely been washed away. But it was determined that she had been repeatedly raped and sodomized by the scarring of the tissue in the vaginal and rectal regions. Only one eyelid remained sewn shut, the other eye socket was void. *Meaning the fish had gotten to it.*

Her breasts were missing, but it could not be determined what instrument was used at that point. Slight ligature marks were found on the wrists and ankles after careful examination, but no threads or fibers were found imbedded in the skin.

No water in the lungs. *So she didn't drown.* Thomas

compared the last photo of Mary Anne, post-autopsy, with the smiling picture of her alive. Floaters were never pretty, but he could see why even her closest relative could not identify her. She barely looked human.

ELEVEN

Meagan was having a great day. Lilah gave her a cupcake with a candle on it and sang "Happy Birthday." Many of her clients gave her cards and gifts. And Stan dropped by, sans appointment, to bring her a sunflower.

She'd scheduled her last client at three that afternoon so she would have enough time to get ready for her date with the girls. They wouldn't tell her where they were going, only that she needed to dress up.

After she'd freshened her makeup, she slipped on a maxi length halter dress with an Indian print. She piled on some silver bangle bracelets, a couple of rings, and finished with a pair of gypsy style earrings.

She was standing in front of the bathroom mirror pulling up the sides of her hair when she heard Theresa, the rowdiest of her friends, yelling through her screen door, "Hey, Birthday Girl! Hurry up, we've got reservations."

"Come on in, I'm almost ready." Meagan put the second comb in her hair. Tiny red curls framed her face, and the rest of her hair hung down her back.

She heard the screen door slam while she applied her red lipstick, then Theresa was at her side.

"You look great. Now get your butt in gear. The engine's running." Theresa latched onto her hand.

"I'm ready. Just let me grab my keys and purse." Meagan yelled goodbye to Godzilla and locked up the house before she followed Theresa out the door. Katy was riding shotgun, and Sarah sat behind the wheel of her SUV. Theresa and Meagan jumped in the back.

"So where are you girls taking me tonight?"

Sarah turned around and said, "Not yet. You'll have to wait until we get there."

"I've gotta say, this is the first time Theresa's ever kept a secret." Meagan eyed Theresa, who had a sheepish grin.

"We threatened her with bodily harm," Katy laughed.

"Hey, I'm sitting right here!" Theresa defended herself. "I'm not that bad, I just get excited."

Meagan patted her knee. "I know, it's cute, that's one reason I love you." Theresa smiled back at her.

When they exited in San Juan Capistrano, Meagan thought they were going to Cedar Creek, one of her favorite restaurants. Instead they turned into the Coach House, a small venue for musical acts.

Katy turned around from her seat. "We know how much you like Chris Isaak and it just so happened he was playing today."

"Oh, my, God! You guys are fantastic!" Meagan beamed

inside and out.

Once inside they were directed to the center table, only four chairs from the stage. Meagan and Theresa sat across from Sarah and Katy. The main floor of the venue was made up of several long tables where everyone sat together. Private tables ran around the back of the club, but if you wanted a seat close to the stage, you shared a table with others.

They drank cocktails and chatted while they waited for their food.

"So, who's the opening act tonight?" Meagan asked.

Katy looked at the program, "The Ravens."

"Never heard of them," Meagan replied.

Once their food arrived, their mouths were busy, and silence ensued. Just as they finished eating, the lights dimmed.

"Ladies and Gentlemen, The Coach House is proud to present... The Ravens!"

The band descended the stairs to the right of the stage and the crowd gave halfhearted applause.

As if on cue, the girls turned their seats toward the stage. The band started with a slow song. The lead singer, who also played an acoustic steel string guitar, was standing front and center.

He was easy on the eyes with his well-trimmed dark beard, eyes that were framed by long black lashes, and height that towered over his band mates. His voice was low and sexy, and Meagan found her eyes riveted to his.

After they finished their first song, Sarah leaned across the table, and yelled to be heard over the applause.

"Meagan, he's singing to *you*."

"Don't be ridiculous. The guy's probably blinded by the stage lights. He's just staring in the direction of the crowd."

But by the end of the set, Meagan noticed that the guy did appear to be singing every song to her.

After the band left the stage, the lights came up. All at once the girls converged on Meagan, talking over one another.

"Did you see that?" Theresa asked.

"I swear he was staring at you the whole time," Sarah added.

"Meagan, he is *so* hot, I bet he asks you out," Katy chimed in.

"Come on you guys," Meagan said, embarrassed. "His girlfriend is probably sitting in the audience somewhere around us."

They fell into easy chatter while they waited for the stage to be set for the main act. Meagan scanned the room. Everyone was talking, drinking, and laughing. A woman walked by with a basket of roses.

"Does anyone ever buy flowers from those women?" Theresa asked.

"I had a guy buy me one on our first date once," Meagan replied. "It lasted a day, which was about as long as the relationship did. It was probably a sign." She laughed.

The lights came down once again, and Chris Isaak took the stage to loud applause. An hour and a half later, the girls were standing to leave.

"That was wonderful, you guys. Thank you so much for the best birthday ever." Meagan hugged her friends.

Just then the flower girl approached Meagan and extended a red rose with a note attached. Meagan accepted the rose with bewilderment. As she read the card, she laughed.

"Very funny, you guys. Who thought this one up?" Meagan stared directly at her friend, "Katy?"

"Not me, I swear." Katy said. "What does it say?"

The girls huddled around Meagan as she read the note.

"Meet me for a drink, I won't take no for an answer.

It's signed *Drew*. Who do you think this Drew is?" Meagan looked around the room.

"I bet it's the lead singer of The Ravens," Theresa answered.

"Oh, it's just like a Danielle Steel novel. He'll get rich and famous, and you'll get married and live happily ever after." Sarah said.

"Then he'll become an alcoholic and get killed one night driving home, taking an innocent child with him. And I'll live the rest of my life in shame. I think I've read that one." "Cynical," Katy said.

They made their way toward the exit. Meagan couldn't help herself from looking around to see if anyone was watching her. They walked out with the crowd to Sarah's SUV.

Meagan was just reaching out her hand to open the car's door, when someone suddenly touched her other arm. Startled, she spun around and came face to face with the lead singer of The Ravens.

"Are you Drew?" At the sound of Meagan's voice, the other women turned to look in her direction.

"You can't just walk out of my life. You're the most beautiful woman I've ever seen." His voice was soft and low.

The timbre made Meagan quiver, but she ignored it.

"Does that line work for you often?" Meagan didn't try to hide the disdain from her voice. "I'm sorry, but I'm not the groupie type. You might want to try that line on one of the younger girls. I'm sure you can find someone that would be more than willing to go home with you tonight."

Meagan turned her back on him.

"Wait." He gripped her arm. "You don't understand." Desperation tinged his voice. "That wasn't a line. Obviously you have no idea how incredible you are."

"Jeez, corny much? Can I have my arm back, please?" Meagan pulled away, and he released her.

Theresa spoke up. "Meagan, one drink won't hurt. We'll all go with you." She turned on Theresa with steely eyes.

"Yes, everyone come, I just want to get to know you," Drew pleaded.

Katy chimed in. "Come on, Meagan, it'll be fun. We'll go down to The Wind and Sea and have cocktails on the water."

"Yeah, we were planning on going there anyway. He can tag along," Sarah added.

Meagan felt cornered.

"Well, it looks like I'm outnumbered. Fine, you can follow us," she told Drew, making clear the resigned note in her voice.

"Great, I'll just get my car. It's parked around back." Turning to Sarah. "You'll wait for me?"

"Of course," Sarah answered reassuringly.

"Don't take too long," Meagan yelled.

The girls climbed into the SUV. As soon as the doors were closed, Theresa turned to Meagan. "Jesus, did you have to be so rough on the poor guy?"

"Believe me, he's not just some poor defenseless guy. He probably pulls this routine on a different woman after every show. Your problem is you trust too easily." Meagan pursed her lips.

"And your problem is you don't trust at all," said Theresa.

"I've met plenty of guys like him and they all have the same goal in mind. You wouldn't know, you've been dating women your whole life," Meagan said.

"Not my *whole* life, I was married once *too*, you know." Theresa said.

Katy turned around. "It's just one drink, then we'll go home."

The car was silent a moment, then Meagan said softly, "I'm sorry, I promise I'll behave. This night's been so great, I don't want it spoiled now."

"That's the spirit", Sarah said. "Now, here he comes."

He followed them in a white panel van to the Dana Point Harbor. Drew got out and crossed the parking lot. Theresa held back and struck up a conversation with him.

They walked through the bar and out onto the patio to sit

by the water. They ordered drinks, and he lit a cigarette.

Katy was the first to speak. "We really enjoyed your band. How long have you been together?"

"Well, the band's been together for ten years, but I've only been with them for three," Drew replied.

"Have you recorded any CDs?" Theresa asked.

"We recorded one on our own, but we haven't been picked up by a label yet. That's what this tour is all about. Before this, we played Los Angeles and next we hit San Diego."

"You're really good, I'm sure you'll have a contract soon. How old are you?" Sarah asked.

Meagan cringed at the obvious interrogation by her friends.

"I'm thirty-two, but I've been playing in bands about fifteen years. There were some record execs in the audience in L.A., but we haven't heard anything yet."

"How long have you been touring?" Meagan finally asked. Drew looked at her and smiled.

"On and off for about three years now. They were already booked to tour when their lead singer got sick. I was a friend of his and was only supposed to fill in until he got better. Unfortunately for him, the band decided to keep me. I was uncomfortable about it at first, but then I reasoned, that's showbiz."

"Where do you live?" Theresa chimed in.

"Right now hotels and motels, but my home is in Northern California."

Meagan was quiet as she listened to the conversation. The

alarm bells that had first chimed through her head had quieted down substantially. Drew didn't appear to be the egomaniac she'd thought; in fact, his personality was more shy and unassuming.

He wore faded jeans and a plaid flannel shirt. The casual look suited him. Now that he was so close, she could tell that the color of his eyes were hazel.

The one drink turned into many, and they ended up closing the bar. As they walked across the parking lot, Drew turned to Meagan, "Can I see you again?"

"I don't see the point, you're leaving."

"We're going to be here 'til Sunday. We're staying just down the street. Next we'll be in San Diego, that's not such a long drive. Please say you'll see me tomorrow. At least let me call you." His brows rose.

"That won't be necessary." Meagan answered and watched as disappointment crossed his face. "I'll meet you here tomorrow night at seven."

He smiled. "Great. You won't be sorry."

TWELVE

Meagan let herself in through her back door. Instantly Godzilla was all over her, and she scratched behind his ears. "I missed you too, boy." In the bedroom, she disrobed and wrapped her naked body up with her red silk kimono. After she washed her face and brushed her teeth, she closed the back door and returned to her room.

Expecting to see the dog waiting for her on the bed, she was surprised to find it empty. "Godzilla?" Meagan walked back out of the bedroom and checked the living room, then stuck her head out the back door.

"Godzilla!" she said in a whispered shout. "It's three o'clock in the morning!"

She spotted him as she rounded the corner of the house. He was at point, growling at the hedge dividing the property. The hairs on the back of her neck stood up, and she circled herself with her arms.

Meagan inched her way toward him. "Godzilla?" A twig snapped somewhere in the dark ahead. She snatched his collar with her right hand. "Come on, boy, there's probably a skunk in there ready to spray you this very minute." She tried to remain calm, but her voice was shaky.

The dog ignored her. A low growl continued at the back of his throat. Whatever Godzilla had cornered wasn't moving now. Meagan tugged on the collar, but he wouldn't budge. A loud bark made her jump, and she pulled at him harder. "Come on, you're going to wake the entire neighborhood."

She grabbed onto his collar with both hands. It took a few good tugs before she was able to get him to move. She kept a hand on him all the way into the house. He fought her the entire time as he tried to whip his head in the direction of the hedge.

Meagan yanked the dog into the house, slammed the door and locked it. She sank to her knees and hugged him close. She didn't know why she was letting herself get all worked up. It was probably just a possum.

***

The man remained hunched in the bushes, his knife tucked in close. Sweat trickled down his face and back, even though the night air was cool. He'd just reached out to grab the fucking dog when *she* rounded the corner. The stupid animal had no idea how close it was to becoming fish food.

She spoke to the beast as if it were fucking human. He hated animals, had no use for them. When she advanced toward him, he jerked back into the shadows and heard that damn snap. She heard it too. He saw the fear in her eyes. It made him hard. She was so close he could smell her pussy.

That robe she wore barely covered her rust-colored mound, and when she moved he caught a glimpse. The cold air made her nipples hard, and they strained against the silky fabric. Fuck. The pain in his groin grew unbearable. He wanted her so bad, he could taste it. Taste her. That motherfucking dog had to go.

He'd been ready to pounce when she pulled the dog away. Two more seconds. Just two more fucking seconds, and the dog would've been dead, and he'd have her all to himself.

He wanted to savor every minute with her. She was special, a thoroughbred. He would make her his own.

He would be back.

THIRTEEN

The next night Thomas arrived at Malone's house around five. The invitations for dinner came often, but he usually declined. Malone's wife, Gail, had a tendency to try and fix him up with all her friends. Either she'd run out of friends, or she'd finally given up, because tonight she promised he would be the only guest. He was more than happy, to say the least. Gail was an excellent cook, and it had been too long since he'd had one of her meals.

Malone had two kids, five-year-old Mandy and Danny, who turned eight today.

Before he knew it the door burst open and Danny rushed out. "Uncle J.J., I missed you!"

Thomas set his package down and squatted to give the boy a hug. "It's great to see you too, Sport." He handed Danny his gift.

Danny ripped off the wrapping paper and squealed. "Thanks, Uncle J.J., you're the best!" He disappeared into the house with his prize.

"Happy Birthday!" Thomas called after him.

Gail walked out from the kitchen drying her hands on a dishtowel. "What did you do, J.J., get him another video game? We can't drag him away from that damn machine as it is. You do know that's considered contributing to the delinquency of a minor. I'm going to have to have my husband arrest you."

She stood up on her tiptoes and kissed him on the cheek. "Glad you could make it, come on in. I'll have John fix you a drink. I'm just finishing up with the salad."

"Smells great," Thomas had just stepped into the house when Malone appeared from the back.

"Hey, get your ass in here and close the door, you're letting all the flies in." He slapped Thomas on the shoulder. "It's good to see you. You want a scotch or beer?"

"Beer, thanks." Malone disappeared into the kitchen, then Thomas heard his booming voice, "It's Corona, you want a lime with that?"

"Yeah, that'd be great," Thomas yelled back, wandering into the living room where Danny was busy playing his new game.

"Hey, Sport, where's your sister?"

"In her room playing dolls, or something stupid like that." Danny concentrated on the screen.

Thomas laughed.

Malone entered carrying two bottles with lime wedges stuck in the tops. "Come on, let's go out back while Gail finishes up with dinner."

Thomas snagged the offered beer and followed his friend

out the sliding glass door to the covered patio. They sat in a couple of rattan chairs that faced the yard. Malone set his beer on the glass table between them and took out a cigarette.

"Want one?" Malone absent-mindedly offered the pack.

"No, thanks. Trying to quit." Thomas had never smoked.

"Shit, what was I thinking? Misery loves company, I guess." Malone lit up and took a long drag, then blew out the smoke. "I think I've quit about a dozen times." He turned to Thomas. "How you holding up?"

"I'm fine, but Harris thinks I should see a shrink." Thomas focused on the swing set straight ahead on the grass.

Malone was silent a moment. "Might not be a bad idea."

Thomas jerked his head in his friend's direction. "I'm not some fucking nut case."

"Whoa." Malone put his hands up in front of him. "I'm just saying, it's gotta be rough, man. I don't know *what* I'd do if I lost Gail. Especially the way Victoria died. I don't think I'd ever recover."

"I don't let my personal life affect my job. If anything, I'm a hell of a lot better detective," Thomas said through gritted teeth. "No distractions, I work twenty-four-seven, and I have the highest arrest rate in the department." He ran a hand through his hair and looked back at the yard.

"That's what I'm saying, buddy. It's time you got a life."

"It's time for dinner." Gail stood at the open screen.

***

After dinner, Thomas excused himself to go out to his car. He met up with Malone on the back patio, a lit cigarette already in his hand and two fresh bottles of beer on the table. He took a seat with the VICAP file in his lap.

"I wanted to get your input on the Sandman case."

"I've seen the photos. This guy's a real piece of work."

Thomas read the four previous cases for him, handing him the crime scene photos as he went. Then he summarized the information on his own victims.

Malone scratched his chin. "Yup, you've got a serial killer on your hands."

"I was thinking of asking Harris if I could have you help me with this case. You willing?"

"Sure, if you can get him to go for it."

"Thanks, buddy. I was looking at the first one, the girl in San Francisco?"

Malone nodded.

"I'm certain it's the same guy, I feel it in my gut. Maybe her death was an accident. It's crude, sloppy. When he realizes she's dead, he panics and takes off. There are marks around her neck as if he strangled her, but she died by blunt force trauma to the back of the head."

"Okay." Malone ground out his cigarette, turned toward Thomas and gave him his full attention.

"Picture this. The guy's on top of her, raping her, he has his hands around her throat. She's screaming, and he's knocking her head against the ground."

"Or a rock," Malone interjected.

"Right, or a rock. He's yelling at her to shut up all the while throttling her neck and slamming her up and down. Finally she shuts up, permanently." Thomas raised his beer to his lips.

"Makes sense." Malone sat up straighter. "That's why the long break between victims. At first he's in shock, scared he'll be caught. Then when that doesn't happen, he realizes he liked it, wants to recreate the thrill."

"Exactly. He could have been raping women all along, just not killing them. Most rapes go unreported. It could have been going on for years, there's no way to know. He's smart, he moves around a lot." Thomas rubbed his hands up and down on his jeans.

"So during the time between the two murders, he's actually busy raping women, except there's no way to tie the two together?" Malone asked.

"That's what I'm thinking. The problem is, rape alone isn't getting him off anymore, so he ups the ante, decides to make the women submissive. He finds a place where he can stash them, then he has his own personal sex slave. But even that gets old or doesn't work anymore."

"The girl with the crushed hyoid bone. He's not able to achieve orgasm anymore, so he tightens his grip on her throat and gets the reaction he's looking for in her eyes, which gives him the ultimate release. But the end result is death," Malone said.

"Now he knows what he needs, so the next time he goes searching for a woman it's with the *intent* to kill," Thomas added.

"Maybe he buries them in shallow graves to intensify the excitement. He knows his victims will be discovered sooner rather than later and he's eager to see his work on the news," Malone suggested.

"Either that or he's just in a hurry. He's taking a big risk carrying these bodies from his vehicle all the way to the beach. I wonder why he feels he has to bury them in sand? It would be a lot smarter to bury them along a deserted road, or in the woods." Thomas tipped back his beer.

Malone lit another cigarette. "Maybe the beach holds some significance for this psycho."

"He may be a psycho, but he's also a smart son of a bitch. Spreading his victims between different jurisdictions is why it's taken so long for anyone to notice what he's been up to." Thomas put the empty bottle down.

"The old sleight-of-hand trick: while you're looking over there, I'll be over here."

"He also knows better than to cross state lines. That would make the case FBI and everyone knows they have the most experience with serial killers."

"Well, he's made a mistake now. If you hadn't stumbled upon that second vic, you wouldn't have looked for more."

Malone pointed to Thomas's empty bottle. "You want another?"

Thomas shook his head. "True, which shows he's getting sloppy. There's more of a chance he'll make another slip-up, and we'll catch this motherfucker. Imagine how long this could have gone on?"

"And this guy's escalating, only two months between his last two kills. He could have another woman now, or at least be searching for one even as we speak."

"This guy's into some scary shit. His methods of torture so far are pretty grisly, I'd hate to see what happens when this fucker totally loses it." Thomas scrubbed his hands down his face.

"Yeah, me too. So what's your plan?" Malone finished his beer.

"I'm going to get Harris up to speed and ask to bring you aboard. Then I'm going to put out a statewide BOLO on similar murders. That way the entire state will be on the lookout, and I'll be notified immediately if this guy kills again in another jurisdiction. I've already faxed the files to my brother, Wyatt. I'm just waiting for him to get back to me."

"Is Wyatt the one who's the forensic psychologist?"

"Yeah, I want to get his take on this guy."

"Are you going to call Cody?"

"Maybe, in an unofficial capacity, I haven't decided. I do know I'm not ready to bring in the FBI yet."

"Well, you've got a lot of help in your family alone. Must be nice to come from a family of law enforcement."

"Sometimes."

FOURTEEN

That same night, Meagan pulled into the parking lot of the Wind & Sea at exactly seven o'clock. Out of the corner of her eye she caught a glimpse of someone coming toward her. Drew approached with a large bouquet of white roses mixed with delicate lavender baby's breath. He helped her out of the car, kissed her on the cheek, then presented her with the flowers.

"You look ravishing," he said with a sigh.

"Thank you, these are lovely, but you shouldn't have."

"Come with me." He led her to a black Rolls Royce parked nearby.

"Where did you get this, is it stolen?" she laughed.

He smiled. "Borrowed."

Meagan ran her hand along the soft leather seat and waited for Drew to get in the car. The moment he was settled, she asked, "Where are we going?"

He smiled at her. "Somewhere special, Theresa told me it was your birthday."

"Blabbermouth, I knew I couldn't trust her." She rolled her eyes. "Did she also tell you how old I am?"

"Thirty-five." He took the flowers from her and set them on the back seat.

"Jeez, is nothing sacred? So you don't mind dating an older woman?"

"Well, I know three years is a long time in a dog's life, but with humans I think it's all right." He started the car.

She smiled and stared out the front window. "Good to know."

They didn't speak as they drove up the coast. Instead he put in a Depeche Mode CD. Meagan laid her head back against the headrest and let the synthesized music lull her as she took in the beautiful night. There was not a cloud in sight. As they passed Laguna Beach, away from the city lights, the sky opened up, brilliant with stars. The full moon reflected on the surface of the ocean.

She could see the white caps of the waves and got lost in their slow steady rhythm as they caressed the shore. The windows were slightly ajar so she could feel the cool ocean breeze on her face and smell its wonderful fragrance. She inhaled deeply and felt such peace.

And to think she'd wanted to cancel this date. It had worried Meagan all day. What stopped her was the fact she didn't know how to reach Drew. She couldn't just not show up; that would be just plain rude. Now she was glad it wasn't an option.

Too soon she noticed the lights of the town up ahead;

disappointment set in at the sight of civilization. The car idled at a signal in Corona Del Mar. Meagan lazily viewed the familiar surroundings, only mildly curious as to their final destination.

On her left stood an antique phone booth in bright red, obviously imported from London. Behind that was the ivy-covered English Tudor which happened to be her favorite restaurant, The Five Crowns. Meagan stared as they pulled up to the valet.

"How did you know?" Meagan gasped. "No, let me guess, Theresa." Drew nodded. "So that's what you guys were whispering about."

"I was pumping her for information. She was quite forthcoming."

"I'll bet. What else did she tell you?" Anger and worry warred with one another in Meagan's head.

"Uh-Uh, that's our little secret." His eyes twinkled, and a sly grin creased his lips.

Meagan suddenly tensed. The valet opened her door, and she let him help her out of the car. They walked to the restaurant in silence. Drew opened the door. "I'm sorry, I shouldn't tease you like that. She didn't say anything else, I promise. After she told me that yesterday was your birthday, I simply asked about your favorite restaurant, honestly."

She relaxed a little, but not much. Theresa's mouth always ran faster than her brain, especially if she'd been drinking. Like a child, she didn't know boundaries. She had a good heart; she just didn't know any better.

Once they were seated, Drew ordered a bottle of their best champagne.

"I don't mean to be uncouth, but as a struggling musician, how is it you can afford all this?"

"I've made some good investments."

She nodded and looked at the menu.

They talked and laughed for hours. Meagan told him about her sisters. And her parents, who were still madly in love after forty-five years.

Drew told her he'd always wanted a family like hers, but grew up an only child. His plans for the future included growing old with lots of children and grandchildren around him. He'd moved around a lot as a child, as his father was career Navy. His parents died a few years back in a car accident, he said.

The night went quickly and soon she found herself back at her car at The Wind & Sea. Drew parked the Rolls, then turned to her. "I had a great time."

"Thanks, me too."

"Can I see you tomorrow?"

"I'm sorry, but I'm going down to my parents' house in San Diego to celebrate my birthday with my family."

"How about the next night?" Drew asked almost shyly.

"I'd like that, but seriously, where do you think this relationship can go? You live in Northern California, and I have a life here. Oh, yeah, and your band is in the middle of a tour."

"The tour is almost over, and I can rent a place down here

and commute when the band needs to practice."

"Be serious."

"Look, I'll figure something out."

He got out of the car and walked around to open Meagan's door. He offered her his hand, when she placed her hand in his, she noticed how small it looked compared to his. He pulled her up and they stood face to face. His eyes were heavy-lidded and spoke of desire. She was certain he would kiss her. Instead, he reached down and grabbed her other hand, then brought them both to his lips and kissed them.

"Thanks again for a great night," Drew almost whispered. He led her back to her car. "Good night." He closed her door and waited for her to drive away before he returned to the Rolls.

Later Meagan lay in her bed, thinking about her date. She had a great time. Drew wasn't anything like she had imagined.

FIFTEEN

The piercing shrill of the phone jolted Meagan from a deep slumber. She snatched it quickly. "Hello." Silence answered her. "Hello!"

Godzilla stared at her. She slammed down the phone. "Dammit, Brad, leave me alone!" She patted the dog on the head. "I'm sorry, boy, some people need to get a life."

She lay back down, but her heart still raced. Twice this week her sleep had been interrupted by the stupid phone. She jumped out of bed and unplugged it.

***

Later that night, the man grew frustrated as he worked to catch the lock on the window above the back door. He only needed to raise the pane a few inches to reach his hand inside and unlock the door. Soundlessly he guided the metal strip up underneath the lock, but the latch was stubborn. Old and rusted, it obviously hadn't been opened in a good long while.

Sweat creased his brow; his fingers were getting slippery. Finally the latch moved a bit, then the tool slithered from his hand and dropped to the concrete below. The thunderous noise ripped through the otherwise tranquil night. He stood still, held his breath, and waited to see a light flick on inside the house.

***

For the second time that night Meagan had been jolted from a deep REM state. Confused, she listened to her surroundings. It didn't take long for her to zero in on the sound. At the end of the bed, tensely staring at the closed bedroom door, Godzilla emitted a deep throaty growl. Adrenaline coursed through Meagan's body. She glanced at the clock. It was just after three.

"What is it, boy?" she whispered.

The dog leapt off the bed and trotted to the door, his deep rumble growing louder.

The hairs on the back of Meagan's neck stood up. She slid out of bed and eased into her kimono, cinching the belt tight. Tiptoeing to the door, she put her ear to it. Godzilla let out an ear-piercing bark. Meagan jumped back, startled, and her hand flew to her chest. She took a couple of deep breaths, then opened the bedroom door a crack to peek out.

Godzilla pushed her aside and ran to the back door. Meagan had to grab the wall to keep from falling down. His barks grew incessant as he scratched at the door. Meagan followed. Without turning on the porch light, she pulled the curtain aside slightly and peered out.

The yard was easily visible by the light of the full moon. Nothing seemed out of place. She inspected the top of the fence for a possum or cat; none were in sight. Not that she really thought a stray animal would make her dog go ballistic.

Godzilla jumped at the door and continued to bark.

Shrouded in dark, Meagan made her way into the bedroom and grabbed the mallet. Weapon in hand, she joined Godzilla at the back door. She peeked out once more before turning the locks. Then she flung the door wide. The screen had barely opened when the dog flew past and raced out into the night. Meagan took off after him.

When she finally caught up, Godzilla was halfway down the street sniffing at some bushes. He seemed frustrated. Frantically he paced back and forth along the thick copse of vegetation. She couldn't see or hear a thing and cursed herself for not grabbing a flashlight before scrambling out the door.

The dog continued to whine and pace.

Afraid of being caught in a stranger's yard in the middle of the night, wearing next to nothing, Meagan began to plead with the dog. "Come on, boy, whatever it was you scared it good."

The dog ignored her pointing stiffly into the darkness.

She patted his head. "Come on, you did your job. The

neighborhood's safe now."

Steadily Meagan's unease grew. She had never seen Godzilla act this way. The dog stood with his tail down, his entire body shook as he growled. Meagan had no idea how long she'd been trying to coax the dog away, but she'd had enough. She was cold and tired.

She reached down, grabbed the dog by the collar and proceeded to drag him back up the street. It was quite a struggle up the small incline, the dog's heavy body resisting the entire way.

By the time they made it back to the house, Meagan was exhausted and out of breath. Sweat dripped down her neck and back. Her nose and cheeks were numb from the cold night air. Just as they rounded the corner, the back door came into view. Meagan stopped. A shiver ran down her spine, she held her breath.

The door stood wide open.

Normally she wasn't the paranoid type, but her otherwise mild-mannered dog was acting peculiar. Gathering her nerve, she eased the screen open and crept in. She clutched the mallet tightly, holding it high above her head.

She flicked the switch and the kitchen was bathed in light. Silently she inched her way toward the living room and peered around the edge of the divider. The room was empty. She turned on her heels and stood in the doorway to the bathroom, which was illuminated solely by a nightlight.

She stared at the closed shower curtain.

Her heart raced, and her breath came in shallow pants.

Club held high, she reached out and clutched the edge of the curtain. In one fell swoop she swung it back and let out a big gasp. The tub was empty. Her relief was fleeting once she realized there was one more place to search. The bedroom.

Spinning back around, Meagan tiptoed toward her room, where the darkness yawned before her. She reached her hand around the wall and fumbled for the switch. Instantly light flooded the room, she quickly scanned the interior, and breathed a sigh of relief. She slid open the closet door even though she knew there was no room for someone to hide; her clothes were crammed in there pretty tight. Half-heartedly she peeked under her bed, not that a grown man could really fit under there either. She collapsed on the side of the bed and sighed before she shoved the mallet back under the covers.

Godzilla, calmer now, stood next to her looking up. Meagan stared back at the dog a moment, then scratched his head. She went over to the dresser and pulled out a pair of old boxer shorts and a tank top. She didn't know what was going on, but if anything else happened that night she didn't want to be caught naked. She climbed in the bed, pulled the covers up under her chin, and stared wide-eyed at the bedroom door.

SIXTEEN

First thing Monday, Thomas went straight to Captain Harris's office with the information he had compiled. He tossed the file on Harris's desk. "Check this out. My hunch was right. We do have a serial killer on our hands." Thomas dropped down in one of the two chairs opposite the captain.

Harris opened the file and thumbed through it. Silence fell as he skimmed the pages before him. "Shit, I was afraid of this."

"I'm going to need a task force, and I'd like to bring Malone on board as my partner."

The captain's brows creased. "You know I can't spare too many uniforms because of the cutbacks."

"Then, give me what you can. This is too big for me to work alone."

"I know." The captain rubbed his chin. "All right, take James and Cooper. They already know the case."

"Fine, and Malone?"

"Malone's caseload is too heavy. If I give him to you, I'd

have to reassign all his cases. We're already shorthanded with you out of the rotation. I need your full focus on this one. I'll distribute your open cases among the other detectives. That means everyone will be carrying about all they can handle."

Harris put his head in his hands and rubbed his temples. A moment later he looked up. "Okay, I haven't received the paperwork on Shadowhawk yet, but we need her now. She had the highest score on the detective's exam and has a good eye for detail. I'd already decided she'd ride along with you and learn the ropes. I'll just bump up the timeline a bit."

"Do you think she can handle it? I mean, being a woman and all." Thomas was concerned by the viciousness of the case. Hell, he was having a hard time with the images himself.

"Don't let the fact that she's a woman fool you. She's got balls of steel, that one." The captain pushed a button on his phone. "Gladys, call dispatch and pull James and Cooper off the street. I want to see them. Then get Shadowhawk in my office."

"Yes, sir."

Turning back to Thomas, Harris said, "I'll have James and Coop check in with you once I've talked to them. Take these three for now and see how it goes. If things heat up, I'll see who else I can scare up for you. But I'm not making any promises."

"It's not like I'm asking for a kidney, for Christ's sake."

"Actually, with the budget in the state that it's in, you'd

probably have better luck if you were."

There was a knock on the open door.

"You wanted to see me, sir?"

Thomas turned around to see an interesting-looking woman walk in. She stood right behind him, ignoring him completely.

Fawn Shadowhawk Quinn was a Native American in her late twenties. She stood around five-foot-seven or eight, and weighed roughly one hundred and thirty-five to one hundred and forty-five pounds with broad shoulders for a woman. Her jet-black hair was pulled back into a tight French braid that reached the middle of her back. Rumor had it that she went by her middle name to honor her great-grandfather, a renowned medicine man.

Shadowhawk wore no makeup. Her jewelry was minimal, a watch and a silver band on her left hand. Her light brown eyes were large and framed with naturally long black lashes. They reminded Thomas of a pair of doe eyes.

Her stance and gait were rather masculine, but when she opened her mouth, a high melodic voice came out. It was such a contrast that he knew it was something he'd have to get used to.

"Yes. I want you to work the Sandman case with Thomas here. It will take me a few days to get you your detective's shield, but I'll put in for that as well as a rush on the paperwork for your promotion. Your raise, such as it is, will probably take a few weeks to catch up, but it will be prorated," Harris said.

"Thank you, Captain." She turned to Thomas for the first time. "Your reputation precedes you, sir."

"Don't believe everything you hear, I started most of those rumors myself." Thomas smiled.

Early that evening, Thomas ate a roast beef sandwich at his desk when he received the phone call he had been waiting for. They had a positive ID on his Jane Doe. Her name was Caroline Bernard. She had resided in Temecula with her husband and two children. The ID came from the husband, Jack. Thomas told the morgue to let him go. He'd grab Shadowhawk and drive down to Temecula in the morning. He thought he'd give the guy a break tonight. Besides, he wanted to get a look at the victim's surroundings. See if anything popped.

SEVENTEEN

Meagan dragged herself through the door and dropped her purse on the kitchen counter. She was so tired she couldn't carry it another foot. Her lack of sleep from the night before made her busy day especially hard. She wandered into the living room toward the flashing red light on the answering machine. There was a call from Katy, one from her mother. And the last was Drew saying he'd call her later.

She turned away feeling a little giddy, then stopped.

Wait, how did he get my home number?

The phone rang, she turned back around and stared at it a moment. What if it were Drew? Should she grill him on how he got her number? Maybe she'd just bring it up like it was no big deal. It was on its third ring when she snatched it up.

"Hello?" There was no answer. "Hello!" She waited a beat and listened to dead air. "Okay, you're busted. The police put a trap on my line. How are you going to explain that to your wife, Brad?" There was a click in her ear. Meagan smiled.

"Gotcha!"

She carried the phone with her to the bedroom while she changed. Then she called her mother, who was just checking in. She returned Katy's call while she made herself a salad. She told Katy about the recent calls and she agreed with Meagan that it probably was Brad. But then she mentioned someone Meagan hadn't thought of. Jerome.

"Do you really think he'd start hassling me at home?"

"I wouldn't put it past him. He's an asshole with a capital A. A guy like that can't imagine a woman telling him no. You've rebuffed his advances on many occasions. This way there's no way to prove it's him, so you can't file charges."

"That's true, but... I don't know."

"You should get caller ID."

"Do you really think it would help?"

"Hell, yes! Then you'll have him dead to rights."

"Okay, I'll call the phone company tomorrow and have them turn it on."

"Good. Crap, I've got to go. I can hear the boys fighting in the other room. I guess I *should* stop them before they kill each other. Call me tomorrow and let me know how it goes."

Meagan grabbed her salad and a glass of milk before heading into the living room to see what movies were on cable. As she tried to focus on the TV Guide, her mind kept wandering back to her conversation with Katy. Could Jerome really be her crank caller?

An hour later, the phone rang. Meagan muted the volume on the TV, then looked around for the phone. Evidently she'd forgotten it in the kitchen. By the fourth ring, she'd snatched it off the counter. "Hello?"

Silence.

"Jerome, is that you?" The phone went dead.

"Dammit. This is getting old fast." The phone rang immediately. She clicked it on. "Get a life!"

"Did I call at a bad time?" Drew's voice was hesitant.

"Sorry, just some kids with too much time on their hands. Is your ear okay?"

"Don't worry about it. I have another one."

Meagan cringed and changed the subject. "Are you in San Diego?"

"Yeah, we got down here last night. Today we unloaded the equipment and did our sound check. The gig starts tomorrow night. Do you wanna come?"

"Sorry, I can't. I've got plans with a friend from work." She and Lilah went to Taco Tuesday every week for dollar tacos and half-off Margaritas.

There was a moment of silence before Drew said, "Bring him along. I'd like to check out my competition. What's his name? I'll put the two of you on the guest list."

"Lilah." Meagan laughed. "Let me talk to her, and I'll call you back tomorrow. What's your number?"

"You won't be able to reach me, I'm going to be in and out. Why don't I just call you?"

"Okay. That reminds me, how'd you get my home number?"

There was a brief pause. "You gave it to me Saturday night, don't you remember?"

"Actually, I gave you the salon number." She never gave out her home number to men anymore.

Silence again.

"All right, I confess. Theresa gave it to me. I was afraid to tell you because I didn't want you to be angry with her. You can't tell her I told you. She made me promise."

"Well that figures."

They ended up talking for a couple of hours. She loved all his stories of life on the road; he was really quite funny. Meagan hung up and found herself humming while she got ready for bed. Suddenly she stopped. It just occurred to her: Would Theresa, with all her faults, really give Meagan's home number to a complete stranger?

EIGHTEEN

With Shadowhawk riding shotgun, Thomas drove the two-hour trip to Temecula, where the Bernards lived. Shadowhawk had studied the file the day before, and they discussed the case. He answered her questions the best he could, and was impressed with his new partner's intellect and insight.

The Bernard's street was a model of suburbia. The track homes with their meticulously manicured lawns could have been Anytown, California. Thomas was having a bad case of déjà vu, like he'd driven down this same street countless times before.

Shadowhawk pointed out the address, and they pulled up in front of a professionally landscaped house with numerous palm trees. Each, placed strategically around the lawn, had a ring of brightly colored flowers around the base, and raised flowerbeds rimmed the circumference. The house itself was a beige two-story Mediterranean with a beige tiled roof. An overturned bicycle lay in the driveway.

As the detectives walked up the front pathway leading to the door, Thomas realized he was not looking forward to this. There was nothing easy about talking to a man who had just lost his wife in such a brutal manner. His mind flashed back to Victoria.

He mentally shook his head, and rang the doorbell. A little blonde girl of about three answered. She had ringlets all over her head and big bright eyes.

"Hi, I'm Kylie! What's your name?" came the perky little voice. Just then a man appeared behind her and put a hand on her shoulder.

"Kylie, what have I told you about answering the door? Now go to your room and watch videos while I talk with my guests." Kylie's smile faded as she turned and did what she was told.

Thomas looked at the shell of a broken man. His bloodshot eyes were swollen, his pallor almost gray. He was in his mid-forties, but today could easily pass for sixty.

"Good morning, Mr. Bernard. My name is Detective Thomas, and this is Detective Shadowhawk." He flashed his ID. "We have a few questions we'd like to ask you. We'll make it as brief as possible."

Jack Bernard moved aside and motioned for them to come in.

"Let's go into the living room where we won't be disturbed. My son Brian is in his room. He hasn't been out since I told him about his mother last night. He's ten. Kylie's too little to understand. Hell, *I* don't even understand." He choked back a sob.

He swiped at a tear that had slipped down his cheek and cleared his throat. "I'm sorry, please sit down. Can I get you some coffee?"

"No, thank you," they said almost in unison.

Mr. Bernard dropped in a chair as if his legs could no longer carry him. Thomas faced him on the couch, and Shadowhawk joined him a moment later. Thomas took out a notebook and pen.

Thomas focused his thoughts, then began. "First, Mr. Bernard, we're sorry for your loss. I know this is very difficult for you, but these questions are important to the investigation."

"I understand. I'll do anything I can to help. And please call me Jack."

"Okay, Jack, when was the last time you saw your wife?"

"It was the morning of her disappearance. Uh, ten days ago, or has it been two weeks now? I don't know, everything seems to be a blur."

"I understand." Thomas looked down. It was hard to stare at the guy, his eyes were filled with unshed tears. Reluctantly he glanced back up. "Did she work?"

"No, I mean, yes. She is, or was, a housewife."

"Do you know what her plans were that day?" Thomas asked.

"She, uh...she dropped Kylie off down the street to play with a friend, and then drove Brian to school. She was going to run errands. You know, the grocery store, stuff like that,"

Jack said with some effort.

Thomas made some notes before he continued. "They found her car parked at a restaurant called The Hunter right off I-5 in Oceanside. Was she meeting a friend?"

"No, I mean, I don't know. I don't understand what Caroline would have been doing in Oceanside. That's a good forty-five minutes from here. We've never been to that restaurant. How would she know it? She usually met her friend Annie at the Soup Plantation here in town. Her time was limited. I can't see her driving that far."

Thomas was aware of the sound of Shadowhawk's pen as she scribbled notes.

"Did she tell you of anything peculiar happening on the days prior to her disappearance? Strange phone calls, someone following her, maybe a man approaching her?" Thomas asked.

"Not that I recall." Jack rubbed his eyes with the palms of his hands.

"Did she have any enemies?"

"No." Jack answered bluntly. "Everyone loved her, she was the most beautiful person you would ever want to meet. She was a great mother, and wonderful wife. I don't know how I'm going to make it without her." He covered his face with trembling hands.

Thomas shoved his pad and pen into his jacket pocket, and stood. "Well, that's all I can think of for now, unless you have anything?" He looked at Shadowhawk, who shook her head.

"Then, I want to thank you for seeing us. If I have any further questions, I'll call, but in the meantime..." Thomas reached into his pocket for a card. "Please call me if you think of anything else, no matter how trivial it may seem to you."

Taking the card, Jack rose and followed the detectives out.

Thomas stopped at the door, "By the way, do you have a recent photo of your wife?" Jack disappeared for a few minutes. When he reappeared, he handed Thomas a photo of a woman on a sailboat caught in mid-laugh, eyes sparkling.

"Thank you," Thomas said. "Again, I'm sorry for your loss."

"Just get the bastard." Jack shut the door with a soft click.

On their way back to Interstate 5, Thomas remained on the 78 freeway and crossed over I-5 to The Hunter restaurant where Caroline's car had been found. Armed with the photograph, the detectives went inside and asked all the employees if any of them had recognized the woman.

No one seemed to know her, but one of the servers did remember a navy SUV parked in the parking lot when she came to work the day Caroline had vanished. She explained the restaurant didn't open before five, so it was the only car in the parking lot when she arrived at work around four-thirty. The vehicle was still there that night after the restaurant closed.

As Thomas and Shadowhawk drove back up the coast, they discussed the case. Was this guy picking his victims at random, or did he select a woman and follow her, get to know her routine? Maybe he spent his days cruising up and down the interstate? They surmised her vehicle had been dumped at the restaurant. Did he have a partner?

What did this guy do for a living? Salesman? Drive a semi or tow truck? Where did he take his victims in between? They hashed out numerous possibilities on their way back to the station.

NINETEEN

Meagan and Lilah left the salon around five o'clock Tuesday and drove to Meagan's house to change since it was on the way. Lilah was up to date on everything Meagan knew about Drew; she'd been keeping her friend informed since the day she'd met him.

"Oh, my, God, this is so awesome! I can't wait to meet this guy. Is he really hot? Of course he is. He's in a band, for goodness sake. And he picked *you* out of the crowd. Of course he picked you, you're gorgeous. It's just so romantic, I can't stand it!"

Lilah chatted nonstop the entire way to San Diego. Meagan couldn't help but smile at her friend's enthusiasm.

They were waiting in the ticket line when Meagan surveyed the crowd. "Maybe we should have gotten here sooner," she told Lilah. "Once we get our tickets, we'll still have to get in that other line to go in and it wraps around the entire building. I'm afraid we won't be able to get a seat."

They inched their way forward for another thirty minutes

before they found themselves in front of the ticket window where Meagan gave the girl their names. She flipped through several sheets on a clipboard before she stopped and asked to see their identification. After studying each driver's license, she crossed out their names and left the window. Meagan and Lilah glanced at one another. A moment later the girl reappeared and told them to go to the door; a guy named Bruce would meet them.

Once inside, Bruce, who resembled a body builder, led them to a table in front of the stage. After they took their seats, he handed them each a menu.

"Order anything you wish, your bill has been taken care of. I'll send your server right over."

After he'd left, Meagan leaned across the table. "I had no idea we'd get the VIP treatment." She glanced around the room; only a few scattered tables were occupied. "The paying customers haven't even been let in yet."

"This is so exciting! A free dinner, too! I can't wait to get a load of your new hunk." Lilah's eyes sparkled.

"Whoa, he's not my hunk. We've only been out on one date." Meagan looked down at the menu.

"Maybe, but he's obviously taken with you, or he wouldn't have rolled out the red carpet."

Meagan looked at her friend over the top of the menu. "Ya think?"

"Are you kidding me? How many struggling artists do you know who would be willing to pay the bill for a woman *and* her friend? Strike that. How many men do you know *period* who'd be willing do that?"

"True." Meagan let Lilah's words sink in while she decided between the teriyaki chicken and the grilled halibut.

They ordered their dinners as the crowd wandered in and filled the seats around them. The waiter had just left when Drew appeared. He bent over Meagan, kissed her lightly on the lips, and claimed the chair next to her. "I'm glad you could make it. Are they treating you okay?"

"Everything's great, thank you." Meagan beamed at Drew. In black from head to toe, he looked like Johnny Cash. His long-sleeved shirt buttoned up the front, and his black jeans and belt matched his black snakeskin cowboy boots. He was, indeed, hot. She felt herself blush.

She wondered if her feelings could be influenced by the attention he was lavishing on her. "This is the friend I told you about." Meagan smiled, remembering how he thought she would be bringing some guy she was dating.

Drew's eyes came to rest on hers, and he smiled as if reading her mind, then he turned his attention to Lilah. He extended his hand across the table to shake hers.

"It's nice to meet you, glad you could come."

"Thank you for including me. I'm looking forward to seeing you perform."

Drew's smile widened. "Hope you're not disappointed." He stood, and glanced down at Meagan. "I've got to get to work. I'll come by for you after we've finished, then we'll see what San Diego has to offer." He lifted her chin and kissed her lips as delicately as before, then disappeared.

Meagan's heart leapt.

Lilah pressed her hands down on the table and leaned forward. "On a scale of one to ten, he's an eleven, and he obviously adores you. You'd better go for it in a big way, or I'll kill you!"

Meagan laughed. Lilah was right. The guy *was* definitely attentive.

A few minutes later, the lights dimmed and the girls turned toward the stage. Their table was literally at his feet. Drew smiled down at Meagan as he sang the first song, his eyes, once again, riveted on her. Occasionally, he averted his gaze, but only briefly, before his focus returned to her and stayed.

Meagan was embarrassed by the attention. She glanced around the room and noticed the angry stares she was getting from other women. She tried to ignore them, and just enjoy the show, but she had to admit it was distracting.

Once the band left the stage, the house lights came up.

"Wow, he's got it bad for you." Lilah grinned at Meagan.

"Stop it." Meagan blushed.

"They were really good. I'm going to go buy their CD." Lilah took off toward the entrance.

She made it back by the time Drew arrived at their table.

"Sorry to keep you ladies waiting. I had to change. It gets rather warm up there under those lights."

Meagan gave Drew the once-over. He looked like he was wearing the same clothes. "What'd you change, your socks?"

Drew laughed. "I ripped a shirt one night when I was

setting up some equipment. I had to borrow one from one of the guys. It was a bit tight, so now I keep an extra set of clothes handy. Come on, ladies, your chariot awaits." Drew led them out the back door of the club to a black limousine.

Meagan raised her brows. "What's this?"

"I don't know the area and could only assume that you didn't either, so I thought I'd hire an expert." Drew opened the door and let the ladies pile in before he joined them.

Once everyone was situated, he grabbed a bottle of champagne from a nearby ice bucket and opened it while he addressed the driver. "So, where are you taking us, Ben?"

The limo driver's eyes appeared in the rearview mirror. "I thought I would take you downtown to the Gas Lamp District where you could have your pick of places to eat, drink and dance."

"Sounds great, lead on." Drew poured the champagne into three flutes and passed them around. He raised his glass.

"I would like to propose a toast. Thank you for gracing me with your presence. I'm lucky to have not one, but two lovely ladies at my side this evening." Drew raised his glass.

"The pleasure is all ours." Meagan raised her glass. "Ditto!" Lilah raised her glass.

They all clinked before taking a sip.

The evening sped past at warp speed. Meagan didn't want it to end, but she had to work the next day. Luckily, she'd danced more than she drank, so driving would not be a problem. Drew was a gracious host. He danced with Lilah almost as much as he danced with her. Not that her friend needed to be occupied. She had more than her share of men vying for her attention.

They were sitting at a table in Johnny Loves when Meagan took off one of her high heels and started rubbing her foot absently. Drew surprised her when he grabbed it with both hands and pulled it onto his lap for an intense massage. Self-consciously, Meagan glanced at Lilah across the table, her friend raised her eyebrows, smiled and shrugged.

His hands were good, too good. Desire crept up on her unexpectedly. Soon she realized her foot was resting on his erection. Meagan eased her foot back and slipped on her shoe while pretending not to have noticed his state of arousal.

Meagan leaned close to Drew to be heard over the band and spoke into his ear, "I'm sorry, it's late, and we have work tomorrow."

He nodded. "I understand, just let me pay the bill, and we'll be on our way." His breath on her ear sent a shiver down her spine. Drew left the table and disappeared through the crowd.

Once in the limousine, Lilah sat on the seat behind the driver, laid her head back and closed her eyes. Drew and Meagan took the seat opposite.

Drew turned to Meagan. "We have a meeting with some record execs in Los Angeles on Friday, so I'll be heading your way Thursday. Do you think we could get together?"

"Sure. Why don't you come by my house, and I'll whip up something for dinner?"

"Sounds great. I don't have any idea about a time yet, but

I'll call you."

"Okay." Meagan searched her purse for one of her cards, then scribbled her address and cell number on the back and handed it to him.

Lilah's eyes opened and she focused her attention on Drew. "Does this mean you're getting a recording contract?"

"That's what the meeting is all about. We won't get our hopes up until we've heard the terms. We had a meeting last year with another label, but we couldn't reach an agreement. The fine print had us practically paying them for the privilege of doing business with them. They also wanted us to sign over the rights to our songs."

"Jeez, did you have a lawyer?" Meagan asked.

"Yeah, Steve, the drummer, his brother's a lawyer. He read it over for us."

"Wow, lucky for you. I bet there are a lot of new bands out there who sign on the dotted line without consulting a lawyer first," Meagan stated.

"Yeah, I know. It could have been disastrous."

They pulled up next to Meagan's car, the only one left in the parking lot. Drew got out, took the keys from Meagan and opened Lilah's door first, then walked around to Meagan's side.

Without hesitation, he took her in his arms and kissed her. The kiss, tentative at first, soon grew deep with passion. When he released her, they were both out of breath. He stared down at her with a seductive look. "I can hardly wait for Thursday."

Meagan's brain was rattled, but she finally found her voice. "Thanks for a wonderful night."

Drew smiled. "Thank you." He opened her car door.

Meagan glanced in the rearview mirror as she drove away. He was still standing where she'd left him, his hand raised in a wave.

Lilah hit her on the shoulder. "Phew, that was some kiss." She chuckled.

Meagan couldn't wipe the smile from her face if she tried, and truth be told, she didn't want to.

TWENTY

Thomas' cell phone rang. He raised his head and found himself at the dining room table surrounded by files and crime scene photos. He must have dozed off. He glanced at the clock. Six in the morning. He cleared his throat. "Yeah, Thomas here."

"Hey, baby brother, did I wake you?" Wyatt's voice echoed through his ear.

"Hey. Thanks for getting back to me." Thomas scooted his chair back and walked into the kitchen to turn on the coffee maker. He rested his back against the counter while he waited impatiently for that first cup. Within seconds, the aroma of fresh-brewed coffee filled the room.

"Yeah, I'm sorry it took so long. I'm consulting on a case for one of the alphabets, you know?"

"Yeah, DEA, ATF, FBI, CIA, DOD. You mean one of those?"

"Exactly."

Wyatt Thomas was J.J.'s oldest brother, a forensic psychiatrist who lived in Maryland. He was quite renowned and often called upon for his expertise from some of the best minds in his field. Of course he never talked about it. Nor did he toot his own horn.

J.J. had learned of his reputation through their other brother, Cody, who worked for the FBI's Violent Crimes Unit. He'd told J.J. that even the SAC—Special Agent in Charge—of the Behavioral Science Unit called their brother for his opinion. That's saying a lot since the BSU were the experts who profiled killers for a living.

"No problem, I'm just glad you found time for me at all. Did you have a chance to look over the file?" J.J. heard paper shuffling.

"Yes, I've got it in front of me now. And I hate to say it, but this is more Cody's area of expertise than yours. Maybe you should call the FBI in on this one."

"Gee, thanks, bro. Nice to see you have so much confidence in me." J.J. poured a cup of coffee and took a big gulp. It would take more than a few cups to get his brain working at even half-capacity today. He was starting at a disadvantage; he'd only had a couple of hours of sleep. Then something occurred to him. He glanced at the table piled high with files and paperwork. An empty water bottle stood on the side.

Dinner wasn't the only thing he'd skipped last night. It was the first time since he could remember that he hadn't woken up with a hangover. He'd come home last night, dropped everything on the table, and worked through till sometime early this morning. He hadn't thought of Victoria once all night. The epiphany was startling.

"Hey, don't take it like that. I know you're a good detective, but this isn't some domestic dispute you have on your hands here. You've got a serial killer in your neck of the woods. Even Cody doesn't close every case he works, and he *is* an expert. I'm just saying that being good sometimes means knowing when to ask for help when you're out of your depth."

"I *am* asking for help. I called you, didn't I?"J.J. put his cup down and rubbed his neck. *This is going to be a hell of a long day.*

"Yeah, I'll give you that." Wyatt chuckled.

"Thanks." J.J. didn't see the humor. "Did you call just to bust my balls, or do you have something for me?"

"No, that's just a bonus." Wyatt chuckled. "Okay, just a second." Paper shuffling. "I didn't have time to write up a complete profile, but I'll give you what I've got."

"I'll take anything at this point." J.J. topped off his cup and took it to the table. He searched under the paperwork until he found a pen, then grabbed the clipboard he'd been using to make notes. "Okay, shoot."

"You're looking for a white male, approximately twenty-five to thirty-five years of age. If he has a job, he works alone, driving a semi, a taxi, a tow truck, working for the county, any kind of job where he doesn't have a boss hanging over his head. Often these types of offenders have a hard time keeping employment because they can't handle authoritative figures telling them what to do. Hot temper, anger management issues.

"He has an extensive collection of pornography, and I'm not talking about the soft core stuff you had under your mattress when you were a kid."

"You mean the magazines I pilfered from you?" He smiled.

"The very ones." Wyatt laughed. "You always were a sneaky little bastard."

"Ha-ha. So, what are we talking about here, S&M?"

"Sadomasochism is the least of it, bondage too. Those are tame for a guy like this. We're talking golden showers, defecating, on up to snuff films."

"So a real sick fuck."

"And that's the clinical term."

J.J. laughed. "Okay, got it."

"More often than not, he lives with a woman who has a domineering personality."

"So, who do you think *she* is, the surrogate he's killing?" J.J. asked.

"She could be his first victim. More probable though, she would be a symbol for his mother, an aunt, a grandmother, whoever raised him. An authoritative figure from his past that let him down. He needs to punish her, degrade and dehumanize her.

"There is a definite pattern here. He's getting back at the same woman over and over again. Whoever she is, she doesn't die for him. He's trying to make *sure* she's dead, but whatever he does she still haunts him. This anger or fear that's building in him could be why he violates her more and more with each new victim, or it's simply because it's getting harder and harder for him to get off. That's why he's taken to cutting the last two victims.

"This kind of rage takes years to simmer," Wyatt continued. "Many times victims of child abuse bury their memories until one day they resurface. It could be little by little, or all at once like a tidal wave. It could be a similar traumatic experience that triggers these memories, like a woman they love leaving them, or often something as simple as a song on the radio.

"If you'll notice, he sewed the eyes shut just prior to killing her. He wanted her to witness the rape and sodomy, wanted her to know who was punishing her. Sodomy has been used over the centuries as a way for one to conquer one's enemies. A degradation that proves who is in control.

"And then, almost as if he were ashamed, he sews the victim's eyes shut so she can't witness the final act. He removes her breasts to eliminate her femininity. Maybe he thinks by doing this, it makes her less attractive to him. As if this were one of the many ways she had of controlling him."

"And the lips?" Thomas asked.

"That symbolizes shutting her up. Either he doesn't want to hear what she has to say, or he's afraid she will tell on him."

"Could it be just to keep her quiet, so she can't scream?" J.J. asked.

"It could be as simple as that, but I doubt it. This guy is a walking textbook, he seems to have deep-seated issues. For instance, take a look at the oldest case you gave me, the one underneath the Bay Bridge?"

"Cynthia Gross?"

"Yeah, that's it. I would say this was probably his first kill. Look at the way he situated the body. Her eyes are closed, her hands are resting peacefully on her chest, as if she were asleep. He probably knew her, cared about her. He wanted to make sure she was resting comfortably. Also, he didn't bury her, he wanted her found right away." Wyatt stopped speaking and took a sip of something. Probably coffee, J.J. guessed.

"So, you do think she is a victim of the same guy?"

"What are the odds, same blood type and a non-secretor? We're talking ten to one. I'd say he hadn't found his niche yet, so to speak. Serial killers usually start with someone they know, even if by accident. So, if I were you, I'd go back to Cynthia Gross. Get to know her inside and out. I'd bet anything he's connected to her in some way.

"He had feelings for this girl. And she possibly had feelings for him, or at least she did in his mind. Maybe he finally gets the nerve to tell her he loves her and she spurns him. Or, maybe they actually *did* start to have sexual intercourse and she changed her mind.

"Whatever the case, you can see that the rage inside him was so great that he couldn't control himself. This murder is personal. Look at the victims head in the photo, the first or second blow would have knocked her out, maybe even killed her, but he continued to bash her head into a bloody pulp."

"So you *do* think these four victims were killed by the

same person?" Thomas asked, seeking some sort of commitment.

"Yes," Wyatt answered without hesitation.

J.J. scratched his whiskered chin. "Okay, so I'm looking for a white male, twenty-five to thirty-five, who's a pervert with mommy issues. That narrows it down *a lot*."

"Maybe you should call Cody, I can only tell you what the guys thinking, he might be able to give you more."

"So you said."

"Your answers are with the first victim."

"Thank you, Obi-Wan."

"Hey, smartass, you asked. Look, I've got a conference call in ten minutes, I've got to go."

"I really do appreciate you taking the time, bro."

"I know, good luck. And call if you need anything else."

"Will do."

TWENTY-ONE

He was sitting up in bed, next to his mother, while she read Goodnight Moon. *He loved the pictures. They were alone in the house. Everything was good. He wished it was always like this. He loved his mother. Someday when he was bigger he would take her away from here.*

The bedroom door burst open and slammed against the wall. They jumped.

"What the hell are you doing, reading him some goddamn sissy book? Jesus, you're turning him into a fuckin' faggot with all this coddling!"

His father grabbed the book and ripped out the pages.

He cried as he watched his favorite book destroyed.

"What the hell are you crying about, you little brat? See, it's all your fault. He's a whiny, sniveling sissy boy."

His father grabbed his mother by the hair and yanked her off the bed. She yelled, grabbed at her hair. The high shrill of her screams filled the room as he dragged her toward the open door.

He jumped off the bed and rushed to his father. "Stop it! Stop it!" He hit the bigger man with both fists as hard as he could.

His father dropped his mother, and grabbed both the boys' hands in one of his. His mother crawled to the far corner of the room and clutched her knees tight against her body.

His father glared down at him and laughed. A wicked menacing sound. "You think you can take me on, kid? Is that what you think?"

"Leave him alone!" his mother's voice rang through the room.

His father's big hand swatted him like a fly. The blow struck him on the side of his head and sent him sailing across the room. He landed in a heap against the wall.

His mother screamed, then lunged and covered him with her body.

The man stood in the doorway, swaying back and forth. He scrunched his eyes up a of couple times, as if trying to focus.

"To hell with the both of you." He waved his hand in dismissal.

Turning around, he lost his balance and grabbed onto the wall in time to stop himself from falling. "I need a drink," he muttered, then stumbled down the hall.

His mother stood, then picked him up. After laying him on the bed, she ran to the door and closed it. Then she pushed the dresser in front of the door, grunting and groaning until it was in place.

At last she joined him on the bed. He felt the side of his face, there was blood by his ear. He couldn't stop crying. She took him in her arms and rocked him.

"Shh, it's all right, Mommy's got you." She stroked his hair. "Shh, he's gone now." She sounded like she was crying too.

***

The man jolted awake. He was hugging his pillow, his heart raced. He jumped off the bed, reached under the mattress and found what he was searching for. The Polaroids of his girls.

He lay back down on the bed and began scanning the pictures. With each girl, a different memory came, a different experience. Soon his heartbeat resumed a normal rhythm, and peace washed over him.

By the time he reached the freshest kill, he had a major hard-on. He shoved the rest of the pictures under his pillow, and held the last one up to his face. The memory had faded; he couldn't taste her fear like before. He gazed at her image as he masturbated. It took longer to come than usual.

He thought about his newest conquest. Although her hair was not nearly long enough, she did have everything else going for her. It was time to claim her. He fell asleep with her image in his head.

Twenty-two

Thomas called the captain the second he got off the phone with Wyatt. He ran down everything his brother had told him, and got permission to drive up to Alameda and interview the parents of the first victim.

Then he called Shadowhawk and told her to pack a bag. The drive was seven to nine hours depending on traffic, so they would probably be spending the night. He would fill her in on the road.

Last he called the San Francisco Sheriff's Department, spoke to the detective in charge of the Cynthia Gross case, and brought him up to speed on the investigation.

Thomas stood in front of the mirror shaving when he noticed his pallor looked more normal and his eyes were no longer bloodshot. It was as if he were greeting an old friend.

He zipped up Pacific Coast Highway to Huntington Beach, and knocked on the front door to what he thought was Shadowhawk's house until it swung open and a young Hispanic boy of about seven stared up at him. Thomas looked at the house number again to make sure he hadn't made a mistake.

"Hello." The boy's voice a high falsetto. "You must be the detective. Come on in." He moved aside and Thomas stepped into the foyer. "He's here!"

Shadowhawk appeared at the top of the stairs wearing black jeans, a tight grey t-shirt and a shiny black vest. He noticed she had a Native American tribal tattoo circling her left arm just below the sleeve. Her jet-black hair hung loose around her shoulders. Thomas realized she was a striking woman.

"I'll be right down," she said to him, then turned to the boy. "Thanks, Dylan. Now go finish your homework." She disappeared down the hall.

Dylan pointed to the living room. "You can sit on the couch; she always says that and then takes another hour to come down."

"Thanks for the insight, buddy. It's a girl thing." Thomas sat down and got comfortable.

"Yeah, like I don't know that. It's tough being the only man in this house." The boy frowned. "Between my sister, my mom and Fawn, it takes *forever* for us to go *anywhere*." His voice raised dramatically on the last word. He sat on the floor cross-legged at the coffee table in front of his homework.

Thomas laughed. "You might as well get used to it. When it comes to women, you'll be dealing with it your whole life."

"Oh, jeez." Dylan put his elbows on the table, his chin in his hands.

Thomas stifled a laugh. Even though the kid was hilarious, it was obvious he wasn't trying to be. He heard someone coming down the stairs and looked up. It was Shadowhawk. She carried a grey blazer over her arm, and an overnight bag in her hand. Her hair was tied back in her usual French braid. Thomas stood.

A petite Hispanic woman followed close behind. When they reached the bottom of the stairs, Shadowhawk introduced Thomas to her partner, Maria. Then she gave her a peck on the lips.

"I'll call you tonight." She turned to Thomas, "Okay, let's go."

Thomas slapped the boy on the shoulder. "Hang in there, buddy. Us men have got to stick together."

The boy puffed up his chest and smiled. "Yeah."

They got in the car and were silent until they reached the freeway. "What was that all about?" Shadowhawk asked.

"That kid cracks me up. He was commiserating with me about being the only man in a house full of women."

She smiled. "Yeah, he's a great kid. I'm lucky."

"He mentioned a sister, is she yours?"

"No, they're both Maria's, but I love them as if they were my own. They've been in my life for the last six years. Hesper is thirteen, and Dylan is ten."

Thomas raised his eyebrows. "Wow, I took him for seven, eight tops."

"He's small for his age."

He filled her in on the call from Wyatt and they discussed

what they were hoping to find in the Bay area. They hit traffic going through L.A., then drove through a McDonald's in Santa Clarita for lunch.

After he'd swallowed his last french fry, he turned to Shadowhawk. "So what made you join the sheriff's department?"

"One night I had a run-in with a homophobic cop. Maria and I were minding our own business, walking down the pier at sunset. Dylan and Hesper were much younger then, they ran ahead of us. And this asshole in a uniform came at us and told us we can't hold hands in public. I told him we could do whatever we wanted, this is America. Well, one thing led to another, and he arrested me for assaulting a cop."

"Did you?"

"I may have shoved him a little. Anyway, the charges were dropped. But the whole time I was sitting in that cell I was thinking: here's this guy who has nothing better to do than hassle us while real criminals are out there breaking the law. So I figured there should be someone doing *his* job."

"So, that was what, five years ago?"

"Give or take."

"Was it hard? I mean, being a woman and all. I hear it can be tough until you prove yourself."

"Yeah, well, I took some shit at first. I was just a dumb rookie trying to do everything by the book. But that changed soon enough."

"What happened?"

"I came across that same asshole, and he started giving me shit. I heard he had six months to go until his retirement, so I decided to make it a six months he'd never forget.

"One night, when everyone was pretty much gone, I took his picture down from the Wall of Fame. I scanned the photo and e-mailed it to myself. Then I Photoshopped his face on some gay porn. I paid this buddy of mine from the academy to get me his locker number. Then I crept into the locker room around three a.m., when it was empty. I picked the lock and pasted the pictures all around the inside.

"The next morning the locker room was full. He opens his locker and yells, "What the fuck!" The idiot drew attention to the photos *himself*. I hear all the guys in the room were crowding around him to see what he was making such a fuss about. By the time he noticed he had an audience, he slammed the door, but it was too late.

"It made him a laughing stock. And I got my retribution." She beamed at Thomas. "I just wish I could have been there to see his face. Man, that would have been priceless." She laughed.

"Anyway, to make a long story longer, rumors spread that I was the culprit. I vehemently denied it, of course. But no one screwed with me after that."

"Holy shit. That was you?" He laughed. "Remind me to never get on your bad side."

She grew serious. "Yeah, well, he deserved it." She looked out the windshield. "It takes a lot to piss me off."

TWENTY-THREE

The detectives arrived at the Gross family home that afternoon. They were led into a small living room that had last been decorated sometime in the early seventies, and sat on a well-worn brown and orange floral couch.

Mr. and Mrs. Gross sat opposite in brown vinyl chairs conspicuously dotted with duct tape, no doubt covering age-old rips in the fabric. The brown shag carpet was worn flat in paths that ran in and out of the room from years of travel. Pictures of the victim at every age graced the hearth, the piano and the walls of the room.

Man and wife looked worn out. Life had hit them with a heavy blow. The image was nothing new to Thomas; all he had to do was look in the mirror.

"I'm sorry to have to put you through this again. We just have a few questions regarding your daughter," Thomas said.

"Did you find the man who killed my baby?" Mrs. Gross' voice shook as she wrung her hands.

"No, ma'am, but we're working on it," Thomas answered.

"I don't understand, what do you people have to do with my daughter's death? It's been years without a word. Now you show up out of the blue from San Clemente? Where the hell is that?" Mr. Gross stared at Thomas.

"It's sandwiched between San Diego and Los Angeles, sir."

"My point exactly. What could you possibly know about Cindy's case?" Mr. Gross' voice was hard. "Well, sir, we believe your daughter may have been just one in a long series of murders." Thomas's voice was soft.

"Oh!" Mrs. Gross covered her mouth with her hand.

Her husband patted her arm. "Norma, honey, why don't you go into the kitchen and get us some coffee?" He watched his wife leave the room, then turned to Thomas.

"As you can see, this is very hard on my wife. Cindy was our only child. We had her late in life. She was a miracle baby. Norma had several miscarriages before she was finally able to carry Cindy to full term.

"The birth was very difficult on her. The doctor advised us not to have any more children. Cindy's death has drained the life out of my poor wife. So let's just get this over with." Mr. Gross looked spent by the time he'd finished speaking.

"Certainly, we understand. We'll try to do this as painlessly as possible. Mr. Gross, can you give us a rundown of Cindy's friends at the time of the incident?"

"She had only one friend."

"And what was her name?" Thomas waited, pen at the ready.

"Roxanne. They met in high school and later worked

together."

"Do you know Roxanne's last name?" Shadowhawk joined the conversation.

"Um, no."

"And where did they work?"

"Some catalog company down town. I can't think of the name right now. I'm sorry."

"Did Cindy have a boyfriend?"

"No, she was shy. She didn't date."

Mrs. Gross entered the room carrying a tray containing four cups of coffee, a sugar bowl and a creamer. She set the tray down on the coffee table and asked everyone to help themselves. The detectives each selected a cup and thanked her. Mrs. Gross added cream and sugar to a cup and handed it to her husband.

She then sat back in her chair and folded her hands in her lap. The last cup sat alone on the tray. Her eyes fixed on the steam rising into the air.

Mr. Gross turned toward his wife. "Hon, what was the name of the company that Cindy worked for?"

"The Frisco Bay Clothing Company?"

"That's right." He glanced at Thomas, then Shadowhawk. "Don't ever get old. The mind is the first to go." He gave a nervous laugh.

Shadowhawk caught Mrs. Gross's eye. "Do you remember her friend Roxanne's last name?"

The woman was quiet a moment.

"Hanover, that's it. Roxanne Hanover."

"Would you happen to have her address and phone number?" Shadowhawk continued.

The woman scrunched up her face. "Oh, dear, I don't know. I..." She put her head down and fidgeted.

Her husband leaned over and placed a hand on her knee. "It's okay, honey, they're detectives. They can find it."

"Right, no need to worry about that," Thomas interjected.

"Would it be possible for us to take a look in Cindy's room?" Shadowhawk asked.

A brief silence ensued as Mr. Gross gazed at his wife.

"I guess that would be okay." Her voice was barely audible. She unfolded her hands and gingerly pushed herself out of the chair.

They followed her up the stairs. She stopped in front of a room at the top of the landing and stared at the closed door. Mr. Gross came up beside her and put his arm around her shoulders.

"It's all right, Norma. They won't disturb a thing." He fixed his gaze on Thomas, who nodded. The man let out a pent-up breath.

"We'll only be a moment," Thomas added.

The detectives passed the couple and walked into the room. Thomas flipped on the light and eased the door shut behind them.

They stopped inside the door to take in their surroundings. The room did not appear to belong to a young woman; instead it held more of a childlike quality. The décor was in pink and white ruffles, including the canopy over the bed. The furniture was white with gold trim.

Stuffed animals littered a shelf along the bookcase. A few sat decorating the bed. Thomas ran a finger across the dresser and found it clean, no dust. Obviously Mrs. Gross visited this room on a regular basis. There were no posters, ribbons or trophies. Instead, pictures of ballerinas graced the walls.

"Jesus, they spared no expense in here," she exclaimed.

"Every little girl's dream." Thomas's hand stroked one of the pictures.

"Not mine," Shadowhawk corrected.

"And what did *you* want to be when you grew up?"

"A race car driver." She stared at him with her hands on her hips.

"Of course you did." He smiled.

Shadowhawk zeroed in on the computer sitting on a desk against the far wall. The moment it powered up, she began scanning the contents. Thomas finished touring the room.

Thomas opened drawers, lifted clothes, and checked between the layers to see if anything was hidden.

He heard drawers slamming behind him, and turned around.

"What are you doing?"

"Searching for a thumb drive, or some empty CDs to copy her files." She located some floppy disks at the bottom of one of the drawers and popped each in, then out of the computer.

"Check this out."

Thomas came up behind her. *Mystery Lovers of America*

flashed across the top. "What am I looking at?"

She started scrolling down the screen. "This is a site she frequented a lot. These are conversations she was having with someone in a chat room for people who liked to read mystery novels. There are pages and pages of these. The guy's screen name is Dark Knight. This *could* be our perp." She reached back into the bottom drawer and picked up a floppy, stared at it, then threw it back. "I think I have a thumb drive in the car. I'll be right back."

Minutes later Shadowhawk returned, connected the thumb drive into the computer and started copying files. Then she searched the room. She peeked behind pictures and under the mattress.

She took out each drawer and flipped it over, sending the contents falling to the floor. She eyed the bottoms, then checked the backs before tossing each drawer onto the bed. After that she slipped her hand into the empty space where the drawer had been, and felt along the top and back.

"What are you doing?" Thomas asked.

"Trying to see if she taped anything in here. I used to hide things all the time. I didn't have the *luxury* of my own room growing up and my brothers and sisters were nosy."

Thomas watched her. "Just so you know, you're going to have to put everything back the way you found it."

"Yeah, whatever," she said, intent on her search. "Pay dirt!" She pulled the satin away from behind the little ballerina in what looked like a child's jewelry box.

He came over and glanced over her shoulder as she flipped

through snapshots. "Hel-lo," Shadowhawk remarked.

Thomas whistled. "Whoa, that is not the same girl we saw in the photographs downstairs."

"No indeedy. She's hot! Looks like our wallflower had a secret life that mommy and daddy didn't know about."

Thomas watched her skim the photos. They showed Cindy Gross in heavy makeup, lying on the bed provocatively in a bikini. A couple of shots showed her without her top, covering her nipples with her arm.

"Who do you suppose took these, a boyfriend?" he asked.

"Probably that Roxanne chick, although she could have taken them herself with a timer. All she had to do was put the camera on the top of the dresser and line the shot up using one of her stuffed animals."

"The next question is why? Who were they for?"

"Yeah, that's what I'd like to know." Shadowhawk slipped the pictures into her pocket and continued her search.

Next, she went over to the bookcase. She read the titles aloud, "*Nancy Drew, The Hardy Boys.* I *guess* you could say she was into mysteries. A little juvenile for her age though, don't you think?"

"This whole room looks like that of a child."

"No shit." She turned back to the books and started picking up each one and shaking it, then thumbed through it.

Thomas put all the drawers back in the dresser, then put the clothes back in. But no matter how hard he tried, he couldn't make them look the way they did before. Let alone close the damn things. Finally he found himself pushing down on the clothes and trying to shove the drawers closed.

Shadowhawk turned around. "I was going to put that all back when I was finished."

"Right."

"Whatever." She picked up a large volume titled *Introduction to Psychology*. The book had a shiny paper cover. She started skimming through it. "What the hell?" She closed the book again and looked at the title. "This book does not resemble anything they gave *me* in school!"

Thomas gave up and joined her on the other side of the room in time to see her remove the paper cover.

"Hel-lo," he said, mocking her, then. "*The Joy of Sex.* I wonder what kind of grade she got in that class?"

"I know, huh?"

"Looks like we'd better track down that Roxanne what's-her-name and see if she can shed some light on our little ballerina."

Shadowhawk went back to the computer, slipped the thumb drive into her pocket and powered it down.

They finished tidying up. Downstairs they met up with Mr. and Mrs. Gross and thanked them for their hospitality. He gave Mr. Gross his card and asked him to call if they thought of anything.

"I just hope it helps you catch this guy," Mr. Gross exclaimed.

"Yes, sir. We'll keep you informed of any new developments." Thomas offered the man his hand.

"Thank you." Mr. Gross smiled as he shook it.

Once the door closed, they walked toward the car. About halfway there, he turned to Shadowhawk. "Well, that was insightful."

"*Very* insightful."

TWENTY-FOUR

Meagan stopped at the fish market on her way home from work Thursday and purchased two pounds of large shrimp for her dinner with Drew. Then she crossed the street to the bakery and snagged a loaf of French bread. It was hot, right out of the oven. The smell filled the car and made her stomach growl.

At home, she sang along with Joni Mitchell while she cleaned the shrimp. She measured out the cayenne pepper, black pepper, crushed red pepper, and the rest of the spices into a bowl, and set it aside.

At precisely seven o'clock, Godzilla barked, and there was a knock on her screen. "Hello?"

"Just a minute!" She placed the last pin in her hair, then hastily pulled down some curls to frame her face. Satisfied, she rushed to greet her guest.

Drew waited with a bottle of wine in each hand. She snagged Godzilla's collar before she opened the screen and invited him in.

"I wasn't sure what we were having, so I bought both red and white." He handed the bottles to her as the dog busily sniffed him all over.

"This is Gozilla."

"Hey." Drew patted him on the head and moved away. He looked nervous.

"Don't worry, he won't bite."

"I'm just not much of a dog person, I guess." Godzilla continued to sniff him as he backed up against the wall.

"Okay, I'll put him in the bedroom." She put the wine on the phone table by the door. "Come on, boy." She slapped her leg and the dog wagged his tail and went to her.

"We're having Cajun shrimp," Meagan said as she returned. "I hope you like spicy food." She grabbed the wine and made her way back toward the kitchen.

"Great, the spicier the better." He followed closely behind.

"Which would you prefer?" She got down a couple of wineglasses from the cupboard.

"I prefer red myself."

"Great, me too." She opened the bottle and poured them each a glass.

They took their wine into the living room where Meagan had lit several candles and strategically placed them around the room. She sat on the couch, curled her legs up underneath her, and set her wine on the end table. Drew sat next to her.

They talked for a couple hours until Meagan noticed the time and jumped up. "Oh, my God, I'd better get dinner on.

You must be starving!"

A few moments later, they were situated on the living room floor, scooted up to the coffee table with their dinners.

"This is really hot," Meagan explained, handing him a bottle. "The beer and bread help to put out the fire. The bread is for dipping into the sauce."

Drew took a bite. "Wow, this is great!"

After about three more mouthfuls his face scrunched up, and he grabbed his beer. "Whoa." He gasped. "This *is* hot." He drank half the beer before coming up for air.

Meagan laughed. "I warned you. Try some bread."

Meagan's heart grew fonder of Drew the more he was in her presence. His eyes lit up when he spoke of his love for his music. The animation of his voice spoke volumes while he described the motivations behind each of the songs he wrote.

When they were in the kitchen she'd noticed his dark, closely cropped beard brought out the green and yellow flecks in his hazel eyes. His lashes, long and dark, made them seem to glitter.

She glanced down his broad shoulders to his strong arms. She hadn't noticed them before because he'd always worn long sleeves. Tonight he was dressed more casual in a Social D t-shirt. The band was one she was also fond of. The memory of those strong arms wrapped around her and the kiss they'd shared sent a shiver down the length of her body. Her eyes roamed further south, then she became painfully aware of the silence that filled the room. Her eyes shot up to his face, and heat filled her cheeks.

"I'm sorry, what?"

A sexy grin played at his lips. He reached over and fingered a curl against her cheek. Her body leaned toward him as if it had a mind of its own.

"I said it's late. I have a long drive ahead of me."

Meagan leaned back and stood abruptly. She mentally shook her head and tried to focus. "Of course."

Drew got to his feet and followed her to the door. Meagan opened it. When she turned around he was close, very close. She looked up and met his gaze. The look in his eyes heated.

"Dinner was great, and so was the company." His voice dipped low on the last word. Meagan's heart skipped a beat.

"Thank you." She swallowed hard.

He wrapped his arms around her and pressed his lips to hers. As the kiss deepened, he let out a soft moan and pulled her body closer against him. She felt his arousal.

Her mind was whirling, she wanted him too, but then again she barely knew him. She knew from experience it was better not to rush things. His fingers found her nipple and pinched ever so slightly. The action made her tingle between her legs. She was finding it really hard to be good right now.

Meagan battled with her conscience. As much as she yearned for Drew, she didn't do one-night stands. Then again, if he were telling the truth, he wasn't looking for that either. He'd told her he was ready to settle down, have a family. That if the record deal went through, he wanted to buy a little cottage in San Clemente. He'd always loved this town.

The longer they kissed, the harder it was getting for Meagan to send him on his way. And just like that he ended the kiss. She wondered if the shock registered on her face.

"I'd better get going before this gets out of hand." He looked down at her expectantly. Her body trembled. The silence between them grew. She knew it was up to her, but she couldn't speak. He took two steps back, his eyes never leaving her face.

Meagan suddenly felt cold where his body had been and wrapped her arms around herself, but still couldn't utter a word. She was afraid that word would be *stay*.

He backed up two more steps.

"I'll call you tomorrow."

She nodded.

He turned around, walked to the van and jumped in. The motor turned over. She watched as his taillights disappeared from sight.

She knew in her head that she made the right decision; now she just had to convince her body. Meagan stood in the open doorway until the cold night air brought her back to reality. Then she sighed and closed the door. This guy was just too good to be true.

TWENTY-FIVE

Thomas pulled into the parking lot of The Frisco Bay Clothing Company an hour later. The detectives strolled into the lobby and asked if a Roxanne Hanover worked there. Without a word, the receptionist picked up the phone.

A couple of minutes later, a sharp-dressed woman appeared through the door. Flashing his ID, Thomas made the introductions and asked if there was somewhere they could talk in private. Roxanne led them to her office.

She smoothed her skirt and sat behind her desk.

"What is this about, detectives?"

"We have some questions about Cindy Gross," Thomas answered.

"I don't know what I can tell you that I haven't already told the police years ago, and I'm very busy. We're getting the clothes in for the summer line. Everything's chaotic at the moment."

"I understand. We'll be brief. What can you tell us about Cindy's boyfriends?" Thomas asked.

"Boyfriends? Cindy didn't have any *boyfriends.* She was too insecure. She was the type of person who faded into the background as if she weren't even in the room, which frustrated me to no end. She could have been cute if she only tried.

"I gave her a makeover once, and she looked really great, but she couldn't wash the makeup off fast enough. It made her uncomfortable. I just wanted her to be happy. She needed to get a life and move out of that house. Her parents were suffocating her. I thought if she started dating it would boost her confidence."

"Did she have any guy *friends* that she hung out with then?" Shadowhawk asked.

"No, I was her only friend. *"*

"What about here at work? Was she friendly with someone here?" Shadowhawk continued.

"No, not really. She was nice and everyone liked her well enough, but she pretty much kept to herself. I was the only person she really felt comfortable being around."

"Did *anyone* ever show her any attention, either here at work or otherwise?" Shadowhawk asked.

"No." She paused a beat. "Wait, there was this one guy who worked in the warehouse. He was quiet and shy like her. They talked once in a while. She told me she thought he had a crush on her but was too shy to ask her out. I told her to ask him. I thought they'd make the perfect pair."

"Did they ever go out?"

"No, come to think of it, he got fired before that could

happen. Wow, I'd forgotten about that."

"Do you remember why he was fired?" Thomas jumped in.

"Oh, yeah. It was a shock, actually. I mean, this guy was so quiet, kept to himself, then one day out of the blue he just goes off on his boss and slugs him. I never saw anything like it before or since. Sure, the boss was an asshole; he got fired a short time later. Too many complaints."

Thomas leaned forward in his chair. Wyatt had mentioned their guy had a problem with authority.

"When was this?"

"Oh, years ago."

His senses tingled. "Do you remember his name?

"Jordan something, I could have someone look him up in the personnel files if you think it would help."

"Please."

Roxanne pushed a button on her phone. "Ginger, get me everything you can find on a guy named Jordan that used to work in the warehouse about five, maybe six years ago. I'm sorry but I don't remember his last name." She turned her attention back to the detectives.

Shadowhawk pulled the snapshots from her pocket and handed them across the desk. "What can you tell us about these?"

Roxanne's eyes grew wide. Her mouth dropped open. "What the hell!" She scrutinized each photo.

The secretary walked in and laid the file on Roxanne's desk.

"Thank you, Ginger." Roxanne's eyes never left the

pictures in her hand.

The secretary hesitated.

Roxanne glanced up. "I'm okay, you can go."

The secretary waited a beat, then turned around and closed the door behind her.

"I don't understand. Where did you find these?"

"Hidden in her room. Very *well* hidden, I might add," Shadowhawk answered.

"But why would she take these? What were they for?"

"That's what we were hoping you could tell us."

Roxanne stared at the last photo of her friend, topless. At last she handed them back with a pained expression. "I have no idea. They're so out of character for her."

"One more question," Thomas said. "Do you know anything regarding Cindy's involvement with a chat room called Mystery Lovers of America? More importantly, did she ever mention a person who called himself The Dark Knight?"

"Cindy may have mentioned the website, I don't know. But she never mentioned this Dark Knight. That I would've remembered. She did get into the internet pretty heavily at one time though."

"When was that?"

She stared up at the ceiling as if trying to remember, then looked back at Thomas before she answered. "About a month before her death. I remember one day she appeared tired. She had dark circles under her eyes. When I asked her about it she said she'd been staying up late on the computer. I thought she meant surfing the net. Do you think her killer was someone she met online?"

"It's possible. We really don't know," Thomas said, then turned toward Shadowhawk. "Can you think of anything else you'd like to ask?"

"Not really."

Thomas glanced back at Roxanne. "Then if you could just give us what you can on this Jordan, we'll get out of your hair."

Roxanne copied the information from the file onto a piece of paper and handed it to Thomas. He slipped it into his pocket and stood.

"Thank you for your time, Miss Hanover." He shook her hand, then reached into his pocket. "Here's my card in case you think of anything else. Please don't hesitate or try to analyze whether it's important or not. Anything, no matter how small, might help."

They were back in the car before Shadowhawk spoke. "It looks like no one really knew our vic."

"Yeah, and now we have two possible suspects. First this mysterious Dark Knight, then Jordan what's-his-name." He looked down at the piece of paper he'd been given. "Roberts, Jordan Edward Roberts. Call that number and see if it's any good. If so, see if we can come right over." He handed the paper to her and listened while she struck out.

"The lady who answered says she's never heard of him."

"Okay, you get internet on that thing?" He pointed to her phone.

"Yeah, why?"

"Check out every Roberts in the Bay Area." He started the car and put the last known address for Jordan Roberts into his GPS. They were going to Oakland.

By the time they arrived, Shadowhawk had called every Roberts in the area to no avail. They got out of the car and walked across the street to an old Victorian house that had been split into apartments.

They knocked on the door to apartment C and were greeted by an African American man built like a linebacker. He informed them he had been living there for three years and suggested that they talk with the landlady across the hall.

After knocking on her door, they waited a few minutes for a response. When none came, they started back down the steps that led to the building. A woman came around from the side of the house carrying a hose. She looked to be in her mid-sixties, wearing a bib apron and curlers in her hair.

Thomas showed his ID and made the introductions.

"What do you want?" An air of caution in her voice.

"How long have you been the landlady here, ma'am?"

"Forty years. My late husband, Dick, and I converted this place into apartments after we were married. Why?"

"Do you remember a tenant by the name of Jordan Roberts? He lived here a few years ago."

"Why, yes. He and his buddy had a hard time paying the rent. I gave them some leeway because Jordan was such a sweet boy, but after three months I had to evict them.

"Even after he got the notice, Jordan was so sweet and

157

apologetic. He was always making excuses for that friend of his. I wished he would give that guy the heave-ho, but what do you do, he wasn't *my* son. But I will tell you this, whatever you think he's done, it wasn't him, it was probably that good-for-nothing Charlie guy that moved in," she said with disgust.

"We just had a few questions regarding a case we're working on. You wouldn't happen to have a forwarding address, would you?" He asked.

"Nope. I have no idea what happened to him after he left here." The hose she was holding was still running. She'd flooded a good portion of the lawn, and the excess water was running toward the street.

"Do you happen to know this Charlie's last name?"

"Nope," she said quickly. "Jordan was who I rented the apartment to. That jerk showed up later and stayed. Jordan told me he had just come for a visit, that he would be moving on, but he never did. That was his downfall I tell you, that Charlie didn't work, never left the apartment. Jordan was supporting them both. That's why he couldn't pay the rent!" Her voice rose with the last word.

They thanked the landlady for her time. Once in the car Thomas asked, "What do you think?"

"The guy sounds like every psycho you've ever read about. nice guy, kept to himself," Shadowhawk said. "But then again, you could describe the vic the same way. Still waters run deep and all that crap," she answered.

While they sat at a signal waiting for it to turn green, Thomas took out his cell phone and dialed a number. It was after six o'clock, and he prayed she'd still be there.

"This is Thomas, is Johnson still around?"

"Johnson," said the voice on the other end.

"Thank God you're still there. This is Thomas and I need you to look up some information for me."

"Where else would I be? You don't *actually* think I have a life, do you? That bastard Brewster made me stay late. I told him he was shit out of luck; I had a concert to go to. But just as I was shutting down my computer, I get a call from the captain. So now I'm going to miss the Nine Inch Nails concert!" Her anger seeped through the phone.

"Oh. Sorry." Thomas replied. He heard a sigh on the other end, then her voice came back softer, "I'm sorry, I shouldn't take it out on you. What can I do for you, Thomas?"

"I really need you to check the DMV computer for a Jordan Edward Roberts, age thirty, birthday June sixth. Last known address, Oakland, California. But that was over five years ago."

"I'll have it in a jiff. Do you want to hold, or should I call you back?"

"Call me on my cell. Thanks." Thomas and Shadowhawk went to the Merritt coffee shop and ate while they rehashed everything they had learned that day. Thomas had a hard time focusing; he was anxious to hear from Johnson. His phone rang as he paid at the cash register.

"I found your Jordan Roberts," Johnson said. "You are so not going to believe where he lives." She didn't wait for a reply. "Laguna Niguel."

"No shit." Then he turned to Shadowhawk who stood nearby. "This guy's looking better and better by the minute." He pulled out his pad and pen. "Okay, give me that address." He wrote it down as she recited it to him.

"Thanks, Johnson. And I'm sorry about the concert."

"No sweat. I'm taking off now. Maybe I'll catch a little Trent Reznor before he finishes."

"Good luck."

"Thanks." She ended the call.

"This guy lives in Orange County."

"Holy crap." Her eyebrows raised. "Coincidence?"

"I don't believe in coincidences."

"Yeah, me neither."

TWENTY-SIX

The following evening Meagan rushed to her answering machine as soon as she arrived home to see if Drew had called. There were no messages at all. Her hopes dashed, she went to her room and changed her clothes.

He had dominated her thoughts all day. It wasn't just the memory of their long kiss goodnight, nor the beautiful flowers he'd sent, but that she was anxious to hear how his meeting went with the record label. Given how he talked last night, it could mean a lot to the future of their relationship. Her heart skipped a beat at the thought.

Meagan had just settled on the couch with a bowl of Cheerios when the phone rang. She jumped up, spilling the cereal, and rushed to get it. "Hello?" She waited for Drew to answer. Instead she was greeted by dead air.

"Hello!" Meagan yelled into the phone, in case the person on the other end was deaf as well as mute. "Damn!" She slammed the extension back in its cradle. She'd been too excited by the prospect of Drew's call to check the caller ID before picking it up. She'd try to remember next time.

She cleaned up the soggy mess, and decided to go to bed since she had lost her appetite. She had just finished brushing her teeth when the phone rang again. She ran into the living room and retrieved the phone from the coffee table. This time she looked at the readout before answering. It read *Out of the Area*. It must be Drew, she thought. "Hello."

All that answered her was silence.

"Son-of-a-B! Listen, creep, my boyfriend's a sheriff so if you know what's good for you, you'll stop playing this stupid game!" Fat lot of good Caller ID was. She gave up for the night. It was after eleven; if Drew called now, he could just talk to her answering machine.

Meagan collapsed on the bed and wearily picked up her book. She doubted she could focus enough to read, but she hoped to get her mind off her mystery caller. Godzilla jumped up and snuggled up next to her. She absently stroked his fur with one hand, while she held the book in the other.

She made it through only a few pages before her eyelids felt heavy. She put the book away and switched off the light.

Sometime in the middle of the night, movement on the bed stirred her awake. She squinted; it was Godzilla. He jumped off the bed and whimpered at the bedroom door.

"You gotta go out?" She shuffled to the bedroom door and opened it. The dog galloped to the outside door and scratched, "Okay, okay, give me a minute." Her body moved on autopilot as she fumbled with the locks.

She propped open the screen and left the back door ajar.

She was too tired to stand there and wait for him tonight. She told herself she would just lie down for a minute. When she felt him jump up on the bed, she would get up to close the door.

***

As he approached the back of the house, he couldn't believe his luck. The door was standing open a good foot. He didn't get it; he was sure she sensed him the other night. Maybe it was a trap.

He peered into the kitchen window and saw no one lurking, waiting to strike. Inching closer, he gently pushed the door wide, and slipped in. The floor creaked; he stopped and waited, barely breathing, but nothing happened.

The kitchen, lit solely by moonlight, made it easy for him to navigate the room, but when he rounded the corner he found it black as pitch. He couldn't tell if the bedroom door was open or closed. He pulled out his small flashlight, turned it on, and got ready to make a mad dash.

The door was open. He shined the light in the direction of the bed. She was sleeping. A gasp escaped his lips. He dropped to the floor quickly and flicked off the light. He heard a rustling on the bed. He waited until her breath resumed its steady rhythm before he flicked the light on again.

There she lay on top of the sheets. Her rust-colored curls fanned out on her pillow; it looked like spun silk. He ached to touch it, and slithered up next to the bed. She hugged the pillow beneath her head, her face at the edge of the mattress.

He lay on the floor looking up at her, close enough to smell her perfume. It made him dizzy with desire. He could feel her warm breath on his face. He lay like that for some time, fighting the urge to touch her soft full lips; the memory of her kiss remained fresh in his mind. The excitement of watching her unawares was almost too much to bear.

He inched his way back far enough to get on his knees so he could inspect her better. She rolled over, onto her back. His breath caught in his throat. The cool night air snuck in through the open door. He watched as her nipples stood erect underneath the thin material of her white tank top. He could just make out the dark pink through her top.

His hard-on strained against his tight jeans; his hand rubbed against his groin. A moan escaped. She stirred, but this time he didn't shut off the light. He watched, his heart pounding in his chest. He dared her to find him in her home, in her room, only inches away. So close he could reach out and touch her.

He took out his cock, imagining what she'd do. Her eyes would open; dreamily she'd move aside and motion him to join her in bed. Her hands would slink down his body, stroke the length of his penis, before taking it fully into her mouth.

Enthusiastically, her warm lips and tongue would work in tandem, while one hand massaged his scrotum and the other pinched his nipple hard. Her full lips would work him eagerly and just as he was about to come she would bite down hard at the base of his cock and—

He groaned deep in his throat, his breathing labored. His

hand worked feverishly along the shaft of his cock. His eyes scanned the immediate vicinity until they zeroed in on a t-shirt peeking out from under the bed. He snatched it in time to expel his load.

Movement on the bed caught his attention. He held his breath, waited to see if she would wake. Her eyes remained closed as she groped for the comforter. She pulled it up under her chin and rolled away. This time he eased up and left the room silently, bringing the soiled shirt with him.

***

The first thing Meagan did when she awoke was reach out for Godzilla. But he wasn't on the bed. She got out of bed and made her way to the bathroom. She noticed the back door wide open. Vaguely she remembered letting him out sometime in the night. She must have been sleeping pretty hard not to notice when he returned.

She closed the door and went to the bathroom. When she finished, she searched the tiny apartment. Godzilla was gone. She opened the back door. The sun had not yet shown its face, but a sliver of light lit the sky. No Godzilla. She walked out and headed toward the street. The cold concrete on her bare feet sent shivers throughout her body. She wrapped her arms around herself in a feeble attempt at warmth, and turned the corner of the house, Godzilla was nowhere in sight.

Meagan ran back inside and changed into a sweatshirt,

sweatpants and her running shoes. She hesitated outside, looking up and down the street. Then she remembered the other night and headed off in the direction that Godzilla had taken.

She walked down the middle of the road. At this hour, there were no cars to worry about. She called his name and whistled. It wasn't until she reached the end of the street that she began to really worry. She thought of the beach and ran down the stairs, then looked in both directions. Nothing. She started toward the pier hugging the hill thickly covered with shrubs.

Diligently, Meagan scoured the bushes yelling his name. By the time she'd reached the pier, a knot had grown in the pit of her stomach. She didn't know what to do next.

Walking back home, she decided to call the county and see if they'd picked up Godzilla. Although he had a dog tag, they may not have had time to call her yet. She reached the top of the stairs and spotted a police car with flashing lights parked in front of a neighbor's house. Her curiosity was only fleeting; she had her own troubles to contend with.

The moment she entered the house, she grabbed the phonebook and was dialing the number for the dog pound when there was a knock at her front door. Phone still in hand, she turned to open it and found a uniformed policeman standing on the stoop.

"Can I help you?"

"Yes, ma'am. Do you have a dog named Godzilla?"

"Yes!" Meagan set the phone down. "You found him?"

"Would you come with me, ma'am?" His emotionless voice sent a chill down her spine.

Meagan followed in silence back down the street, her mind whirling with possible scenarios. She couldn't imagine what Godzilla had gotten himself into that would have pissed off the officer this much. He led her into the backyard of her neighbor's house. The first thing Meagan noticed was an elderly couple, both dressed in robes, huddled together. They looked solemn.

Meagan followed their gaze, and noticed a strawberry blonde ball of fur. She stood there a few seconds not understanding. Then, as if a switch turned on in her head, she ran over and dropped to her knees.

"Godzilla?"

"Is this your dog, ma'am?"

She couldn't speak, couldn't turn around. Meagan lifted his head. Tears slid down her cheeks. She looked at the dog that had become her child, her companion, her best friend. The one she loved most in this world.

His soul had departed. He no longer resembled the exuberant partner with whom she had shared her life. His mouth and eyes open, his tongue lay limp toward the ground. She set his head down gently, then inspected the rest of his body. Her hands buried deep within his fur stroking him lovingly. Then her eyes came to rest on the gaping wound at his throat.

Meagan looked up, her gaze following the bloody path that led to the back of the house.

"Ma'am, is this your dog?"

She couldn't answer, instead she collapsed on Godzilla's chest, her body jerked up and down as she sobbed, her arms clung to him tightly.

She barely remembered the policeman lifting her by her shoulders and leading her back to her house. She didn't acknowledge him when he told her he would be back to ask her some questions. Instead she collapsed facedown on her couch, and remained there until the policeman returned.

Meagan managed to sit up and dry her eyes when she heard his first questions.

"Do you have any enemies? Any arguments with the neighbors? Have you received any threats lately?"

Meagan told him about the hang-ups, but he didn't seem interested. The cop told her that animal control was on its way and handed her a card. After reminding her to call if she remembered anything, he left.

She managed to close and lock the door behind him. She had no idea how long she had stood staring at the closed door when she suddenly remembered work. There was no way she could go in today. She called in sick, then shuffled off to her bedroom and collapsed on the bed.

TWENTY-SEVEN

The detectives had elected to drive home the night before, so by ten a.m. Thomas was dressed for the day and ready to check in with Shadowhawk. "How's it going?"

"I just sat down at the computer, so I don't have any answers yet," she said.

"Okay, you work on the Dark Knight. I'll go see if I can talk to this Jordan guy."

"Are you sure you don't want me with you?"

"Yes. I want you to follow up on that lead."

"I was hoping you'd say that. Call me the minute you leave him, I'm dying to know what his story is."

"Will do. Catch ya later."

Thomas headed to Laguna Niguel. He pulled into the Hidden Hills apartment complex and drove around until he found the building, then parked.

The apartment was on the first floor. After knocking on the door repeatedly, it was finally answered by a woman of indeterminate age, perhaps somewhere in her late thirties? It was hard to tell; she looked like she'd been ridden hard and put away wet.

The cigarette pressed between her lips expelled smoke in Thomas' direction. He waved his hand. She let out a phlegm-filled cough, exposing a pierced tongue. The makeup surrounding her eyes was so dark, it was hard to determine their color, brown. The dark purple lipstick she wore clashed with her pale skin and reminded him of a corpse.

"Well, Hel-loo good lookin'." Her eyes roamed the length of his body, and a smile tugged at her lips. "And what can I do for you?"

He ignored the suggestive remark and introduced himself, flicking his ID open.

"Does Jordan Roberts live here?"

Her expression turned sour. "You're shit out of luck, he ain't here. He's working, or so he says. What do you want with the little worm anyway?"

"I just needed to question him regarding a case I'm working on."

"Uh huh." She flicked her ash on the floor.

Thomas was losing his patience. "And you are?"

"Sharon, his wife."

"Do you mind if I ask you a few questions?"

"Sure." She stepped back.

Thomas walked into a cave. It was dark; the curtains were drawn. It reeked of smoke, and a dirty litter box. On his right stood the kitchen. Dirty dishes filled the sink and spilled out over the counters. The trash can overflowed with fast food bags and beer cans. Flies buzzed around the contents.

Sharon Roberts led him into the living room, then picked up a load of laundry off the couch and tossed it on the floor so he could sit down. He stared at the spot she'd cleared; it was covered with long white cat hair. She made a feeble attempt to brush it away; it stuck like glue.

Thomas eased himself down on the edge of the sofa and attempted to hide his grimace. He already knew he'd be sending his suit to the cleaners to remove the stench that undoubtedly started seeping into the fabric the moment he entered the room. A few cat hairs wouldn't make much of a difference either way.

She sat next to him; any closer, and she'd be sitting on his lap. It took everything he had in him not to run for the door. The odor alone was bad enough, but the woman herself made his skin crawl. This was going to be the fastest interview in history.

"How long have you been with your husband, ma'am?"

"I've been with him about two years. But I'm thinking our relationship has run its course. He's too jealous, too possessive. He's cramping my style, if you catch my drift." She gave him the once-over again and licked her lips.

He hoped his poker face remained intact.

"I mean, just look at this place." She waved an arm around the room. "He doesn't do a damned thing, he expects me to do his laundry and pick up after him. Well, I'm done. Finished, I tell you. I'm not his mommy. I got me a job too, you know."

He could only imagine the kind of work she did, but had to ask. "What kind of work do you do?"

"I'm a bartender down at OJ's. You should come in and see me sometime. I'll give you a drink on the house." She leaned into him.

He feigned a smile and leaned back. "I just might do that." He made a show of taking out his notebook and pen. "And where is this OJ's?"

"San Clemente."

She leapt from the couch and headed for the kitchen.

The action startled him.

"You want a beer?" she yelled back.

Thomas looked at his watch. It was barely eleven in the morning.

"No, thanks. I'm on duty."

Peeking her head around the corner, she winked. "I won't tell if you don't."

"No, really, I'm fine."

"Suit yourself!" She appeared with another cigarette clenched between her lips and a can of Coors in her hand.

"When will your husband be home, around five, six maybe?"

She laughed. "Hell, no. He just left yesterday."

"What does your husband do for a living?" Maybe this wasn't a bust after all.

"He drives a truck. You know, one of those big ones? He's gone anywhere from three days to a week at a time."

Bingo! He sat up straighter.

"When is he due back?"

"I don't have a clue. He comes and goes as if I'm running a damn hotel. He doesn't exactly hand over his schedule to me."

Thomas scribbled some notes. "What's the name of the company he works for?"

"I don't know that either." She displayed an exaggerated pout. "I'm just the wife, he doesn't tell me anything." Sharon Roberts rubbed her hand down his thigh.

Thomas stood abruptly. "Thank you for your time." He rushed toward the door. "I'll let myself out."

She ran after him and stood in the open doorway.

"Come back anytime!"

As he drove toward the station, he thought about the interview. Talk about torture. He wondered how anyone could stand to be in the same room with that woman for any length of time. It gave him even more incentive to meet this guy. Then his brother's words ran through his head: "He will live with a domineering female."

He checked in with Shadowhawk.

"Hey, you got anything?"

"Not yet, I'm still sifting through the conversations. So far it's boring as shit. What about you, how'd your interview go?"

"He wasn't in. I met his lovely wife though."

"That good, huh?"

"I'd rather eat tar than go back to that place. I think I need a shower."

"I'm intrigued." Shadowhawk laughed. "So when do we go

back?"

"Apparently he has a job that keeps him out of town… a lot, and he lives with a very dominant female. So far he fits the profile."

"Sounds promising. What does he do?"

"That's where I really hit the jackpot. He's a trucker."

"So, this could be our guy. When do we meet him?"

"That's where I hit a snag. His wife has no idea when he'll be back in town. Evidently, their communication skills are lacking. I'm going to have to call all the trucking companies in the area to see if I can find the one he works for. Maybe then I can narrow down when he's due back in town. I'll catch up with you later."

When Thomas arrived at the station he went directly to Johnson's office. "Tell me you've got something good for me."

"Phew, what's that smell?" She leaned away from him.

"Don't ask." He took off his jacket and slung it over his arm. He reminded himself to take it to his car afterward.

"Nasty."

Thomas backed up a foot. "Sorry."

"Well, all I found on this guy were some speeding tickets, and a DUI from about ten years ago. He's pretty clean. Do you want me to keep looking?"

"If you don't mind. I'm really liking this guy for it. Shit. I was expecting an attempted rape, peeping, exposure, something that would show his escalation."

Thomas spent the afternoon calling all the trucking companies in the phone book looking for the one with Jordan

Roberts on the books. He finally lucked out with The All American Trucking Company in Santa Ana, and jumped in his car and made the trip in record time. His interview with the boss was brief. He'd already known that Roberts had been fired weeks before, but he wanted to get a feel for the guy from his boss. Gauge his reaction to the questions.

Bill Bower seemed like a decent man; his complaints justified. He said he had no problem with Roberts's attitude. His problem with the boy, as he called him, was that his loads had been coming in late more often than not for the past few months. Bower's reprimands seemed to have fallen on deaf ears.

He hated to have to cut Roberts from the crew, he said, but in this economy, finding able-bodied men to do the job right was far too easy. Bower told him he was sorry, that it was just business. He had to keep the customer satisfied.

Thomas replayed the interview in his head while he sat in the drive-through line at Arby's waiting for his roast beef sandwich. He wondered if Roberts was indeed their perp? The way the guy seemed to be escalating, it was possible that his little side hobby took precedence over his paying job these days.

TWENTY-EIGHT

When Meagan opened her eyes, the room was dark. She sat up slowly. Her brain was fuzzy as if she'd been drugged. She shuffled into the kitchen, regretting the light the moment she flicked the switch. Her eyes burned, and she rubbed them. It took a moment to adjust to the brightness before she could fill the teakettle with water and pop a slice of bread into the toaster. She felt as if she were sleepwalking. She had to concentrate on the simplest of tasks.

While waiting for the water to boil, Meagan went to the bathroom. She didn't recognize the woman in the mirror; her red eyes were so swollen they were mere slits. She splashed her face with cold water. It felt so good, she continued to do so until the tea kettle called to her from the other room.

Just as she'd turned off the burner on the stove, she remembered that she had to call Lilah and make sure she had a ride home from work. She was surprised to see the light flashing on the answering machine, then she remembered that she'd unplugged the one in the bedroom.

There were two hang-ups, a message from Katy just calling to say hi, and the last was Drew.

"Sorry I didn't get back to you yesterday. We made the deal and the boys and I went out to celebrate. I lost track of time. I called the salon, and they told me you were sick. I hope you're okay. I'll call you later."

She called the salon. Darlene, the senior receptionist, answered.

"Oh, hi, baby. How are you feeling?" Darlene's warm, motherly concern was a welcome sound. Meagan almost broke down just hearing it.

"I'm better, thanks. Where's Lilah? I was worried because this is one of the nights I normally drive her home."

"She didn't show up for work today. She didn't even call. Jerome is livid, says he's going to fire her."

"He can't do that. I'm sure there's a good explanation."

"Oh, he's just being a pest. I doubt he'd really fire her."

"I hope you're right," Meagan said. "I guess I'll call her at home and check in on her. I'll talk to you later."

Meagan quickly dialed Lilah's number. Lilah's father answered on the first ring, "Hello!"

"Hi, Bill, it's Meagan. Is Lilah around?"

"No, she's not here," he sounded wrung out.

Confused, Meagan asked, "Isn't she sick?"

"No, she didn't come home last night, never called. I don't know *where* she could be."

"That doesn't sound like her. Who did she go out with last night?"

"No, you don't understand. She never made it home from work! I'm worried sick and I don't know what to do." His voice cracked.

"But I thought you were picking her up." Meagan's heart picked up a beat.

"No. She called and told me a friend was bringing her home. I never thought to ask who."

"What did the police say?" Meagan scratched her head.

"They said they couldn't file a report for at least twenty-four hours. I didn't go to work today. I've been sitting here by the phone."

"Look, I'll check into this, and call you right back." Meagan disconnected the call, then dialed the number for the salon. "Who closed with Lilah last night?" she blurted out the second she heard Darlene's voice.

"Let me check the books." After a brief pause, she was back on the line. "Sarah, Mi Ling and Jerome. Why, what's wrong?"

"Lilah didn't make it home last night after work and her father still hasn't heard from her. You know as well as I do that's just not like her. Something's wrong. Go ask them if they saw who she left with." Meagan talked so fast that she forgot to breathe.

"Okay, hold on. I'll be right back."

Darlene came back a few agonizing minutes later.

"Sorry, Meagan, no one saw anything. She left out the

front door. They were either having a cigarette in the back or finishing their cleanup. What are you going to do?" Darlene's voice went up an octave on the last word.

"I don't know." Meagan stared at the ceiling as if it had the answer.

"Call me if you hear anything," came Darlene's worried voice.

Meagan hung up and called the police. Her words tumbled over themselves. She wasn't sure the woman on the other end understood what she was getting at until she asked for Lilah's address and promised to send an officer over to take a statement from the father. By the time she hung up, Meagan felt better, but not much.

She called Bill Carpenter back, told him the police were coming by, and asked him to call her the minute he received any news.

Meagan disconnected the call and collapsed in the nearby chair. It seemed that the day from hell just wouldn't end. Then she remembered her tea and got up. When she entered the kitchen, she noticed the toast standing in the toaster. She tossed it into the trashcan; she wasn't hungry anymore.

The phone rang, Meagan ran into the other room.

"Hello?" Silence. "Hello, Hello, Hello!" By the last word she was yelling. "Dammit!" She slammed the phone down.

Carrying the handset of the cordless phone with her, Meagan curled up on the couch and wrapped a blanket around her. She stared at it, willing it to ring with good news about Lilah, and fell asleep praying she was all right.

She was jolted awake by the ringing phone right next to her head. Her heart hammered in her chest. She swung her legs around and sat up before answering it. "Hello?" The clock above the TV read two-fifteen.

At first there was nothing but silence. Just as she was about to hang up, Meagan heard something. She put the phone back up to her ear.

"Hel-lo Mea-gan my pr-et-ty. Iee- le-ft yo-u a pre-sent. Iee ho-pe yo-ou li-ke it." Click.

Goosebumps enveloped Meagan's body. "What the hell was that?" The voice was mechanical, the words broken up. She jumped up, looked around, then scurried through the house shutting and locking windows, yanking the curtains. She checked the locks on the front door, then raced to the back.

But when she tried to lock the door, it wouldn't click into place. She was going to have to open and slam the old door hard. The wood warped sometimes. She turned off the kitchen light, then pulled the curtain back just enough to peek out. She didn't see anyone lurking, but that didn't mean they weren't there. Then a twinkle caught her eye.

There was something sitting on the table between her two chairs. She couldn't quite make out what it was, but there was a tiny spot on it that glittered in the moonlight. She eased the door open a crack and quickly scanned the yard to make sure she was alone, then her hand groped the inside wall for the switch on the porch light.

It took a moment for her brain to catch up with her eyes. Then a bloodcurdling scream echoed through the quiet night.

Her knees gave out; she crumpled to the ground in slow motion. Then everything turned black.

Twenty-nine

Thomas glided through the crystal clear aquamarine water, the wind in his hair, salt spray on his face, enjoying the speed and freedom. He was flying, not a care in the world. He handled the 25-foot sailboat with an expertise he didn't know he had.

He loved the tranquility. Victoria stood on the beach beckoning to him. Just a few more minutes, he thought. Slicing through the water so fast gave him a rush. He looked to his right where dolphins playfully raced the boat. He smiled; he wanted this ride to never end.

But Victoria stood among the palm trees, her arms waving more frantically with each second he delayed. Not wanting to, but knowing he should, he started toward the beach and his wife.

Thomas awoke with a start. His phone was ringing. Sluggishly, he reached for the receiver, then searched for a pen and paper. He hung up, and dropped his head back down onto the pillow. He didn't want to get up; he wanted to go back to that tropical island with Victoria. He laid there for a minute, fighting sleep, the conversation running through his head.

She said she knew he wasn't on call, but couldn't reach any of the other detectives. They were either out on other cases or sick with the flu. The captain said he was to take the initial call, then they would see about getting someone else to work the case so he could focus on the Sandman. But one phrase kept rolling through his head, "They had a body, sort of." He was sure he had misheard that.

By the time Thomas pulled up outside his destination, the place was lit up like a Christmas tree. Black-and-whites littered the street, their lights flashing red and blue. The coroner's van was there, along with CSU. He had to park way down the street. As he walked up to the crime scene tape, he had to flash his badge to gain admittance. The rookie standing guard didn't know him.

He lifted the tape, and let Thomas through, pointing to the side of the house. The klieg lights they had set up made the area as bright as day. He turned the corner, but all he saw were people busy at work. No body yet. Cheryl's assistant, Brody, bent over to examine something Thomas couldn't see. Light bulbs flashed like strobe lights. The moment they noticed Thomas, a hush came over the crowd, and they backed out of the way.

Brody was the only person to speak. "We waited for you before we took her away."

Thomas didn't answer, because now he could see the vic. The "her" in question was sitting on top of a plastic outdoor table. At least, her head was. She was a young woman, probably early twenties. Her eyes were wide open in terror, her mouth frozen in mid-scream. Her hair was blonde, about chin-length, and her pierced nose held a small diamond that glinted in the light. That tiny speck of beauty amid the monstrosity of the scene perverted it even more, if that was possible.

He stared at the abomination for a moment. "Okay, talk to me. Did this woman live here? Where is the rest of her body?"

The officer standing nearby—his name tag read Harrison—filled him in. "The woman who lives here found the head. The neighbor lady heard a scream and ran over to find the lady of the house on the ground. She had fainted. Her name is Meagan Laurel McInnis. It was the neighbor, Lisa Willis, who called 911. Her husband took her home the moment we arrived. Ms. McInnis hasn't said a word."

"Did anyone get the neighbor's statement?"

"I was on my way when I saw you pull up."

"All right, thanks."

Thomas made his way through the wave of people and stepped into the house. He found the witness sitting on a couch.

Her arms were wrapped around her legs; her chin rested on her knees. She looked as if she wanted to disappear, and he couldn't blame her. The redhead's eyes were bloodshot and swollen, staring straight ahead without blinking.

Thomas retreated to the kitchen and searched the cupboards until he found the liquor, what little there was. He snagged a glass and poured two fingers of brandy, then returned to the other room. He grabbed a blanket off the couch, wrapped it around her shoulders, then sat next to her.

He brought the glass to her lips and told her to drink. She took a big gulp, then coughed.

"So, you are alive after all." He smiled.

"What are you trying to do, drown me?" She wiped her mouth.

Her eyes focused on him. "Who are you? What are you doing in my house? Where'd the cops go?" Her body trembled.

"They're still around. My name is Detective J.J. Thomas." He pulled the blanket around her tighter. "It's okay, you're safe. I just need to ask you a few questions."

She looked uncertain at first, then her shoulders relaxed.

"Can you tell me what happened?"

Her eyes began to glaze over again. He picked up the glass and put it to her lips. This time she took a sip without much prompting. After she swallowed, her face screwed up, and her body did a little dance.

"That's awful. I think you like torturing women." She shivered again.

Thomas couldn't help but laugh. "You've got me pegged. I love getting up in the middle of the might and wreaking havoc on poor unsuspecting women."

Turning serious again, he asked her if she was ready to talk to him. The story she told was more than he'd bargained for. It seemed that the woman had a stalker who'd been tormenting her for weeks. First with phone calls in the middle of the night. Then the morning before, she'd found her dog murdered.

As if that wasn't bad enough, she discovered the decapitated head of a friend in her back yard. Thomas really felt for the poor woman; she'd been through hell. But he could tell she was strong. A lesser person would have turned stark raving mad by now. Instead she told the story in a calm voice, staring down at her painted red toenails. He noticed she wore a couple of toe rings. Her eyes were dry; she obviously had no more tears left.

"So he'd never spoken before tonight?"

"No. Like I said, the calls have been increasing over the last few days, but this is the first time someone actually spoke."

"Tell me again what the voice sounded like."

"It was a deep mechanical sound, he spoke really slow. Not like a stutter, but he seemed to hold the words out. Like Maaaa-gunnn," she mimicked the caller. "You know what I mean?" She looked up at him. Her crystal blue eyes searched his face. He was stunned into silence.

He cleared his throat. "Um, I'm trying." *Trying to get my thoughts back on the case that is.* "Tell me again what he said."

"Hello, Meagan, my pretty. I left you a gift. I hope you like it."

"So this guy knows your name."

She shuddered. "Do you think I'm next?" He watched as she started shutting down again.

Thomas put his hand on her arm. "I won't let that happen."

He listened to himself say the words, and inwardly cringed. How the hell was he going to manage that? He had his hands full with the Sandman case. The captain flat-out told him that there were no uniforms to spare. But there was just something about this woman that made him want to protect her at all costs.

He noticed Harrison standing at the entrance of the room, and led him into the kitchen to talk. The CSU had packed up and left. The coroner's van had gone.

"Do you need me for anything more?" Harrison asked.

"No, thanks, you go on ahead. I'll finish up here." What Thomas didn't say was he couldn't leave, and it wasn't just because he thought she might be in danger. He stood at the entrance to the room and gazed down at Meagan McInnis. She looked so lost, so broken. Life had smacked her hard.

For some reason he wanted to pull her into his arms and comfort her, but for the life of him he couldn't figure out why. He'd been around plenty of victims, some even more attractive than her, but never once had he felt this pull. He just wanted to be near her, to gaze at her, to take care of her. Make sure nothing bad ever happened to her again.

The thoughts running through his mind unsettled him to no end. Maybe it was the dream he was having before coming over here, but he never felt that way about Victoria. She didn't *need* him. He ran a hand through his hair and sighed. What the fuck was he going to do?

Thomas went back into the living room and walked over to where Meagan continued to study her feet.

"I'm going to stay here for the rest of the night."

THIRTY

Meagan's head shot up and she stared at him.

"You're staying here?"

"That's the only way I know of to protect you."

"So you do think I'm in danger." It wasn't a question.

"I'm just being cautious. Unless, of course, you have somewhere else to stay?"

"I have friends and family, but if you truly think this guy's after me, I wouldn't want anyone else hurt."

Thomas glanced at his watch. Five-thirty.

"It'll only be for a couple more hours. I'll be right here in the living room. You'll be safe. Why don't you go see if you can get some sleep? In a little while I'll call my partner. She'll stay with you today. That should give us time to figure out what to do until we catch this guy."

She stared at him blankly, but didn't move. He crossed the room and held out his hand. She focused on it, then up at his face. His heart galloped in his chest. A moment later she took his hand and let him help her up. When she unfolded herself and stood, he was surprised to see that she was much taller than he'd thought, five-feet-ten, maybe five-eleven, but she was still dwarfed by his six-five frame. He watched her walk away until she was out of sight.

Thomas mentally shook his head and got to work. He called and ordered a trace put on Meagan McInnis's phone, as well as a record of all incoming calls to her number for the past month. He would have someone drop off her statement later for her to sign after he'd finished typing it up. He'd call Shadowhawk and have her work here today. He would wait until seven; no need to wake her entire family. At least one of them would get a good night's sleep.

**

Meagan climbed under the covers and waited for sleep. She stared at the window, a sliver of light seeped through a crack in the curtains. The sun was starting to rise. Although exhausted, her brain wouldn't shut down. Her mind kept replaying the events of the last twenty-four hours over and over again like a scratch in a record.

Her eyes burned. She rubbed them, then covered her head with her pillow as if she could block it all out. She prayed she was just having a bad dream from which she'd soon wake.

**

Thomas checked in with Cooper and James. He told them to set up a stakeout on the apartment. He had dispatch connect him to their cruiser.

"James, here."

"James, it's Thomas. How's it going?"

"Nothing yet. The wife arrived home around four this morning toting some guy. He was too tall to be our perp. Either she doesn't expect the husband home, or she doesn't give a shit either way."

"Takes all kinds. Keep your eyes peeled, and call me the second the guy shows up. The DMV picture is fairly recent, he shouldn't be difficult to recognize."

"Cooper is spelling me at six. I'll let him know."

"Great, catch ya later."

Thomas hung up and looked around for something to read. He noticed an array of magazines on the coffee table. He had his choice of In Style, Cosmopolitan or People.

Sighing, he picked up the People with Angelina Jolie on the cover. Anything that included her couldn't be all bad.

An hour later he called his partner and filled her in. Then he asked her to come down to San Clemente and spell him.

"How's it going with the Dark Knight, you come up with anything yet?" Thomas asked.

"He could be our perp. Sounds like she was falling for the guy in a big way. He even asked her for a photograph. So that's one mystery solved. Did you notice a computer at Ms. McInnis's house?"

"No. You'd better bring your laptop to be on the safe side."

"Okay, see you in about an hour."

By the time Shadowhawk arrived, Thomas was relieved. He'd read all three magazines and had learned more than he needed to know about the importance of exfoliating skin, what men wanted in bed, and he was still pissed off about the score he received on the What Kind of Mate Are You? quiz.

The minute he heard the knock at the door, he threw the Cosmo on the coffee table, and jumped up so quickly he got a head rush. When he opened the door he must have looked like a deer caught in the headlights because the first thing out of Shadowhawk's mouth was, "Is everything all right?"

"Yes." He must have said it too fast because she still stared at him, hard. His cheeks flamed as if she'd caught him with his pants down, instead of reading a bunch of women's magazines. "Ms. McInnis is still asleep."

She seemed satisfied with the answer, because she let it drop and entered the house. He grabbed his jacket off the couch and told her that he was going to talk to the father of the victim. He promised to get someone else to cover the girl so they could return their focus to the Sandman case.

Thomas headed home. Once he entered the house, the first thing he smelled was coffee, and he veered straight for it like a beacon in the night. He filled a cup and took it with him upstairs. A hot shower beckoned.

He was drying himself off when his cell rang.

"Thomas."

"Detective, it's Cooper."

"Is the husband back?" That was sooner than he expected.

"No, there's been another murder. The detective I interviewed last week in San Diego just called. He said the MO is similar, but not exact. He's still convinced it's our guy all the same. The woman was found on the sand this time, the perp didn't bother to cover her up. He said it was as if he wanted her found right away."

"Shit, this guy is escalating."

"Detective Chase said that too. He thinks you're going to want to see this vic and asked if you could get there ASAP."

Thomas wrote down the information before hanging up, then dressed and was out the door in five minutes flat.

He called Detective Chase from the road, but couldn't get much else from him. He told Thomas he wanted him to look at the scene with a set of fresh eyes and get his take on it. By the time he reached the beach in Oceanside, things were winding down. It looked more like a sideshow than a full-blown circus. The CSU had already left and only a few uniforms stood around guarding the site.

But the looky-loos were out in full force standing behind the tape trying to catch a glimpse of a dead body. He found Chase waiting for him by the parking lot and he led him to the body. Thomas stared down.

"Shit, this guy has snapped." Thomas swallowed hard.

He was quiet a moment while he collected his thoughts. Before him lay the body of a naked woman, her arms and legs had been hacked off, then crudely placed together again like a broken doll. Blood soaked the sand around her. Her breasts were missing. So was her head.

Thomas scrubbed his hands down his face. "This is no dump site. He killed her where she lay. I don't think he held her for any amount of time, either. There are no ligature marks on her wrists and ankles. He chopped her body parts off while she was still alive. Too much blood." He pointed while he talked. "I'd say the head was last, not much blood pooled there. She'd pretty much bled out by then. Shit, he's gone from months to days between kills. I hope he fucked up this time and left us some evidence we can use."

"There's no sign of the head or breasts. I think he took them with him," Chase said.

"I think I can help with that. Well, at least the head."

Chase looked at him, his eyebrows raised. "No shit?"

"No shit." Thomas filled him in on the events from the night before.

Chase walked Thomas to his car, promising to keep him in the loop, and vice versa. Thomas was speeding north on I-5 toward Orange County when he called the captain to bring him up to speed.

"Sir, I really need more people. I can't cover the girl, the primary suspect, and follow leads with the small task force I have."

"I'm sorry, Thomas, but I wasn't just blowing smoke up your ass. I really can't afford to give you anyone else right now. The county doesn't just shut down because we have a single priority-one case. This guy's all over the map; let's hope he's moving on. Besides, I've got Sanchez out on his honeymoon, Benton in New York at a funeral, and half the squad out because of that damn flu going around.

"Lost another one last night: Riker heaved in his cruiser and had to be sent home. Seems this flu is a nasty one, gets you from both ends. They're still trying to remove the stench from his ride. Do what you can with the manpower you have. If anyone becomes available, I'll send them your way."

"Great," Thomas said.

THIRTY-ONE

When Bill Carpenter opened the door, he looked shell-shocked. His face was covered in gray stubble, he had bags under his eyes, and his hair stood on end as if he'd been running his hands through it countless times. Thomas decided that he'd better get his questions out of the way before he broke the news about his daughter.

He asked about Lilah's friends, boyfriends—past and present, as well as any contact information he might have.

Mr. Carpenter disappeared and returned a few minutes later with her address book. He told Thomas he could copy it and return it later. He didn't know his daughter would no longer have any use for it.

"Sir, why don't we sit down?"

"Huh, what?" He looked at Thomas as if he were speaking a foreign language.

"I have something I need to tell you, and I think you should be sitting when you hear it." Thomas ran his hand through his hair.

The father's eyes widened and he shook his head. "No."

"Sir, I really think—"

"Oh, God, no." His face screwed up and his eyes implored Thomas to correct his assumption.

Thomas stared at the man a moment. He didn't want to be the one to deliver the crashing blow, but he had no choice. He steeled himself for the man's reaction.

"We found your daughter. I'm afraid she's dead."

The man let out a heart-wrenching wail and his knees gave out. Thomas caught him before he collapsed to the ground and half-carried, half-dragged him over to the nearest chair.

Thomas was at a loss. He didn't know what to do for the man, so he knelt beside Bill Carpenter while he cried, hunched over in the chair, hiding his face with his hands. Thomas patted the man's back every so often.

After a time Thomas asked, "Is there someone I can call for you? Someone who can come over and be with you right now?"

At first Bill Carpenter just shook his head. Then after a moment he wiped his face and looked at Thomas with a pained expression. "I just want to be alone."

Thomas nodded. "I'll let myself out."

"Thank you." His head dipped back down.

Thomas made it to the door before he turned back. "I'm sorry for your loss."

Thomas tried to shake his somber mood as he stopped by

his house to pack a bag before returning to Meagan's for the night, but he couldn't get the image of poor Bill Carpenter out of his head. He wondered if that's what he looked like after finding Victoria.

Shadowhawk answered his knock, lowered gun by her side. Obviously she'd looked through the peephole first. When he walked into the room he noticed a pizza box on the table and an old black and white movie on pause.

"What are you girls watching?"

"*Rebecca*," Meagan answered through a full mouth. She swallowed before she continued. "You want some?" She pointed to the box.

Her smile warmed him. He couldn't hide one of his own. A moment of repose, no matter how fleeting, was always welcome. He knew from experience after Victoria died. Once in awhile he would actually forget she was gone, for about a minute—two if he was lucky—then it would all come crashing down on his head. A simple thing like reaching for the phone to tell her he'd be late could turn his whole world upside down.

He noticed the swelling around Meagan's eyes had retreated, her face more relaxed. At the moment, she looked like a kid. She was sitting on the couch with her legs crossed, plate on her lap and a glass of milk beside her. Suddenly he realized he'd been staring too long. "Yeah," he said. "I don't remember the last time I ate."

Then she asked, "Are you moving in?"

He glanced down at the bag, then back at her, "I thought it

best I have a few things with me tonight. It looks like it's just Shadowhawk and I watching you for the time being." He gave his partner a pointed look, and she gave a slight nod. She understood that they had to talk.

Meagan jumped off the couch and disappeared into the kitchen. "Do you want anything to drink?"

"Coffee, if you've got it," he yelled back.

"Coffee with pizza? Yuck. You and Fawn both," her voice rang out.

Shadowhawk lifted her mug in mock salute. Thomas smiled and took a seat in the overstuffed chair. He let the girls have the couch to themselves.

"I suppose you want it black too?" She yelled again.

"Please!"

Meagan returned with a paper plate and a cup of coffee. They ate quietly while they watched the end of the movie. The moment the credits rolled, Shadowhawk took her plate and empty coffee cup to the kitchen. When she returned, "I'd better get home." Looking at Thomas, "You want to walk me out?"

"Sure." He got out of the chair and turned toward Meagan. "I'll be right back. Lock the door behind me."

She nodded and followed them to the door.

Thomas waited until they got across the street to Shadowhawk's black F150 truck before he asked, "Did you get anything more out of her?"

"Oh, yeah." She filled him in on Meagan's boss, the prince, Jerome Banks, and former boyfriend/stalker Brad Landis.

When she finished Thomas said, "I can top that." Then he brought her up to speed on his day.

"Holy, crap, Batman! So, *you're* telling me that Meagan's stalker, and the Sandman are one and the same?"

"Unbelievable, huh?"

"Shit, this girl is a major creep magnet. Hell, her creeps trump all my exes combined, and I've dated some pretty crazy chicks."

"You and me both." Thomas blew out a breath. "I'm going to have to delve deeper into Meagan's history and see what I can come up with. You go ahead and interview everyone at the salon tomorrow."

Shadowhawk unlocked the truck's door and opened it before she turned back. "What are we going to do with her?"

"Good question." He looked up at the sky, then back at her. "I guess we're on double duty till we catch this guy."

"What about Cooper and James, have they come up with anything yet?"

"No, there's been no sign of Jordan Roberts."

"Do you think the wife tipped him off?"

"Hard to say. She talks a good game, says she finds the confines of marriage a little too *restrictive*."

"The more I hear about this woman, the more I can't *wait* to meet her." Shadowhawk laughed.

He smiled. "She's some piece of work, all right." Then he turned serious. "Of course, I've seen women beaten to a bloody pulp go back to their husbands time and time again, so there's no telling what some people will do."

"Ain't that the truth." She started the engine. "Well, I should get going, it's nine-thirty. I'm sure Maria's getting a little anxious by now."

"Tell her I'm sorry to keep you late—"

She interrupted him. "But until this case is over, it's going to happen more often than not."

"Pretty much."

Shadowhawk drove off. Thomas walked back to the house and knocked. Meagan opened the door, but she was no longer smiling. He walked in and noticed she'd cleaned up and topped off his coffee.

She returned to the couch and drew her legs up tight. No longer playful, she'd reverted to trying to disappear. He wasn't sure if she was uncomfortable with him or going through the memory crash. Either way he'd try to get her mind off her troubles.

He decided to start by asking harmless questions. They discussed movies, books, authors, and music. They had a lot in common, so the conversation flowed easily for the next couple of hours.

They fell into a debate about the reality of the scene in the movie *Swordfish,* in which the bus was lifted by the helicopter.

"It's not possible!" Thomas enjoyed getting a rise out of her.

"Who cares, it's entertaining. I don't go to the movies for reality, I go to *escape* it!" She was sitting cross-legged again on the couch and leaning forward, her eyes sparkling with passion as her voice rose.

They were interrupted when the phone rang. They stared at it a moment before either moved. Meagan looked at Thomas. He nodded, then followed her over to the table. She lifted the phone, and he lifted the extension he'd set up next to it. Once he was ready, he nodded and she answered.

"Hey, gorgeous, sorry it's so late. Were you still up?"

Thomas put the extension down and walked away. He grabbed his coffee cup and retreated to the kitchen. Meagan took the phone to her bedroom and closed the door. He felt weird. He was actually pissed at the guy for interrupting them, taking her away. Was this what it felt like to be jealous? Whatever it was, he didn't like it.

***

Meagan was thankful that Drew called. She hadn't talked to anyone she cared about regarding what was going on. She didn't dare. Whether family or friend, they'd insist she stay with them. She couldn't put anyone else in danger. After all, Lilah was dead because of her. She'd been avoiding Katy's calls all day; Meagan was afraid she'd be able to detect something wrong by her voice.

She told Drew all that had happened since last they talked. She tried hard to hold back the tears, but she lost the battle in the end.

"Oh, honey, I'm so sorry," Drew said. "I can't believe everything you've been through. The record company wants us to start recording tomorrow. Let me see what I can do. Maybe under the circumstances they'll give me a couple of days off. In the meantime, I'm glad you have someone there with you. I'll call you tomorrow, okay?" His sympathetic voice made her cry even harder. She realized that she wished he were there.

"Okay," she finally managed.

After Drew hung up, Meagan felt lost and abandoned. She set the phone on the nightstand, then blew her nose and wiped her eyes before returning to the living room. She sat back down on the couch.

"Was that your boyfriend?"

"Sort of," she answered without looking up.

"Tell me about him. What's his name?"

"Drew Jackson."

Thomas laughed. "As in Andrew Jackson?"

Meagan scowled at him.

"How did you two meet?"

For the next hour he heard the story of Meagan and Drew. Her voice was animated in the telling, and when she was done, a smile came to her lips. For the second time that night he felt jealous. He wanted to be the one to put that smile on her face.

"So you haven't known this guy all that long." Relief washed over him.

"Well, no, not exactly."

"I see, and does he feel the same about you? After all, he *is* a musician." Thomas reminded himself to rein in the sarcasm.

"He's not your typical musician." Her words cut right back.

"And how do you know that? You've only had a few dates with him. That's not long enough to set up a track record."

"Because I know him!"

Thomas knew he was upsetting Meagan, but he couldn't stop himself. "You do, huh? Let's just recap, shall we? He lives somewhere up north, you don't know where. His parents died in a car crash and he's been on the road for the last three years. Yeah, you know him very well." He sounded angry even to himself, he should quit while he's behind.

"I mean, you've never met him. He's gentle, giving and considerate."

"Oh, so you mean he makes sure you have your orgasm first before he gets his rocks off?" *Dammit all to hell, I just said that out loud!*

She jumped up, her eyes as wide as saucers. Her mouth opened and closed, then she turned on her heels.

He leapt at her and grabbed her wrist, "Wait! I'm sorry, Meagan, I didn't mean that. *Please* don't go."

Her face turned three shades of scarlet before she jerked her hand back and stormed off to her bedroom. The door slammed.

Thomas scrubbed his hands down his face. What the fuck was wrong with him? He couldn't *believe* he'd just said that. He never talked that way to a woman, yet he just did. He was out of control. What was it about this redhead that got him so worked up?

"Meagan, I'm so sorry. Really, I swear I'm not normally like this. I just haven't had a lot of sleep for the past week. Please say you'll forgive me." He stood there in silence, waiting.

Finally the door swung open, and Meagan stomped out past him. She went straight to the cabinet at the end of the hall, opened it, grabbed some sheets and a blanket, then shoved them at him. Without a word she went back to the bedroom and slammed the door.

Thomas stared at the door a moment, wishing Meagan would open it again. After a while he gave up and walked back into the living room. He didn't blame her; he deserved it. In fact, he even respected her for it. He dropped the bedding on the couch and went into the kitchen to make a fresh pot of coffee. It was going to be a long night.

He was pulling the case files out of his bag when the phone rang. He waited until the ringing had stopped to make sure Meagan had answered, then he carefully hit the talk button on his end. He heard the low mechanical voice she had described. "Hel-lo Mea-gan, did you like my lit-tle gi-ft?You shoo-uld be mo-re care-ful when pic-king yoo-ur fri-ends." Then the phone went dead.

Meagan flew out of the bedroom and ran smack dab into his chest. She wore a mask of fear. He wanted to put his arms around her; instead he laid his hands on her arms and gently pushed her away far enough so he could see her. All the color had drained from her face.

"That was him! Did you hear it?" She was breathless; her voice trembled.

"Yes. Come over here and sit down." He set her in the chair, then called to check in on the trace.

He hung up and looked at her. "They couldn't get it. Next time you're going to have to talk to this guy. See if he'll answer any questions, but more importantly, keep him on the line as long as you can."

"He friggin' terrifies me!"

"I know, but you have to try."

Meagan stared at him a moment. "Okay." She got up and left the room. He heard the bedroom door close behind her.

Thomas fell into the chair she'd just vacated and ran a hand through his hair. *What the hell is going on with me?*

THIRTY-TWO

November 1, 1985

The woman dragged her son through the house by his hand.

"Mommy, you're hurting me." His frantic cry made her stop. She turned around and squatted in front of her son. "I'm sorry, baby, but we've got to get out of here before your daddy gets back!" She picked him up and ran toward the front door.

She hadn't bothered to pack. She'd seen her chance and took it. When she'd woken up on the kitchen floor, the room was dark. The house was suspiciously quiet. She'd searched each room in case her husband was lurking somewhere.

It was twilight. The sun had already dipped behind the trees at the edge of their property. Their long shadows reached across the barren farmland where tumbleweeds danced in the breeze. The porch light was still on from the night before.

The woman raced around the car, kicking up dirt from the driveway along the way. The Chevy Impala's rusty door complained loudly when she wrenched it open. Hastily, she deposited her son in the front seat and fastened his seatbelt. She ran to the other side, jumped in, then locked all the doors, climbing over her son in the process.

"Mommy, I'm scared." His lower lip trembled.

"I know, honey, but everything's going to be all right from now on. We're going to live at Grandma's house." She spoke quickly while she searched the car. "You'll love it there, she has chickens and ducks and even a pond. And everything is green, nothing like this dirt park your father calls a farm." She looked in the back seat.

"Dammit!" She forgot her purse. She unlocked the door and started to get out.

"Mommy, don't leave me!"

The woman stopped, turned around and took her four-year-old son's face in her hands. "Honey, Mommy would never leave you, I love you. You're the most important thing in the world to me. That's why I'm taking you away from here. Do you understand?"

The little boy nodded, and his mother kissed his forehead.

"Now Mommy has to go get her purse. The car keys are in it. It will only take a second, baby, then we'll get out of here, okay?"

He nodded and sniffled as he watched his mother disappear into the house.

The keys weren't in her purse. Her husband must have hidden them. Sweat trickled down her face and her back as she searched every drawer in the kitchen. Her heart hammered in her chest. She ran to the mantle and dumped out every jar. She stripped the cushions off the couch and tossed them across the room in a frenzy.

***

His mother was taking forever. The little boy jiggled his legs to make her hurry. A thud to his right made him jump. He turned toward the window, where his father's angry face glared at him. The boy screamed. His father jerked the door handle and tried to get it open. His bright red face got screwy; the veins in his neck and forehead bulged. His giant fist beat against the window. The boy leaned away as far as his seatbelt would allow.

"Open the goddamned door, you little brat," he bellowed into the night. "Do you hear me?" He hit the glass so hard the boy was sure it would break. "Open." Pound. "This!" Pound. "Door!" Pound. With each thud the window vibrated.

He'd never been so scared in his life. His body trembled. His father hit him when he did nothing wrong. What would his father do to him now that he was disobeying him?

The pounding abruptly stopped. His father backed away. The little boy breathed a sigh of relief. He watched his father stagger around the front of the car. He tripped and disappeared from sight.

"Fuck!" The boy heard his father's muffled curse.

First one hand appeared on the hood, then the other. His father climbed up the front of the car and stood up. Blood dripped from his nose; he wiped it off with the back of his hand. His father staggered around the hood of the car to the other side. His mother's door stood wide open! The boy tried to unbuckle his seatbelt, but his hands were shaking something fierce. His fingers couldn't find the button. He had to reach that door before his father.

***

The woman stopped, held her breath and listened. And heard her son's screams.

"No!" She raced toward the front of the house and paused in the open doorway, gasping for breath. Her husband was bent down in the driver's side of the car yanking on her son's arms. His little body was still secured by his safety belt.

The woman took a running leap onto his back and wrapped her arms around his neck. "Leave him alone, you bastard!"

The man jerked back from the car and tried to buck her off.

"Get off me, you bitch!"

He swung around the yard, but she held on tight as if she were in a rodeo.

"I'm gonna kill you!" her husband bellowed.

She tightened her grip around his neck, but he wasn't slowing down.

"Get off me, now!" He whirled his body in circles. It made her dizzy, but she hung on.

She started biting anything she could sink her teeth into. She bit his ear so hard that it tore. Blood spilled down his neck. He howled like a wild animal. His arms flailed about in a futile attempt to free himself.

Her teeth sank into his shoulder, and she squeezed her arms as hard as she could around his throat. He had to pass out soon. He bent his head forward; she thought she'd finally won. Then his head whipped back fast and hit her in the forehead. Hard. She felt her hands loosening their grip; she was falling. The last thing she heard was her son yelling her name.

***

The boy watched his mother fall and her eyes close.

"Mommy!"

His father stormed off toward the shed. The boy struggled with his seat belt, and finally it came loose. He scrambled out the driver's side of the car.

He knelt down next to her.

"Mommy, get up." He nudged her.

"Please, Mommy, please get up!" He shook her body frantically.

The little boy grabbed his mother's arm with both hands and tried to drag her to the car. "Come on!"

Her eyes fluttered open and she rubbed her forehead.

"Okay, baby, Mommy's awake. You go on and get in the car, I'll be right there." She got up on her hands and knees.

The boy turned toward the car and jerked to a stop. His father stood right behind him. He carried something in one hand. The other reached back and hit him with such force that he flew through the air. His head hit the concrete steps with a crack, and everything went black.

The little boy groaned. He eased his eyes open and winced in pain. His hand flew to the back of his head where it hurt. It was wet, and he looked at his hand and realized he was bleeding. He stared at his bloody hand and wondered what had happened. It took only a moment before his head shot up. His father stood with his back to him, his head bent toward the ground; the axe he used for chopping wood dangled from his right hand. Blood dripped from the blade.

The boy stared at his father's feet. He blinked a couple times.

"Stupid cunt." His father dropped the axe, then turned. His face was splashed with blood; his clothes were soaked in it. He started toward the boy. The little boy scrambled out of the way and breathed a sigh of relief when he passed him on the stairs.

"I need a drink." He disappeared through the open door.

The boy stared at the ground. He barely recognized his mother. There was blood everywhere. She was hurt really bad. The boy jumped off the stairs and ran toward her, ignoring the boo-boo on his head. It hurt, but Mommy looked like she hurt more. He dropped down beside her and shook her arm.

"Mommy, wake up." She didn't move.

"Mommy, please wake up, you're scaring me."

He heard the coyotes cry in the distance and shivered.

He looked up at the moon. "Come on, Mommy, it's time for bed." Maybe Mommy wanted to sleep outside. The little boy laid down next her. He needed to guard her. He heard a hoot owl from the direction of the barn and something rustled in the bushes not far away. He was scared, but he had to be brave for Mommy. He needed to protect her from the creatures of the night.

THIRTY-THREE

Thomas awoke with a start; the bathroom door had softly clicked shut. He was slouched down on Meagan's couch, with the files spread out before him on the coffee table. He rubbed his eyes with the palms of his hands and heard the toilet flush. He scooped up the photos before she could see them and headed to the kitchen to make a fresh pot of coffee.

The scent of burnt sludge permeated the air. He'd left an almost empty pot on the burner all night. He opened the window and back door hoping to air out the place before Meagan noticed. As if that were possible.

He was vigorously scrubbing the pot with an SOS pad when he heard the bathroom door open. His hands froze; he turned his head. Meagan glared at him a moment before she went back into her bedroom and closed the door.

Thomas let out a pent-up breath. He glanced down at his

shirtsleeves shoved up past his elbows, his hands deep within the pot, and realized he must look ridiculous. He heard the door open and turned in time to see her in a skimpy red robe before the bathroom door shut behind her and the water go on in the shower.

He set about making coffee, and grabbed the filter filled with grounds and laid it gently on top of the trash can under the sink. The can was full. He finished putting the pot on, then took the trash outside to empty it. He thought he remembered seeing garbage cans out on the side of the house.

As soon as he stepped through the back door, he noticed the small plastic table where the head of a dead woman had lain. The blood had baked in the sun.

After dumping the trash, he grabbed the hose and turned the water on. He stood above the table and adjusted the nozzle to high. The force of the water peeled the blood away from the plastic like paint. Behind him he heard a loud thud, and swung around. The window to the bathroom was open; a gentle breeze blew the curtain. Thomas caught a glimpse of Meagan's naked body as she stepped into the shower.

He quickly turned his gaze back to the table and tried to concentrate on the task at hand, but his mind wouldn't listen. Instead it filled with the image of her porcelain skin, her auburn curls cascading down her back, the curve of her well-rounded hips and the swell of her heart-shaped bottom. He swallowed, hard. And that wasn't the only thing that was hard.

He tried to clear the vision from his head and focus. He looked down at the table and noticed it was clean. The yard was getting flooded. He released the pressure from the nozzle and the water stopped. He carried the hose back to the wheel attached to the wall and started to roll it up. Thomas wrestled with it a couple of minutes before he realized why the hose was winning: he'd forgotten to turn the water off.

"Get a grip." He turned off the water and wrapped the hose the way he'd found it. He snatched the trash can up on his way back into the house and this time kept his eyes glued to the ground.

He poured himself a cup of coffee and headed into the living room to make a call. Johnson picked up on the third ring.

"It's Thomas. I need all the information you can get me on an Andrew Jackson, thirty-two, resides somewhere in Northern California. Parents died in a car crash and he's in a band called The Ravens. They've been touring small venues, the last in San Diego. I'm sure they have a website."

"Got it. Call you later." Johnson hung up.

Meagan walked out of the bathroom in that skimpy red robe, her hair wrapped up in a towel. Her long legs were sleek and sinewy. He jumped off the couch and met her in the kitchen. He stood by as she prepared her coffee, then turned and walked past him as if he were invisible.

"Are you going to stay mad at me all day?"

She stopped, hesitated a second, then turned around.

"I haven't decided yet." She disappeared in the direction

of her bedroom.

He knocked on the bedroom door. It opened, and she jutted her chin out in defiance.

He ignored the look. "I'm going to jump in the shower. I don't want you to leave the apartment or open the door to anyone. Even if it's someone you know." He was dead serious.

"Okay."

"And if you hear or notice anything strange, come get me. You got that?"

"Fine." Meagan planted her hands on her hips. "You plan on spending the day in there?"

"No, but it's been my experience that if something's going to happen, it'll be when you least expect it."

"Fine." She pushed past him, reached into the closet and thrust a towel into his hand. "Go take your shower."

"Thanks." Thomas grabbed his bag and hit the head.

***

Meagan closed her door, put on a pair of jeans, a royal blue sweater, and her well-worn hiking boots. The day was cool and cloudy. It looked like rain. While she combed through her wet hair, her stomach growled, so she went to the kitchen to find something to eat. She searched the refrigerator from top to bottom, and couldn't find anything to fix for breakfast. She needed to go to the store.

The bathroom door opened. "Whoa, it's hot in there."

Meagan turned in time to see a cloud of steam rush out, then noticed the detective wrapped only in a towel.

"Do you have a blow dryer?"

His dark brown hair was wet, a curl had fallen across his forehead. His heavy black whiskers made his blue eyes appear darker, the three-inch scar across his cheek more pronounced. His shoulders were broad; his chest hair just heavy enough to be sexy.

And his body, my God, his body was rock-hard and sculpted. Damn. His left shoulder bore a scar the size of a bullet. Her eyes skimmed the length of him, down his tight abs to the trail of hair that disappeared beneath the towel.

When she realized what she was doing, her head jerked up and met his stare. Heat rushed to her cheeks.

"I'm sorry, what did you say?" *Oh God, I think I'm going to die right here, right now.*

A slow grin lit his face. "I asked if you had a blow dryer."

"Right." She turned away and pulled out a drawer under the hall cabinet, and handed him the dryer.

***

Thomas noticed Meagan's appraisal. He felt the warmth of her gaze like fingers stroking him down the length of his body and settle on his groin. His cock turned hard as if on command. Then she looked up, their eyes locked.

The electricity in the air was almost palpable.

He wanted nothing more than to taste those full luscious

lips, to slip deep inside her with those long legs wrapped tight around his waist. All his senses were on high alert.

He didn't understand what was happening to him, but whatever it was, the timing sucked. He hadn't thought about another woman for years, not since he'd met Victoria. He still dreamed of making love to his late wife every night.

Then out of nowhere he's blindsided by this siren. She reminded him of a painting he'd seen long ago on a trip with Victoria. It was of a red-haired maiden staring out to sea, a storm is brewing and there was a ship in trouble. The image was haunting. The painter's name was something like Walterhouse or was it Waterhouse? Whatever was going on here, *this* red-haired Meagan had sure cast a spell on him.

Her hair was damp and hung in corkscrews. It was all he could do to keep himself from reaching out and fingering one of the curls. The swelling had disappeared from around her big blue eyes and they sparkled. She was more gorgeous than he ever thought possible. Dammit. This was very inconvenient.

Thomas mentally shook his head, grabbed the blow dryer, mumbled a thank-you, and shut the door.

***

Meagan quickly spun around, feeling feverish. What was she thinking? She had no right to be lusting after this man who simply saw her as a job. Or did he? She could almost swear for a second there he was going to lean down and kiss her.

And what if he did? Would she have kissed him back? Oh, hell, yes! Oh, no, this wasn't good. Just the other night she'd stood at her front door kissing Drew. Now she's looking at another man like he's something on a menu. She was so confused. Here she thought she was starting something with Drew. She remembered the way he kissed her and attempted to convince her that he should stay. What if it was Detective Thomas kissing her, seducing her, caressing her with those big, strong hands, could she turn him away as well?

Um...

THIRTY-FOUR

Thomas entered the living room adjusting his tie. His suit was perfect, not a wrinkle in sight.

"Did I miss something?" Her anger had disappeared. "You're dressed like you're going to work."

"No, you didn't miss anything. I just haven't gotten around to telling you the plan for today. I have some interviews I need to conduct and you're going with me."

"Does that mean I have to get dressed up too?" She scrunched up her face.

"No, you're fine. Besides, you'll be staying in the car."

"No way. I'm supposed to ride around with you all day and sit in the car while you work?" She ended with her hands on her hips.

"Look, I'm sorry it has to be this way. I have Shadowhawk conducting the interviews at your salon, so I can't have you with her. The only other people I have on this little task force of mine are doing surveillance on a suspect.

So, it looks like you're stuck with me. You can't go inside because you're not law enforcement. I don't want to take the chance that someone might complain and compromise this case. Besides, on the off chance that we actually *do* come across the killer, I don't want you anywhere in sight."

Meagan's body crumpled into the chair. "Great. I get to trade one prison for another."

"We really should get going." He started toward the kitchen. "Do you have anything we can grab and eat in the car?"

"Sorry, I missed grocery day. Looks like we're going to have to go out for breakfast." She smiled broadly.

"Okay, where's the nearest McDonald's or Jack In The Box?"

"Oh, hell, no. We're not eating fast food. I want a *real* breakfast." Meagan grabbed her purse and dragged him out the back door.

***

When they got to his BMW, he opened the door for her.

She glanced over at him. "Gee, homicide detectives make more money than I thought."

"I've made a few investments," he said.

"Boy, it seems everyone has investments except me." She looked like a sullen child as she got into the car. He smiled and shut the door without comment.

Meagan directed him to a local eatery called The Sugar

Shack, a cute little café where the surfers hung out. She ordered ham, eggs, hash browns, a half-stack of pancakes and a large milk. Thomas ordered black coffee and a Denver omelet, hold the toast.

"Wow." He raised his eyebrows. "Do you eat like that all the time?"

"I haven't had much of an appetite lately. I guess you could say I'm making up for it." She sounded apologetic.

He looked her up and down. "I don't know where you're going to put it."

"What about you? Are you on a diet?" she said defensively.

The waitress dropped off their drinks.

"If it's not fast food or donuts, I don't have much use for it." He smiled and took a sip of his coffee.

She rolled her eyes. "Don't you be eyeballing *my* food, then."

"You mean you won't share?" He put his hand over his heart dramatically.

"Not on your life, buster. You had your chance." She ripped off the top of the paper on her straw and shot it at Thomas. He caught it before it landed in his coffee. She put the straw in her milk.

He laughed. Then he turned serious. "Look, Meagan, we have to talk."

"I don't like the sound of that." She took a sip of her milk.

"We have to try to figure out who's doing this. Lilah's murder isn't the first. We seem to have a serial killer on our hands and he's been at it for several years."

***

Meagan winced at the mention of her friend's name, the image of her head flashed through her mind. Somehow she'd pushed the whole nightmare from her thoughts; now, all at once, it played back in her mind. She stared out the window while he talked. His story sounded familiar, she looked back.

"Are you talking about the Sandman?"

"So you've heard."

"Who hasn't?" She stared down at her lap and played with her napkin. Then she remembered something, her head shot up. "Wait. Didn't you say you have a suspect?"

"Possible suspect. We haven't had a chance to interview him yet. We don't have any strong evidence on him right now. He could have alibis for all or some of the murders. He's linked to the first victim. We really have to find out how you tie into all this."

"I've dated some creepy guys in my time," Meagan said, "but I don't think any of them were crazy enough to commit murder."

"I need you to make a list of everyone you've dated in the last five years. Also a list of men who maybe asked you out, but you declined." He handed over his notebook and pen.

"Are you kidding me? In my line of work I get asked out at least once a week. It would be impossible for me to remember everyone in the last five years, especially the walk-ins."

"Walk-ins?"

"People who walk in without an appointment. Maybe they're new to the area or just passing through. Some of them never come back, especially men who get shot down for a date."

"Just do your best. Try to think of anyone who stands out in your mind, maybe he was overly persistent. And speaking of work, I'm going to need a list of all your male clients too."

Her mouth dropped open. "Are you out of your mind?"

The waitress set their food on the table.

"Okay, just stick with white males between the ages of twenty-five to thirty-five. That should narrow it down a bit." He smiled and took a bite of his omelet.

"Do you have any idea how many clients I need to maintain in order to make a living in this business? Then factor in that about sixty percent of those clients are white males and maybe fifty percent of them are between the ages of twenty-five to thirty-five. By the time I get these lists together, the killer will have died of old age. That is, of course, if I don't first." She layered her pancakes with syrup.

"Don't you have records on your clients?" He grabbed a hold of his coffee and waited for her answer.

"Well, yeah, sort of. They're not exactly up to date, clients come and go." She took a big bite of her pancakes.

"Do the best you can. We're talking about your life here and the lives of more innocent women."

***

Thomas interviewed five different male acquaintances of Lilah's, but each was a bust. They had solid alibis. He would be verifying them just the same, but he wasn't really surprised. He knew that the key lay somewhere in Meagan's past, and she wasn't familiar with any of the names on the list. Then there was the fact that none of them fit the profile. For one thing, they were too young: early twenties.

By the time they'd finished for the day, it was nearly six o'clock, and they were heading back toward Meagan's house. She reminded Thomas they needed to stop at the grocery store. As he exited the freeway, she gave him directions to where she did her shopping.

They had just pulled into a slot in the parking lot of Trader Joe's when his cell phone rang. He turned off the car and took the call. When he'd finished, he put the phone back in his pocket and turned to Meagan. "We need to talk."

"Not that again. I hate it when you start a sentence like that." He knew she was kidding, sort of.

"Remember when I told you the killer is probably someone you know, maybe even dated?"

"Yeah." She stared at him expectantly.

"I'm just saying that *everyone* in your life is a suspect. You're going to have to accept the fact that this guy Drew, the one you think you're in love with, just might be the killer."

"That's not possible. Besides, I never said I was in *love*

with him," she countered.

"Fine. The guy you're *madly* in like with then. You're the one who was defending him so passionately last night."

"I wasn't defending *him,* you idiot. I was defending myself! You insinuated that I don't know the difference between good sex and a meaningful relationship." Her response was just short of a shout.

"That's not what I meant. What I meant to say was that *he* didn't know the difference. After all, where is he now?"

"He can't help it. He has people depending on him." Her face was beet-red.

"I'm just saying if you were *my* girlfriend, I would have moved heaven and earth to be there for you!"

The car was suddenly quiet.

Meagan stared at him mouth open, she closed it, hesitated a moment, then got out of the car slamming the door behind her.

Meagan didn't know why she was defending Drew. It wasn't as if the same thought hadn't occurred to her. But when it had, she immediately felt selfish. He really did have people depending on him. He couldn't just drop everything to be at her side. Could he? Then hearing Thomas repeat those thoughts out loud felt like a slap in the face. She pulled out a cart and entered the store. And what did he mean, if she was *his* girlfriend? Did he mean that literally?

***

Thomas sat in the car trying to compose himself. He couldn't believe he had voiced the very thought that had been plaguing him all night. *Dammit.* This woman really got under his skin. By the time he caught up with Meagan, she had already filled her cart with fat-free bran muffins, coffee, fresh vegetables, fruits, cheeses, organic 1 percent milk and wheat bread. He looked around. "What is this, a health food store?"

She smiled. "You could say that."

"Then, after you're finished, we're going to a *real* store."

Meagan laughed.

He noticed some cookies above the frozen foods and made a beeline for them.

When they were loading the bags into the trunk, Thomas spied a Ralph's grocery store across the parking lot. They drove over and Meagan followed him around the store. He filled the cart with his favorites: cinnamon rolls, more cookies, Coke, steaks, a bag of potatoes, sour cream, green onions, butter, whole milk and Sugar Frosted Flakes.

Meagan cupped her hands around her mouth like a megaphone.

"Heart attack, aisle seven!"

"Hey, these are all-American staples."

"Yeah, maybe in 1950."

"I'm a traditionalist."

By the time they reached Meagan's house, the sun had been down a couple of hours. They filled their arms with groceries and headed for the back door.

Meagan stopped. "That's funny, why is the porch dark?

The light is on a sensor. It goes on the minute it starts getting dark out."

"Stay here." Thomas set the groceries on the ground. He pulled out his Glock, held up his palm signaling her to stay, then cautiously approached the back of the house.

When he reached the kitchen window he ducked until he got to the other side. He was about a foot from the back door when his shoes crunched on something. He glanced up and noticed someone had broken the bulb of the porch light. His senses tingled.

Thomas reached the other side of the door, then with his left hand tried the knob. It was unlocked. He turned it silently and peered in, but everything was dark. He took out his penlight and flashed it around the kitchen then entered the house. He did a cursory check of the bathroom and hall before moving into the living room. So far the house was clear.

Keeping his back to the wall, he made his way toward the other side of the unit. If the perp was still in the house, Thomas knew he had the guy cornered. Peering around the corner, he directed the light into the bedroom.

Seeing nothing, he leapt across the hallway into the small bathroom to check behind the closed shower curtain. He clasped the edge of the curtain then dramatically swung it open. It was empty.

***

Meagan stood at the side of the house, nervous energy making her bounce up and down on her toes. Her heartbeat echoed loudly in her ears. Her impatience grew worse with each passing second until she couldn't wait a minute more. She had to see what was going on inside.

She crept up along the side of the house, ducking under the kitchen window as she had seen Thomas do. Once she reached the other side of the open door, she peered into the darkened abyss. *Fat lot of good that did, I can't see a damn thing. Maybe if I just take two more steps into the kitchen, I'll be able to see what he's doing.*

***

Thomas took a deep breath. Adrenaline pumped through his body. Out in the hall again, the flashlight beam danced over the bedroom. Everything looked clear. He entered the room, gun first, and quick as lightning, something hard came crashing down on his hand. Pain. Numbness. His gun dropped to the floor. He turned toward his attacker, but the room was too dark. The attacker had the advantage since Thomas had a bit of light behind him.

Thomas jumped into the darkened room and shot out a jab. It landed on something soft, probably the guy's stomach. The guy countered with a left hook that hit Thomas in the jaw. Thomas moved behind the guy so that *he* was now backlit. He charged the black shadow, slamming him up against the open door.

Their bodies tumbled to the ground and rolled. They were stopped by the closet door, and the attacker ended on top. He jumped up and fled.

Meagan heard the gunshot. She jumped and yelped at the same time. Grunts and groans followed. It sounded like a fight, but she didn't know what to do. As she pondered her next move, a dark figure burst through the doorway, knocking her backward into the flowerbed. While she lay on her back, the black-clad figure disappeared into the night.

It took her a moment to catch her breath. With the aid of a wooden lawn chair, she helped herself up. Meagan rushed into the house, searching for Thomas flicking on lights as she went. She found him on the bedroom floor, a broken lamp beside him.

"What happened?" She offered him her hand. He waved it away and got up on his own.

"He got away." Thomas rubbed his jaw.

"Did you shoot him or did he shoot you?" She searched his body for blood. "I heard a gunshot."

"No one got shot. He was hiding to the left of the bedroom door. He meant to clock me with that lamp, got my wrist instead. The gun went off before I dropped it. Dammit! I can't believe I let him get away." Thomas rubbed his wrist.

"It's not like you *let* him. It looks like you did your best to stop him." His clothes and hair were mussed; blood dripped from his nose. She grabbed a tissue and handed it to him.

"Thanks." He wiped up the blood and felt the bridge of

his nose. "Not broken, at least that's something."

Thomas glanced around the bedroom. He hadn't been in there before. His eyes came to rest on a framed poster. It was a reproduction of the haunting painting he thought of yesterday. The one that reminded him of Meagan. Now that was just plain weird. But what disturbed him even more was that the red-haired maiden staring out to sea in *this* picture had a bullet hole in her. Right where her heart would be.

THIRTY-FIVE

Meagan whipped her head around and scanned the room.

"What the hell?"

Thomas followed her gaze. Lingerie was scattered everywhere.

She moved to the edge of the bed and picked up a black lace teddy. It had been shredded. "Who would do such a thing?" Her voice was barely audible.

As he walked toward her, his foot kicked something. He bent down to see what he'd just shoved under the bed. A large carving knife poked from under the coverlet.

Thomas pointed. "Does that belong to you?"

Meagan bent down next to him. "Yes, that's one of my knives."

He left the bedspread up so the CSU wouldn't miss it. "Don't touch anything else. Let's get out of here before we contaminate the scene further." He dragged Meagan out of the house.

Thomas put his hands on either side of her arms and focused his attention on her. "Did you get a look at the guy?" His voice was hopeful.

Meagan hated to disappoint him, but she had no choice.

"No, I'm sorry. He was wearing a black ski mask."

"Dammit!" Thomas took out his cell phone and requested a crime scene unit as well as some uniforms to guard the scene.

Thomas was still talking when Meagan's phone rang. She looked at the screen and noticed it was Katy. She waited until she'd left a message, then retrieved it. Katy had heard Meagan's home address broadcasted over her police scanner and needed to know if she was okay.

Meagan had to call her back. She couldn't have Katy worrying about her needlessly. She strolled to the end of the driveway and made the call. She assured Katy she was fine and told her she'd simply had a break-in. It still took her some time to calm her friend down. God only knew what would have happened had she told her the whole truth. Only by promising Katy she would keep her in the loop was Meagan finally able to end the call.

She glanced up and noticed Thomas waiting for her. He did not look happy. Meagan walked back to where he stood.

"Who were you talking to?"

"My girlfriend, Katy. She listens to a police scanner; it's kind of a hobby of hers. Anyway, she heard my address and was worried about me." She felt like a child in the principal's office.

He glared at her. "What did you tell her?"

Meagan tried to keep her cool.

"I just told her I had a break-in and that I was all right. I didn't want her to worry. It's a good thing too because that freaked her out enough." She laughed trying to get a smile out of him. It didn't work.

"Good. We don't want her unknowingly tipping off this guy. He could be in contact with someone in your inner circle, so whoever she tells could tell someone else and so on. We can't risk anything about this case getting out."

"But I don't know anything."

"You know more than any other civilian and you need to keep a lid on it for now. Do you understand?"

Meagan nodded.

"We're going to spend the night at my house. Let's go inside so you can pack a bag. We better hurry before everyone gets here, because after that we'll be barred from the residence."

He went to the open trunk of his car were the rest of the groceries waited to be unloaded. He reached into a box and pulled out two pairs of latex gloves, handing her one. "I know your prints are all over the house, but we can't risk smudging any he may have left behind. So remember to touch as little as possible."

"But he was wearing black leather gloves," She countered.

"When you saw him, but who knows, he could have taken them off at some point so he could feel the silk or lace of your garments." He put his gloves on.

Meagan shivered. "That's just plain creepy."

"Yes, it is, but you never know what's going to get some of these guys off."

She scrunched up her face and put on the gloves.

***

It was after nine when they pulled into Thomas' garage. They entered the house to a set of stairs that led to the kitchen.

They passed what she thought was the living room on the left, the English Tudor home was filled with antiques and tapestries. Not what she expected to find in a cop's house.

Meagan followed him up another set of stairs, then down a long hall to the last door on the right. He opened the door, switched on the light, then motioned her to go in before him.

Meagan entered the room and stopped.

"This will be your room." He set her bag down on the inside of the door, then pointed to a closed door on the right. "You have a private bath through that door over there."

She wandered over to the window framed by chintz curtains and peered down. The tumultuous sea crashed below; the white caps glowed in the moonlight. She took in the canopy bed with its matching bedspread and curtains.

"Some investments," she said with awe.

"I'll start dinner. You should find fresh towels and everything you'll need in the bathroom. In case you don't, just let me know." He left the room closing the door behind him.

Meagan ambled over to the window and cranked it open. A cool breeze rushed in and filled the room with the wonderful scent of the ocean. She took a deep breath and sighed. The sound of the waves crashing against the rocks below was amplified. In the distance she heard a foghorn. This was the home she'd always dreamed about.

She unpacked her bag and hung what little she'd brought in the closet, then changed into a caftan. She put her hair up and washed her face. Feeling half-human again, she went in search of her host.

When she turned the corner at the bottom of the stairs she found herself in the warmest, most enticing room, lit by a crackling fire. There was an overstuffed couch and matching chairs, each with its own ottoman, all upholstered in the same English rose material. She imagined herself curled up in one of the chairs in front of that fireplace, engrossed in a gripping novel.

The floors were a dark hardwood, so shiny they looked wet. A large square area rug in deep burgundy, forest green vines, and pink roses covered a giant portion of the floor. The antique furnishings were all mahogany. Paintings surrounded the room, each with its own special light above. They were not pictures, but actual paintings. She had no doubt they were worth a bundle.

Meagan ogled each one as she made her way around the perimeter of the room. Her favorite was a ship being tossed about on the waves in the middle of a bitter storm. It reminded her of the picture in her room, *Miranda-The Tempest* by John William Waterhouse. It had the same moody vibe.

After making the full circle, she found herself in front of the fireplace again. She gazed up at the portrait of a beautiful woman holding a violin. Her long straight hair flowed over one shoulder; it was too dark to tell if the shade was black or brown. Her velvet gown was a deep forest green that brought out her exquisite green eyes. Her ears sparkled with diamond and emerald earrings. She was the most stunning woman Meagan had ever seen, and she just couldn't take her eyes off her.

When she was finally able to tear herself away, Meagan wandered into the kitchen where she noticed an open bottle of wine with an empty glass next to it. She poured herself a glass, and gazed out to the deck where she spied Thomas in front of a barbecue grill.

She opened the sliding glass door. The aroma of the steaks on the grill filled her senses and made her stomach grumble. He was just turning them when she walked up beside him.

"Your home is *amazing*."

"It was my wife's home. It's where she grew up."

She hoped the shock didn't register on her face.

"Where is she now?"

"She's dead." His tone was hard and flat.

"Oh, I'm sorry. Do you mind if I ask how she died?" The

second the words flew out, she wished she could take them back. She scrunched up her face, covered it with her hands. "I'm so sorry. Forget I said that."

The silence was deafening.

She braved a look, the muscles in his jaw clenched. Then he shocked her with his words. "She was a gifted violinist, she'd played her entire life. It's all she'd ever wanted to do.

"Then she began having problems with her fingers. It got to the point where the pain was so great, she finally went to the doctor. She was diagnosed with rheumatoid arthritis, the kind that cripples you. Her hands would eventually turn into claws. She was only thirty-eight.

"I took her to countless specialists, for second, third, even forth opinions. Her depression was so great, she wouldn't leave our room. She withdrew from the world, withdrew from me. She slept all the time. I felt helpless, nothing I said or did made a difference. I begged her to seek help, to see a psychiatrist. She argued that a psychiatrist couldn't fix her hands.

"Then one night I came home and found her on our bed. She had swallowed an entire bottle of Xanax. The note she left simply read *I'm sorry.*"

Stunned, Meagan focused on his profile. Thomas stared straight out at the sea. Unshed tears stood in his eyes. She put her hand on his arm. "I'm so sorry. When did this happen?"

"Two years ago last month." He swiped a hand across his eyes and cleared his throat. "How would you like your steak cooked?"

"Well done, thanks."

Silence ensued. Meagan hung over the railing, sipped her wine and watched the waves below while she figured out a way to change the subject. Then it came to her. "What does the J.J. stand for?"

He looked at her and smiled. "Jesse James."

"I can see why you'd go by your initials then. Sandra Bullock's ex-husband pretty much sullied that name, huh?" Meagan laughed nervously.

"Actually, I've been J.J. my entire life. It was a nickname that kind of stuck. My dad was a big fan of the Wild West. All my siblings are named after famous people: Wyatt, for Wyatt Earp. Annie, for Annie Oakley. Billy, for Wild Bill Hickok. And Cody, for Buffalo Bill Cody.

Meagan got a sudden attack of the giggles. It really wasn't that funny, but she couldn't stop herself. Chalk it up to stress or lack of sleep. Whatever it was, it felt good to laugh. The levity seemed to relieve the tension hanging in the air.

When her laughter finally died, she wiped the tears from her eyes, cleared her throat and patted him on the back. "I like it. Jesse James Thomas, it's a good solid name for a good solid guy."

His warm smile made her tingle down to her toes, as did the grateful expression in his eyes. For what she wasn't sure. But after the loss of his wife, it was a wonder he could smile at all.

THIRTY-SIX

The phone woke Thomas early the next morning. His hand shot out and fumbled around until it closed on the receiver, then he answered without opening his eyes.

"Thomas." He cleared his throat. "What's up?"

"It's Cooper. The husband just pulled up."

"What time is it?" Thomas looked around.

"It's six-fifteen. What do you want me to do?"

"Just stay put. Where's James?"

"He left about ten minutes ago."

"Okay, I'll get there as soon as I can. Call me on my cell if he moves."

Thomas hung up and scrambled to get dressed. He was pulling on a pair of pants when it struck him: what was he going to do about Meagan? Then the answer came: nothing. No one knew where she was. She should be safe. He tied the second shoe, then rushed to her room. After a couple of swift knocks, he threw the door open.

Meagan bolted straight up. "What is it? What's happened?"

Thomas was speechless. Her hair was wild and extremely sexy. The white tank top she wore was practically sheer, he could see her erect nipples right through it. Instantly he was aroused. He noticed the chill in the room and looked toward the window. It was wide open.

Mentally he shook his head, then found his voice.

"I've got to go interview the guy we've had under surveillance. I'm going to leave you here. You'll be safe. I have a state-of-the-art alarm system. I'll arm it when I leave." Thomas flew out of the room as quickly as he'd entered. After he closed her door he took a deep breath, then looked down and adjusted himself.

By the time he'd arrived at the apartment complex, the rain was coming down in sheets. He parked his car next to Cooper and quickly jumped in beside him. "Bring me up to date."

"The subject pulled in around six-fifteen in that old beat-up Ford LTD over there." He pointed to a car on the left. "DMV records show it's registered to the wife, as is the Mini Cooper that she drives."

"Is the wife home?"

"Yes. James recorded she pulled in at three-ten, alone. Do you think she was expecting him?"

"She claims she's not privy to his schedule. But your guess is as good as mine."

"I talked to a couple guys at the station who'd been out

here a few times for domestics," Cooper said. "Seems that twice the neighbors called 911 because of some horribly loud fights. The third time, the wife called claiming he'd roughed her up.

"When they got there, it looked like it was the other way around. Jenks, one of the officers at the scene, said the husband was pretty docile. The wife didn't have a mark on her. But Roberts had a bloody nose, black eye and scratch marks down his left cheek. He wouldn't press charges. Jenks said he thought the wife was an attention-seeker," Cooper said in disgust.

"Everyone I've talked to so far acts like this guy's a real saint. I called Shadowhawk. She should be here any minute. I want to see what her take is on him," Thomas said.

Cooper nodded.

As they waited, Thomas brought Coop up to date on the case. By the time he'd finished, Shadowhawk had arrived. He got out of the car to greet her. The rain had calmed to a heavy drizzle. The detectives made a run for the shelter of the overhang outside the Roberts's downstairs apartment.

Most of the residents were bustling off to work, or school, but no one stirred in the darkened apartment before them. Thomas knocked on the door, waited. When there was no sound from within, he rapped again with more purpose. Before long he was pounding on the door when it was finally yanked open.

"What!" Sharon Roberts stood in the doorway in an oversized T-shirt with a picture of a rubber duck floating upside down. Her features softened when she noticed Thomas.

"Oh, it's you, come on in." She moved away from the door.

The moment Shadowhawk appeared from behind him, her expression turned to a scowl.

"This is my partner, Shadowhawk. We'd like to talk to your husband," Thomas said.

"Whatever." She slammed the door then yelled toward the back of the apartment. "Jordan, get your ass out of bed. You got company!" She left them standing in the doorway and disappeared into what he could only assume was the bedroom.

A minute later the same door opened and a man wearing boxer shorts and a t-shirt shuffled into the room scratching his butt.

He stared at them through sleepy eyes. "Who are you?"

Thomas made the introductions. "We'd like to ask you a few questions."

"'Kay," he said, groggily. He opened the fridge, then glanced back. "Want something to drink?"

"No thanks, we're fine," Thomas said.

He grabbed a Coke, slammed the door and popped the top.

"So, what do you want?" Jordan Roberts led them into the living room and plopped down into a chair. He drank half the Coke before he looked at them.

His curly dark brown hair hung past his shoulders; his

beard was closely cropped and his brown eyes were sad like those of a basset hound. His manner was docile.

"Can you tell us about your relationship with Cindy Gross?" Thomas asked.

"I worked with Cindy *years* ago at a clothing company up north. Why?"

"Have you seen her or been in touch with her at all since you left that job?" Shadowhawk asked.

"No, I have no idea what she's up to. We weren't that close, didn't keep in touch."

Thomas took out his notebook. "Can you tell me where you were on—" Thomas read a string of dates.

Jordan stared at him a moment. "No, can you tell me where *you* were on those dates?" he countered. "What the fuck is this about?"

"Murder," Shadowhawk answered.

The room fell silent.

"I'll get my log." Jordan left the room. When he returned, he handed a black book to Thomas, who immediately skimmed it.

"This covers all the dates but one. I talked to your boss; he said you were fired. What have you been doing since?"

"I'm renting a rig. I work for myself now."

"I'll be checking that out."

"Go ahead."

"That still leaves the first date. Where were you?"

"Shit, I don't know. I was living down here. Probably working."

"Where?" Thomas asked.

"OC Sportswear."

"So, you're telling us you didn't make a *special* trip up north to visit your *friend?* See if you could rekindle some of those old feelings? But maybe she didn't feel the same, so you killed her!" Shadowhawk countered.

"Yes. No. Shit, I don't know. I didn't kill Cindy, why would I wanna do that? I barely knew her!"

"That's what we're trying to find out, Ace. We know you liked her." Her voice softened. "We're not saying you did it on purpose."

Jordan squirmed in his chair.

"If you can't give us a solid alibi for the date in question, we may have to haul your ass downtown and book you." Shadowhawk threatened. "I suggest you think long and hard on that."

Thomas stood and Shadowhawk followed his lead. "If you get your memory back, call me. I wouldn't plan on any out-of-state trips in the near future. We'll be checking out your alibis in the meantime." Thomas handed him a card.

Jordan took the card, but didn't get up.

By the time they stepped outside, the rain had stopped altogether. They walked in silence toward Cooper's car and stopped within earshot of his open window.

"Well, what do you think?" Shadowhawk asked.

"I don't know. His alibis for the other murders are pretty strong, if the log is correct. Looks like he was in other states when those girls went missing. I'm curious what he'll come up with for the TOD on Cindy Gross. It's possible she's not tied to these other murders."

"Oh, she's tied in all right," Shadowhawk said with confidence.

"What makes you say that?" Thomas asked.

"Call it a hunch."

Thomas raised his brows. "Okay, Sherlock, tell me what *you* think of this guy."

"He's hiding something. A couple things stood out. First of all, he was calm, too calm. If you accused *me* of being a murderer, I'd be all over you like white on rice. At the very least, I'd be defending myself vehemently. The only girl he said he didn't kill was Cindy and I've got to admit, he wasn't very convincing at that. He acted like he knew we were coming and why. He answered our questions as if they were rehearsed."

"Cooper did say they were used to having cops over. There had been a few domestic abuse calls."

"So he beats his wife, I'm not surprised."

"Actually, no, she beats him."

"Now that's a twist."

"It bodes well for the overbearing woman in his life, though. You said there was something else?" Thomas said.

"He lied about how well he knew Cindy. So it makes me wonder what else he's lying about?"

"Yeah, I was thinking the same thing. I want you to interview his former boss at the trucking company." He handed her the log.

She nodded. "Do you think he could be our Dark Knight? Maybe that's how he lured her to meet him. Maybe he thought she wouldn't go if she knew it was just plain old Jordan from the warehouse. So he makes up this phony persona. This Dark Knight knew how to get her attention, told her everything she wanted to hear."

"You're right. Keep on it. What did you pick up at the salon?" Thomas asked.

"A whole lotta nothing. No one saw anything. The businesses around them were closed when Lilah left, so no witnesses there. No one knew any of her friends. The boss, Jerome, is a major asshole. I'd love nothing more than to pin all of this on him, but his alibis are solid. He was safely tucked away in one salon or another. Several witnesses corroborate his story."

Thomas nodded. "What about Meagan's ex-boyfriend? Did you come up with anything on him?"

"He's *another* piece of work." She took out her notebook. "He's been married for the last twenty years. His wife is fifteen years his senior. His affairs seemed to have started pretty much right after the wedding.

"No documentation stating that either one of them had ever filed for divorce. They live in one of those expensive houses in Laguna Niguel; it's got to be worth close to a million even in this market. No priors. He's VP of sales for some Fortune 500 company and travels a lot up and down the coast.

"I was going to interview him yesterday, but when I called

his office the secretary told me he'd died three months ago. I checked into it. Suicide. Allegedly ate a bullet. No note. Cleaning crew found him in his office."

"But you don't buy it."

"No. A guy like that is a narcissist with an ego the size of Texas. I can't see him killing the one person he loves the most, himself. He may not be our perp, but he could be one of his victims. I thought I'd check into it further. What's your schedule like?" she asked.

Thomas continued. "Meagan's currently dating this guy who also fits the profile; still looking into the overbearing female. He's a musician, travels a lot. Everything she's told me about him doesn't check out. If this Roberts doesn't pan out, it's possible that Jackson will. I've got Johnson learning everything she can about him and his band, The Ravens.

"His address is in Eureka, California. He claimed his parents died in a car crash, but there are no death certificates for either one. He was arrested for assault and battery on a girlfriend in 1991, but the charges were dropped. I want to check him out further."

THIRTY-SEVEN

When Thomas arrived at OC Sportswear, he showed the receptionist his ID and asked to see the head of Human Resources. While he waited, he wandered around the lobby looking at the giant posters depicting athletes in every sport. All at once, he had that prickly feeling of someone watching him, he turned his head. The blond receptionist smiled at him, he smiled back, then pretended to be engrossed by the runners in a track event before him. A woman's voice broke the silence.

"I'm Sally Braverman."

Thomas turned around. A petite brunette in her fifties stood behind him, offering him her hand. He shook it and introduced himself.

"What is this about, detective?"

"How long have you been working here, ma'am?"

"About fifteen years, why?"

"Do you remember an employee by the name of Jordan

Roberts? He worked in your warehouse four years ago. Five-ten, brown curly hair, brown eyes, on the quiet side."

"Yes, I do remember him. My daughter worked here that summer in shipping and she had a big crush on him. She was a high school senior. She'd come home from work and everything was Jordan this and Jordan that." She smiled. "He wasn't here long, maybe about six months or so.

"At first, he was a sweet boy, very charming, a good worker, then that changed. He became moody, problematic, calling in sick for the dumbest reasons. The last was for a sunburn, can you believe that?" She laughed. "Not too bright, that one. I had to let him go. Why all the interest. What has he done?"

"He's a person of interest in a case I'm working on. Would it be all right if I take a look at his file? I'm particularly interested in his attendance."

"I guess that would be okay." She glanced over her shoulder to the receptionist. "Heather, get Judy on the line, will you?" The receptionist picked up the phone, dialed, said a few words, then handed the phone over to Sally.

"Judy, I need the employee file on a Jordan Roberts. He worked here about four years ago." She was quiet as she listened to the woman on the other end. "Right. I forgot. Thanks." After she hung up, she turned to Thomas.

"Our computer system crashed last year and we didn't bother to enter the past employees, just the ones currently working here. We only have the hard copies of the files of ex-employees dating back about two years. The rest are stored at our old building down the street. We moved into this larger facility in '09. I'll need to send someone over to search. I'm sorry, but it could take a little while."

"This is very important," Thomas said. "If you could get someone on that right away, I would truly appreciate it. Here's my card. Please call the minute you have that file in your hand." He was disappointed, but at least Sally Braverman was cooperating and didn't ask for a warrant.

The moment Thomas arrived at the station, he headed to Kim Johnson's office. "How's the background check going on our Mr. Jackson? Have you learned anything new since we last spoke?" He slumped down into the chair next to her desk.

Johnson clicked her computer. "To begin with, your boy was in the Navy, but only a short time. Dishonorable discharge. Evidently, our government decided he wasn't mentally stable enough to kill people. After that he did six months in a VA mental ward before he was released, supposedly cured. Which is just another way of saying that they were out of beds and needed the space.

"Then he vacillated between jobs. Construction here, roadwork there, bartending, never staying in one place long. He was living with the girlfriend that had him arrested for assault and battery. That was up in Sausalito on her houseboat. She threw him out after that. Smart girl. He returned to Eureka, then nothing for a few years until he resurfaced as the lead singer in The Ravens three years ago.

"There's a little mystery behind that. It seems the original lead singer, David Neusbaum, was a 'friend' of this Andrew Jackson." She did air quotation marks on the word *friend* before she continued. "He became mysteriously ill and had to drop out of the tour. He almost died. Doctors never did find out what was wrong with him.

"So, in stepped our boy. Then, just as suddenly and without explanation, David regained his health. But by the time he was ready to perform, the band had decided to keep Jackson as their front man."

"So you think Jackson poisoned his friend so he could take his job?" Thomas asked.

"It crossed my mind, but proving it is your department."

"Yeah, lucky me. Do you think you can track Jackson down for me in L.A., maybe find out where he's staying? Allegedly, his band is recording with JWI, that label that Josh Whitman started."

"No problem."

Thomas headed to his office. The last time he'd checked in with Meagan was around noon, so he decided to give her a call. She didn't answer after five rings and the phone went to voicemail. He shoved all the case files into his briefcase, then called again. When she didn't answer a second time, he got that prickly feeling that something was wrong. He grabbed his briefcase and headed out.

THIRTY-EIGHT

Thomas stepped into the house and noticed the alarm was still set, so he punched in the code, disarmed it, and called out to Meagan. When there was no reply, he took a deep breath and searched the lower level of the house. No success.

Once he reached the base of the stairs, he yelled up. No luck. A niggling feeling at the back of his mind made him draw his gun. He tried to reason with himself: the alarm was still on, no one had gotten in. But it was no good. He was worried. Soundlessly, he proceeded up the stairs with his back to the wall. He was able to keep an eye on the bottom floor, and cover the top as it came into view.

The moment he reached the landing, he set about opening doors. The first room on his left was his own; he had moved out of the master bedroom the day he'd found his wife. Carefully he turned the knob, peered in, and saw that nothing had been disturbed. He proceeded down the hall repeating the process with all the rooms until he came to the last one.

Meagan's door stood wide open.

He peered in, gun ready. The moment he had the entire room within view he entered. The bed was made; there was no sign of a struggle.

He stood in the center of the room perplexed. He walked over to the window to check the latch when suddenly a loud crash sounded behind him. He spun around, gun poised to shoot.

Meagan was dressed in that skimpy red robe, her hair wet. She quickly grabbed the handle of the bathroom door and slammed it shut. He laughed. The tension left his body. He returned his gun to its holster and waited for Meagan to remerge. When she didn't, he strolled over to the door and knocked. A moment later, he was still staring at the closed door.

What's taking her so long?

"Are you okay in there?" he shouted through the door.

Finally he heard the lock turn. The door burst open and Meagan flew into his arms. She held on tight. Her body trembled. He could feel her rapid heartbeat against his chest and wrapped his arms around her. "Hey, it's okay. I've got you."

Her body relaxed, molded against him. Suddenly he was acutely aware of her close proximity. She smelled like fresh-cut roses. His body began to respond. He felt like a shit for the images rolling through his mind and pulled away before she guessed what he was thinking.

He placed a finger under her chin and tilted her head up, she was crying. Wiping the tears away. "Hey, what's wrong?"

She peered up at him with such sad eyes that he melted on the spot. "I saw a man standing in the room with a gun. I thought it was him. I thought I was dead." She wiped her face with shaking hands and looked down.

"I'm sorry I scared you, but I phoned you from the station and you didn't answer. I continued to call all the way home. Then when I finally got here I yelled out to you several times and you didn't answer. I was concerned. That's why my gun was drawn." He swiped a damp curl from her forehead.

"I was taking a shower." Meagan laughed nervously.

"I see that." He smiled down at her. "Look, what do you say I take you out for dinner?"

"Okay," she answered, sniffling.

"What do you feel like eating?"

Meagan gazed at him through long dark lashes. "I could use a good stiff drink." She giggled.

"How about the Royal Hawaiian?"

"Perfect!" Thomas was rewarded by a broad smile.

"Good. I'll go get changed."

***

Meagan was sitting on the edge of the bed tying her boot when Thomas appeared in the doorway. She raised her eyes and stopped. He was wearing jeans and a navy sweater that strained across his broad shoulders. Deep blue eyes sparkled at her, and his normally tame hair was wild with curls.

Why the hell does he straighten it?

"Are you ready?" he asked.

She ducked her head and stared at her boot, her cheeks flamed. *Damn, he looks hot! Better make it two stiff drinks.*

"Let me just grab my jacket in case it starts to rain again." Meagan got up, forcing herself not to look at Thomas, and headed to the closet.

When they reached the bottom of the stairs leading to the garage, Thomas showed her how to work the burglar alarm and gave her the password.

Soon they were speeding north along PCH through the heart of Laguna Beach. Thomas' BMW pulled into the parking lot, and the valet opened Meagan's door. They were quiet as they strolled toward the restaurant. She eyed the windows of the shops along the way.

They passed by the hand-carved Tiki God that guarded the restaurant, then walked between the lighted Tiki torches on either side of the giant wooden door. The sound of Hawaiian music welcomed them as they entered.

Since it was Friday night, the place was packed, but they managed to grab seats at the bar while they waited for a table to open up.

The bar was intimate, lit only by the salt-water aquariums and a single candle on each table. The minute they sat down, a waitress appeared in a sarong and asked for their order. Thomas requested a beer, Meagan a Lapu Lapu.

After the waitress disappeared, Thomas glanced at Meagan.

"You weren't kidding when you said you wanted a *stiff* drink. I guess I'll be carrying you out of here tonight." He smiled.

She jutted her chin up. "I can hold my liquor. Don't you worry."

"I'm not worried, but if you rip off your top and start dancing on the tables, I *will* carry you out." He laughed.

"If that happens, I give you permission to carry me out of here as quickly as possible." She returned his laugh.

For the next hour they talked. Meagan had started her second drink. Thomas listened while she talked incessantly, obviously feeling the effects of the alcohol. It made her all the more endearing to him. He'd stopped after the first beer.

He couldn't help but laugh and tease her while she regaled him with stories of her disastrous dating life and what it was like to be a single woman over thirty.

"Let me get this straight, you were twenty-eight and he was what... twenty-three? Hell, he was still a kid then. What were you thinking?" He shook his head.

"I went out with him on a whim. I never dreamed it would turn into a relationship," she countered.

Thomas heard his name over the loudspeaker. He picked up Meagan's drink, grabbed her hand, and followed the hostess to their table. They ordered, and he peppered her with more questions regarding this ex-fiancé of hers, Jay.

"Okay. You said you didn't expect to get serious about this guy. What changed your mind?"

"Well, like I said, he was different from the men I'd been dating. They all came with so much baggage. Besides, I was having fun and wasn't ready to end it. I never *dreamed* I would fall in love and cast all common sense aside."

"When was it that you knew it was getting serious?"

"After about six months, we were always together so he moved in. He'd been talking marriage since practically the first date. I told him after my first marriage failed, I promised myself I wouldn't marry again without living with that person first. I needed to see what happened after the honeymoon phase was over."

"What *did* happen when the honeymoon phase was over?"

Meagan quieted when the waitress approached the table with their salads and another basket of bread.

Again they were silent while they ate. Thomas finished first and watched Meagan enjoy hers. He loved what a voracious eater she was. Most women ordered a large dinner, ate two bites, then announced they were full. Not Meagan. She would clean her plate, then start on his. He also loved how down to earth she was, nothing pretentious about her. She held nothing back.

When she was almost finished with her salad, she glanced up. "I'm making a pig out of myself again, aren't I?"

"Nope. I was just thinking." Before she could ask him about what, he continued. "So when did you know it wasn't going to work out with this Romeo?"

"To tell you the truth, I think I always knew I was kidding

myself. But I'd have to say it was probably after he was fired from his sixth job. After that, he decided he didn't want to work anymore. He claimed he was looking for a job, but how would I know. I had to open up my schedule and work six days a week just to break even. Thank God the salon's open Mondays.

"As far as I could tell he did nothing all day but eat. Then he'd leave the mess for *me* to clean up. He gained fifty pounds in six months, stopped shaving, and stayed up all night watching TV.

"He hadn't allowed me to cut his hair in about eight months. I knew he couldn't get a job looking the way he did. No way was he going on interviews. I was angry, constantly nagging. In short, I was a shrew. I didn't like the person I'd become. The relationship was more like that of mother and son, than lovers. He became obsessed with pornography. He was renting adult movies from pay-per-view and I was paying for them! His laziness repulsed me.

"Then one evening I just snapped. I'd arrived home after ten, exhausted. He was lying on the couch, watching a porno movie and drunk on beer. The sink was full of dishes, the dust on the furniture was about an inch thick, and the floor needed to be vacuumed." Meagan stopped talking the minute the waitress appeared.

She set their meals in front of them and disappeared taking their salad plates with her. Meagan took a big bite of her seared Ahi.

"Then what happened?" Thomas asked around a bite of

steak.

Meagan swallowed. "I told him he was going to have to move in with his buddy. I wouldn't put up with his crap anymore." She took another bite.

"Good for you," Thomas exclaimed. "So, did he go quietly?"

She finished chewing and swallowed. "Not exactly. He got all up in my face and blamed *me* for all his shortcomings. To top it off, he smashed all of my grandmother's china. I'm still heartbroken over that. He left only after I picked up the phone to call the police. That night I packed up all his stuff and put it on the lawn, then called a locksmith. He came back the next day and picked up his things. I never heard from him again."

"How long ago was that?"

"Well, let me see." Meagan stared at the ceiling while she calculated it. "Just over five years now."

"Wow, you really have dated some real winners." He shook his head.

"Just lucky I guess." She sucked on her straw and finished her drink.

Thomas was flummoxed. How could one woman attract so many lunatics? Then he thought about how his own behavior had changed since he'd met Meagan and had to wonder.

What is it about this woman that drives men insane?

Will the real Sandman please raise his hand?

THIRTY-NINE

When they got to the house, it was Meagan's turn to disarm the alarm system.

"Do you remember the code?" Thomas asked.

"I think so. Are you sure you want me to do this? I mean, what if the alarm goes off?" She was afraid she'd make a fool out of herself.

"Better for that to happen when I'm here. Don't you think?" He smiled.

Meagan nodded and stared at the keypad. She was so nervous, her hand shook. The second they entered the house, the stupid machine started beeping. It took her a couple tries, and in her haste, she kept hitting the wrong number. Finally, she entered the code correctly and the infernal noise stopped. She took a deep breath.

"In case you don't get it in time, do you remember the password?" His voice was calm, patient.

"Skipper. Why Skipper? Do you have a boat?" She

followed him into the kitchen.

He stopped in front of her and turned around. "Skipper was the name of our first dog when we were kids. Annie, the youngest, wanted to name him Ariel, after *The Little Mermaid*. We told her she couldn't because he was a boy." He tossed the mail on the counter.

"So, how did that turn into Skipper?" she asked.

"*Gilligan's Island*. That was Wyatt's favorite TV show growing up. He's the oldest. Originally he was named Little Skipper, and it got shortened through the years." He put his briefcase on the counter next to the mail.

"What kind of dog was it?"

"Dalmatian. My poor mother hated that dog. He was always chewing up something. He especially liked her shoes. She desperately wanted to get rid of him, but she was outvoted." He laughed.

"You must have some old photos around here. I want to see you as a little kid." Her curiosity was piqued. She couldn't imagine this rugged man as a child.

Thomas shook his head. "Oh, no. I don't need *that* humiliation. You just want to see me as a little buzzhead. I'd never hear the end of it."

"I won't tease you, I promise," she pleaded.

He stared at her a moment, then relented. "Okay, I think they're upstairs. Why don't you go into the living room and get comfortable? I'll see if I can find some for you."

After he left the kitchen, Meagan searched the cupboards for a glass. She was in desperate need of a drink of water.

Meagan heard his heavy footfalls on the stairs. When he was about halfway up, the phone rang. "Shit," he mumbled, then yelled. "Would you grab that and tell whoever it is I'll be right there? I'll get the extension in my room." He ran up the remaining steps.

She picked up the phone. "Hello?" There was a few seconds of silence, then she heard the mechanical voice.

"Hel-lo Meag-an, you did-n't thi-nk yo-uu coo-uld hi-de fro-m me did yo-uu?"

Thomas picked up the extension and was about to say something when he heard the caller. He stopped and listened.

"I-ee tho-ught yo-uu were dif-fer-ent." The mechanical voice continued slowly. "Bu-ut now I se-ee yo-uu ar-e a who-ore just li-ike the re-est. Yo-ou to-oo must di-ie." Then the phone went dead.

Thomas was next to her in an instant.

"Are you okay?" He grabbed her face with both hands, stared into her eyes.

"I...can't...breathe," she said in-between gasps.

"You're hyperventilating." He found a paper bag, then pulled her over to a kitchen chair and made her sit. "Here, put your head between your legs and breathe into this." He squatted next to her, rubbed her back.

Once her head came up, he asked, "Better?"

"I think so. How did he find me?" Her voice shook.

He racked his brain. "He could be following you, but that doesn't explain how he got my number. It's unlisted. Did you notice anyone outside the house today? Someone familiar, maybe you couldn't quite place him?"

She shook her head.

"Were there any cars parked on the street with someone just sitting in them? Think Meagan, this is important. You may have seen something, but don't know what it was. You have to jog your memory." He needed to get to the bottom of this. Fast.

"I don't think so."

"What did you do today?"

"Nothing. Read my book." Her eyes implored him to come up with an answer.

He thought once more. "Did you call anyone?"

A shadow crossed her face, her head dipped down.

"What? Tell me, Meagan, what did you do?" He tried to keep the panic from his voice.

"I had to tell him I was okay. I didn't want him to worry," her voice was just above a whisper.

"Who did you call, Meagan?" But deep down he knew. She couldn't be that stupid, could she?

Thomas shook her by the shoulders. "Look at me." He was letting his fear get the better of him.

"I called my answering machine to retrieve the messages. There were several from Katy, one from my mother, and..."

"And, Drew? Is that who you told?" Anger boiled up inside him.

"Well, you should have heard him, he was so worried. I had to call him!"

"Jesus Christ, what the hell were you thinking? Whether you'd like to believe it or not, he *is* a suspect. I told you that. What did you do, give him my number? Draw him a map? Shit!" Thomas ran his hands through his hair.

"No, nothing like that," Meagan yelled back. "I just told him what happened at my house and that we had to leave. I didn't even say what town I was in!" She glared at him.

He jumped up and started pacing in front of her. "You do *know* there are ways to get an address from a phone number, don't you? It's called a reverse directory. All you have to do is look up the number, and there's the address plain as day. Hell, nowadays you can do it on the internet for free!" He scrubbed his hands down his face.

"But I didn't give him the number." She squirmed in her seat. "He didn't ask." She looked down, her lip quivered.

"He must have some kind of advanced caller ID," he said more to himself. He glanced at Meagan and noticed she was about to cry. He dropped back in the chair next to her, drew her to him and held her face against his chest.

"I'm sorry," Thomas said in a hushed tone. He stroked her hair and felt her relax against him. They came together like two pieces of a perfect puzzle.

After a couple of minutes she pulled away, her wet eyes gazed up at him. He wanted so much to kiss her that it hurt. Instead, he stood. "We can't stay here. Go upstairs and pack. We're going to a hotel. Do you still have his number?"

Meagan got up, walked over to her purse on the counter, and pulled out her wallet. After riffling through it a few seconds, she handed him a slip of paper.

"I'll be up in a minute, now go." He swatted her behind, then cringed at the familiarity of the act. As soon as she was out of sight, he picked up the phone.

They drove up the coast to Newport Beach. He kept an eye on the rearview mirror to make sure they weren't being followed. As an added precaution, he got off PCH several blocks after their turn and took a lot of side streets. When he was satisfied they were indeed alone, he doubled back and made his way to a sleepy little bed-and-breakfast he knew.

They took a private tree-lined road up a hill and drove between two statues of lions on either side of a driveway. Meagan stared as a huge French villa covered in vines, came into view. It sat alone on a cliff overlooking the Pacific Ocean.

When they entered through the giant door, Meagan felt as if she'd jumped back in time. She found herself standing in the foyer of a beautiful mansion. The floors were an effervescent hardwood that gleamed in the soft light.

Above her hung a dramatic crystal chandelier, before her a wide sweeping staircase with a floral runner in deep hues flowing up to the second floor then split in opposite directions. The walls surrounding the foyer were lined with flickering sconces as if lit by candles, but at closer inspection, cased bulbs for modern day convenience. The chandelier was dimmed for the hour.

Thomas rang the bell at the desk and checked them in while she ogled the decor.

"This is breathtaking." Meagan brushed her hand along

the ornate banister.

Thomas carried the bags up the stairs, while Meagan lagged behind, inspecting the remarkable paintings along the wall. He'd stopped at the end of the hall and slipped the keycard into the lock. He pushed the door open to allow Meagan to enter first.

She found herself standing in an elaborate sitting room with dark wood furniture and a large bouquet of fresh flowers resting on a claw foot table in the center of the room. She spun around taking in her lavish surroundings. To her left the bedroom. It too contained a floral arrangement, next to the bed stood an ice bucket, with champagne, two crystal flutes sat on the nightstand next to it. A giant king-sized bed filled the room, a fireplace sat at the foot.

"All they had left was the honeymoon suite," he said by way of an explanation.

Meagan turned when he spoke. He dropped his bag on the floor, then took hers into the bedroom. She twirled around and her eyes came to rest on the French doors that led out to the balcony. She ran over and opened the doors. Her eyes closed as she felt the cool ocean breeze wash over her.

Meagan took a deep breath.

"Jesus, close that thing. It's freezing out there!" Thomas complained.

Meagan rolled her eyes and did as he asked, making her way out onto the balcony. She leaned over the railing and looked down at the tempestuous sea as it pummeled the cliff below. It was only a couple of minutes before she rushed back in, her arms wrapped tightly around her. After securing the double doors, she noticed Thomas exiting the bedroom with a pillow.

"You can have the bed. I'll take the couch," he said. He tossed the pillow to one end, and lay down, shifting his body back and forth trying to get comfortable.

"I wouldn't hear of it..."Meagan disappeared into the bedroom.

Thomas' head rose and he followed her with his eyes. She couldn't possibly mean what he *thought* she meant.

She reappeared a moment later.

"Not without a blanket." She finished the sentence with a wide, toothy grin, and dropped the blanket on Thomas's stomach. She turned back and exited the room.

"Good night!" she called cheerily over her shoulder.

"Good night," he grumbled. His head flopped back down on the pillow as he watched the doors close behind her.

FORTY

Meagan awoke to the sound of voices murmuring in the other room. She couldn't imagine whom Thomas was talking to. She swung her legs over the side of the bed, and reached for her robe. When she opened the double doors, she spied Thomas sitting next to Fawn on the couch. She was running her finger down a sheet of paper and speaking in a hushed tone. Paperwork littered the top of the coffee table before them.

Fawn was the first to notice her. "Good morning." She smiled.

Thomas' head came up and he smiled broadly.

"Good morning," Meagan said. Not feeling quite awake, she rubbed her eyes and looked around.

"Good morning. We have coffee if you'd like some. How did you sleep?"

"Okay, I guess." Meagan flicked a look at one detective, and then the other, trying to figure out what was going on, then she tried to read the papers on the table upside down.

Fawn noticed and started scooping them up.

"We have somewhere we need to be today, so I'm going to leave you in the capable hands of Officer Cooper." Thomas glanced at his watch, then back up at Meagan. "He should be here any minute now."

Meagan frowned. The thought of sitting in these close quarters with yet another stranger made her feel uncomfortable.

"Are you okay?" Thomas asked her.

Meagan noticed she'd been staring off into space and focused on him. "Yeah, sure. Just not awake yet. I need my coffee." She smiled at him and made her way over to the coffee service on the sideboard. Without another word, she headed out onto the balcony. She couldn't wait to enjoy her coffee while she gazed out at the sea.

The minute the doors closed behind Meagan, Shadowhawk resumed her explanation of what she found in Meagan's phone records.

"We have the names and addresses for most of the numbers. These come from friends, family and some clients." Shadowhawk's finger slid down the page. "I've looked into each number individually and they all check out. Then we have these here."

She pointed to some numbers highlighted in yellow. "All of these came from phone booths starting in northern California and ending down here in San Juan Capistrano." The last number was highlighted in orange. She looked expectantly at Thomas.

They were interrupted by a knock on the door. Shadowhawk jumped up to let Cooper in, and Thomas brought him up to date. He collected the phone records and placed them into his briefcase. By the time they were ready to go, Meagan was still out on the balcony.

Thomas walked over to the glass doors and gazed out at Meagan. He got a knot in his stomach and realized that he didn't want to leave. He took a deep breath, strolled out onto the balcony, and came to rest at the banister before he turned around.

He looked down at Meagan. "Cooper's here. We're going to be taking off." He had to speak loudly to be heard over the cries of the seagulls.

Meagan put her cup down on the table beside her and glanced up at him. "But it's Saturday. I didn't think you'd have to work today."

"Unfortunately, I don't have that kind of job." He noticed he was wringing his hands, and shoved them in his pockets.

"Can you at least tell me where you're going?"

"I'm afraid not. I'll fill you in tonight."

"I'm part of this investigation too, you know. Or did you forget?" Her eyes implored him.

"No, I haven't forgotten, but we can't talk about it right now." She looked so forlorn that it about broke his heart. He didn't like keeping things from her. But he had to play things close to the vest right now. He couldn't trust her; she'd proven that already.

When Meagan remained quiet, he said, "I'll see you tonight." Then he started toward the door. He'd just reached out for the handle.

"Wait!"

He turned back. Meagan jumped up and ran to him. She gazed up into his eyes and his heart did a little dance. She dipped her head down and made a pretense of straightening his tie.

"Be careful," she said to his chest, then her eyes locked on his once more. She rose up on her tiptoes, and grazed his lips with her own.

"Make sure you *do* come back tonight." She stepped back.

He was stunned into silence. He wanted to grab her, to kiss her. A real kiss. A kiss that would get her attention, and keep her from thinking of that Jackson character ever again.

Instead he just nodded and left.

The detectives drove north heading for the freeway.

"The APB hasn't turned up anything on Jackson yet, and the number Meagan gave me is a prepaid cell phone. There's no way to trace it. He could be anywhere between here and L.A. Johnson got the number to the hotel where the band is staying.

"I've called several times since last night with no luck. When I phoned the recording studio, I found out the band is due in there around ten this morning. I contacted the West L.A. Sheriff's Department to let them know about the arrest since it's in their jurisdiction. I don't want to be stepping on

273

anyone's toes here," Thomas said, staring straight ahead.

They sped up the freeway toward the City of Angels. Thomas was glad this thing was almost over. He wondered how Meagan would take the news that her new *boyfriend* was a serial killer. She'd probably still be in serious denial. Not only was he the only one who knew where she'd been staying, but all the band's play dates coincided with the disappearances of each girl.

The Humboldt County Sheriff's Department was searching his residence in Eureka right now. Thomas was certain they would uncover some serious evidence that would tie the case up tight.

They walked off the elevator that opened up to the recording studio around nine-thirty. Thomas introduced them to the receptionist and asked if they could speak with Drew Jackson. He simply told her they needed to question him regarding a case they were working on. The young girl stated that although some of the band members were already waiting in the studio, that Mr. Jackson was not one of them. He had yet to arrive.

Thomas and Shadowhawk sat in the lobby and waited. Ten o'clock came and went, still no sign of Jackson.

"Do you think he knows we're on to him?" Shadowhawk asked, looking at her watch.

"That's not possible. Just wait, he'll be here."

"Yeah, well, the rest of the band has shown up." She countered.

Thomas didn't say a word.

Forty-five minutes later, the elevator doors opened and Jackson rolled in. His red eyes carried a pair of matching luggage underneath. He'd obviously not been sleeping much of late.

The detectives stood and faced him.

Thomas started reading him his rights, as Shadowhawk cuffed his hands behind his back. The receptionist was on the phone immediately. Before they were out the door, a man came rushing from the back, yelling.

"What are you doing? Where are you taking him? You can't *do* this, we have a recording session!" The man stopped when he reached them, bent over with his hands on his knees trying to catch his breath.

When neither detective answered him, he said, "At least tell me what you're arresting him for."

Thomas stopped halfway through the door, turned and looked the man straight in the eye. "Murder." Then without another word they entered the elevator. When he turned back around to hit the button for *Lobby*, Thomas spied the man staring at them, his mouth wide open.

Jackson was surprisingly quiet until the elevator doors closed, then the yelling began, "What the *hell* are you talking about? I haven't killed anybody. You're making a *huge* mistake and you'll pay, believe me. My lawyers will eat you for lunch!"

FORTY-ONE

Meagan had finished her coffee and was starting to get cold, so she headed back inside. Upon entering, she noticed the officer sitting on the couch reading a newspaper.

He was about six feet tall, with a large belly. She guessed he was in his mid-fifties. At the sound of the door, he put the paper down. His smile was warm. "Good morning. I'm Myron Cooper, but you can call me Coop, everybody does." His boisterous voice took her by surprise. He stood up and reached to shake her hand.

Instantly she felt comfortable and joined him on the couch. He was extremely friendly and told her all about his wife of thirty-five years, their children and grandchildren. She couldn't help but smile at the man's enthusiasm. His stories of the misadventures of his kids were not only overly dramatic in the telling, but had her in stitches as well. He obviously enjoyed talking as much as she enjoyed listening.

Around two that afternoon they were sitting at the table

and eating lunch. Well, she was finishing her club sandwich and fries, but Coop had been finished quite awhile. His cell phone rang, and he excused himself to answer it. Meagan listened to the one-sided conversation.

"Coop, here. Yes. Okay, you got it. Thanks." He hung up and looked at her. "Well, little lady, it looks like you're going home."

Meagan stared at him in disbelief. "You mean it's over?"

"Apparently so. Now get your gear together, and I'll give you your own personal police escort."

"I'll be ready in no time, just watch me!" She squealed with excitement, then sprinted into the other room. Within minutes she was standing by the door.

"You're sure you're ready?"

"Yup."

"You didn't forget anything?"

"Nope." She was out of breath.

On the ride to her house Meagan grilled Coop about the Sandman. Who was he? How did they catch him? But the officer didn't know any more than she did. He told her he was sure that Detective Thomas would contact her with all the details later.

When they pulled up outside her house, Meagan saw the yellow crime scene tape and her face fell. She wondered if she'd ever feel safe in her little cottage again. As much as she loved the place, she might have to move. Too much had happened.

She unlocked the back door and walked in. When

Godzilla was nowhere in sight, an inexplicable sadness overwhelmed her. She dropped her bag. The room was suddenly stifling. She started to open a window, then stopped. "You're sure I'm safe?"

"Don't you worry your pretty little head. They've got that guy safely tucked behind bars. Detective Thomas is probably interrogating him as we speak."

Meagan went about opening the windows and letting the fresh air in.

"Well, I guess I should be getting back to the station. Can't wait to get a look at this scumbag myself."

"Thank you so much for everything, Coop." She kissed him on the cheek.

He placed his hand on his cheek and smiled shyly. "It was nothing." He ducked out the back door, closing it behind him.

Meagan took her overnight bag into her bedroom. Her eyes captured the total chaos. She dropped her bag on the bed, then returned to the kitchen where she grabbed a box of trash bags. She started filling them with all her ruined lingerie. After she'd tossed the last bag in the garbage outside, she set about the task of cleaning the mess the crime scene people had left behind. Black dust coated every hard surface.

The fingerprint powder had even ruined some of her belongings, but she supposed it was a small price to pay. At least she was alive. By the time she had cleaned the entire apartment, it was getting dark and she had to put the lights on to survey her work. Grimy from head to foot, Meagan jumped into the shower.

While the hot water ran the length of her body, it eased the stress that had built up since she'd arrived home. Her thoughts went back to Thomas. She wondered if she'd ever see him again. And what about Drew? She would have to have a talk with him. She couldn't continue to see him, now that her thoughts were dominated by the tall, dark, handsome detective.

But did Thomas feel the same? There were times when she felt electricity between them, but it's not like he acted on it. Perhaps he was still mourning the loss of his wife.

Or maybe he's just like that around all women? The idea dashed her spirits. Could she really be that wrong about him?

Meagan pulled on a pair of sweatpants. No, surely he had feelings for her too. She'd bet on it. She reached into her dresser, pulled out a t-shirt, and slipped it over her head.

 Meagan was standing in the bathroom in front of the mirror, combing out her wet hair, when she heard a knock on the front door. Maybe it's him! Her heart fluttered.

She raced to the door and snuck a glimpse through the peephole. Her heart sank; it wasn't the detective. Still her curiosity was piqued. She flung the door open. "My God, I haven't seen you in years!" She found herself looking into the face of her ex-fiancé.

"Oh Meggie, can I come in?" he asked through his tears.

"Of course. What's wrong?" She stepped aside.

He said nothing as he entered. Meagan shut the door and wrapped him in a warm hug. He grabbed her, tight, and sobbed on her shoulder. She'd never seen him so distraught. They stood like that a few minutes while she let him get it out of his system.

Finally, she pulled out of his grasp, looked him in the eyes. "What's happened?"

He brushed the tears from his cheeks before answering her.

"My wife is dead."

"What? That's horrible! Come here and have a seat. Can I get you anything?" She walked him over to the couch.

"I could use a drink. Do you have anything stronger than soda?"

"Sure. I'll be right back." Meagan hurried to the kitchen, poured a shot of whiskey and rushed back in to hand it to him.

He downed the shot and put the glass down. After a few minutes, he seemed to have calmed down enough for her to talk.

"I didn't even know you were married."

"I met her not long after we split. I guess you could call it a rebound kind of thing. The night we met I went back with her to her apartment and never left. One weekend we went to Vegas, I was drunk, she persuaded me to get married in one of those cheesy little chapels. It was the second dumbest thing I've ever done. The first was losing you."

He turned and looked at her. "I love you, Meagan. I

always have and always will. I just didn't know what a good thing I had in you. I was stupid and thoughtless, I'm sorry." He placed his hand on her knee.

Suddenly uncomfortable, she jumped up, walked to the middle of the room before she turned back around and stared at him.

"Meagan, I want to come back. I know it could work this time. I've had the same job for years now, I make good money. I want to buy you a house. You could stay home and have all the kids you want. I've been saving, I have fifty thousand dollars and it's all for you!" He leapt from the couch, knelt at her feet, and clasped her hands in his.

"Meagan Laurel McInnis, would you do me the honor of letting me love, honor and cherish you for the rest of our lives?"

She pulled her hands away, stunned. "You're distraught. You don't know what you're saying."

He stood up, took her hands again, and gazed into her eyes.

"No. I'm *not*. I never loved her, she was a whore." He shook his head and smiled. Then he spoke to her like she was a child. "You misunderstood. Those were not tears of pain, but tears of joy."

Meagan pulled her hands free and stepped back. A chill coursed through her body. Her memory replayed all the times he had accused *her* of cheating on him. Every time he'd answered the phone and the person hung up, he would say it was her boyfriend. If she came home late, he would grill her about her whereabouts. Now he was calling his recently deceased wife a whore. She didn't know what to think.

"Actually, I'm seeing someone," she blurted out.

"If you mean that singer, he's been arrested for murder. I don't think you'll be able to carry on a decent relationship from a jail cell."

"How, what—" Icy fingers played along her spine, and she inched her way backwards all the while keeping her eyes on his.

He closed the gap between them. "Or were you talking about that detective?"

"Jay, how did your wife die?" Her voice shook.

"Dear, sweet, Meggie." He reached his hand out to stroke her hair.

She jerked away, stared into his black soulless eyes.

"The *Sandman* got her." The grin that spread across his face was pure evil. She didn't know this man at all.

Meagan's heartbeat quickened, her body trembled. Her mind began swimming with flashbacks: Jay flirting obscenely with Lilah at the Fourth of July party; the disgusting magazines she'd found under the bed six months after she'd thrown him out; the time he'd asked her to beat him during sex, then recanted saying he was only kidding. Maybe she never really knew this man at all.

Without much thought, she kneed him in the groin. When he doubled over, she raced for the back door.

"You bitch! You're going to pay for that!"

She got the lock undone and was just turning the knob

when she felt him grab her by the hair and yank. She screamed as her neck snapped back, a jolt of pain whipped through her body.

"I should have *known* you'd be like all the rest. All those years of loving you, working *hard* for you, and this is the thanks I get!" Jay dragged her backward.

Meagan tried to keep up with him before he pulled her hair out by the roots. Finally she found her footing, whipped her elbow around and connected with his eye.

He let go and screamed, "You cunt!"

She fled to the bedroom and slammed the door. Holding it closed with her body, she searched the room. Her eyes locked on the chair in the corner. She dragged it over and lodged it up underneath the doorknob tightly to secure it. He pounded on the door, screamed obscenities. She prayed her neighbors had called the cops.

Unexpectedly she heard a loud thud. The door shuddered. Jay was trying to kick it in. She watched in horror as the top hinges started to give way. Frantically she searched the room for a weapon, and found the mallet. She plopped down into the chair. The next time he rammed the door, it barely budged.

Suddenly the phone rang and all went quiet. He'd stopped trying to gain entrance to the room. Meagan looked back at the door, then at the phone. Her mind was buzzing. What do I do? What do I do? Finally she leapt from the chair and raced toward the phone. Just then a loud crash startled her, she turned. The door had collapsed on top of the chair and he climbed over it toward her. She picked up the phone in mid-ring and screamed "Help!" Then felt a sharp pain on the back of her head.

Everything went dark.

FORTY-TWO

"I already told you, I don't know anything. I just met the woman!" Jackson yelled.

"So you just wanted a little piece of ass while you were in town, then you moved on?" Thomas was bent over the table, resting on his hands. The muscles of his arms were tight, his jaw set, his face mere inches from Jackson.

"Look, she's a tasty morsel, but she wouldn't put out. I called her a couple of times to see if she'd changed her mind, but when I found out all the shit happening to her I bailed. Hell, who wouldn't? I mean, that's some crazy shit, man, you know? No chick is worth it." Jackson shook his head.

Thomas threw Jackson up against the wall and placed his arm across his throat. "You want us to believe that you took no for an answer, that was just fine with you? You didn't take any of these women and hold them somewhere, maybe to teach them a lesson?" Thomas said through clenched teeth. "Because women don't say no to you, do they, stud?"

"I want my lawyer," Jackson eked out.

"Thomas." Shadowhawk had her hand on his shoulder.

The phone on the wall rang. He ignored it.

His partner picked it up. "Yeah, okay." She whispered into Thomas' ear, "Harris wants to talk to us." Then she started toward the door and stood waiting for Thomas. Finally he let the jerk go and left the room.

Captain Harris was waiting for them in the viewing room.

"Doesn't look like you guys are doing so good." Harris had his arms crossed over his chest.

"He's just playing us. He was in every city when the girls went missing. Women are just playthings to him. Just look at his history, for Christ's sake."

"Thomas, that's just circumstantial evidence. You have nothing that will hold up in court. You don't have a witness, you don't have a fingerprint, and you don't have anything that puts this guy at any of the crime scenes. The sheriff's department up in Humboldt recovered nothing of significance from his house.

"The only thing you have on this creep is that he's a cocky son of a bitch. If that were a crime, we'd have to lock up half the men in Orange County. Admit it, you're shooting blanks. The sooner you realize it, the sooner you can go out and get some solid evidence.

Harris continued. "If you and Shadowhawk know in your gut that this is the guy, then let him go and put a tail on his ass. He'll incriminate himself, trust me. What do you think Shadowhawk. Is this the guy?" The captain turned his attention to her.

"Everything does point to him, but there's just one thing niggling at me. We can't put him with that first victim," she answered.

"Let's swab the guy. We check the blood type and find out whether or not he's a secretor. If we have a match, we nail the son of a bitch. We don't have to wait for DNA," Thomas quickly interjected.

"You guys have been interrogating this bozo for hours. Now he's lawyered up. No lawyer worth his salt will let you swab his client. Besides, we can't hold him on blood type alone, and we can't wait until the DNA tests come back. I think it's time to call it quits, guys." Harris left the room.

Shadowhawk turned to Thomas. "Maybe he's right. We cut the guy loose, tail him, maybe even catch him in the act. What do you say?" She patted him on the back and followed the captain out.

He stood there staring at Jackson. It had to be him, he thought. Thomas didn't believe in coincidences.

The door opened and Cooper walked in. "How's it going with that scumbag?"

"What the *hell* are you doing here?" Thomas yelled.

"What do you mean? I was told to take Meagan home and return to the station. They said you caught the guy. That's him, isn't it?" Cooper hooked his thumb at the suspect.

"Who gave you those orders? I'm the one running this damn investigation!" Thomas slammed his fist down on the desk.

"I don't know. Some guy from dispatch called. He told me you were busy interrogating the suspect." Cooper hitched up his belt.

"I never gave that order. What the hell is going on around here?" Thomas flew out of the room toward the nearest desk and picked up the phone. "Shit!" He slammed it back down, got out his notebook and started skimming the pages. He found Meagan's number, then picked the phone up again and dialed.

It rang four times. "Come on, come on, come on. Pick up the goddamned phone!" Finally someone picked up, but before he could say anything, he heard Meagan scream for help. Then the line went dead. Cooper was standing next to him.

"Get some cruisers over to Meagan's house, and tell Shadowhawk to meet me there immediately!" Thomas raced toward the door.

Once in the car, he took out his cell phone and dialed Meagan's number again. This time the phone just kept ringing. His mind was reeling. If the Sandman had her, would she still be alive?

His car sped down the highway weaving in and out of traffic. He was passing San Juan Capistrano when his cell phone rang. He answered, "Talk to me."

"Detective, this is Kowalski. I'm at the residence, sir. There's no one here and no sign of a break-in, but there are signs of a struggle. What do you want us to do?"

Thomas' heart sank.

"Start canvassing the neighborhood for witnesses. I'm almost there." Thomas hung up.

When he pulled in front of the house, the scene was all too familiar. There were black-and-whites all around her driveway, their lights flashing. He jumped from the car and raced toward the house, but when he walked in, he found he was alone.

He found the signs of the struggle in the bedroom. The door was caved in, and a chair was toppled on its side. The phone was ripped out of the wall. On the floor lay a broken lamp, and beside it, a puddle of blood.

Someone came up behind him, but he couldn't tear his eyes away from the blood, Meagan's blood. That crazy motherfucker had her.

"The CSU should be here soon."

Thomas turned around. The officer's name tag said Darby.

"Thank you. Has anyone touched anything?"

"I don't think so, sir."

"Good. Secure the scene and keep everyone out. I need to think."

The officer disappeared, then after a moment Thomas left the bedroom. He couldn't look at the blood anymore. He wandered into the living room, his eyes darting around. They settled on the coffee table where one lone shot glass sat.

Just then, Shadowhawk came bursting through the front door, panting. Thomas jerked his head up.

"What have you got?" she asked, anxiously.

"Nothing, yet. It was obviously someone she knew." He pointed down at the table. "The rest you can see for yourself. Check out the bedroom." He put his hands on his hips and looked around.

She made a beeline for the bedroom.

A few minutes later she was back by his side. She laid a hand on his shoulder. "She's still alive."

"I hope you're right. I was a fool, I jumped the gun. Because of that, I just may have gotten her killed." His eyes came back to the glass on the table, and he shook his head.

The screen door slammed and Officer Kowalski walked in.

"Detectives, I think I've got something." He had his notebook in his hand. "The woman across the street, is one Mrs. Mary Kline, widowed. She has MS and is confined to a wheel chair. She doesn't get out much, so she spends a lot of time in front of the window.

"Anyway, she saw a large dark car pull up in front of the house around six-thirty. A guy got out, walked up to the door and was let in. About an hour later, he came around from the side of the house and put what looked like a rolled-up carpet into his trunk and pulled away."

"Did she get a look at the guy?" Thomas asked.

"As a matter of fact she did. She said she saw him under the porch light as he was waiting for the door to open; he turned around and looked at the street. Then when the door opened he turned back around. "Let me see," He consulted his notes. "Here we go. He's about five-nine or five-ten,

Caucasian, late twenties to early thirties, with long curly dark hair, and a possible beard, or at least whiskers. From a distance she said he looked a bit like Jesus Christ."

"Roberts," Thomas said to no one in particular.

"What about the car? Did she give you anything more on that?" Shadowhawk asked.

"Yes, ma'am, she did. The car was a dark color. She couldn't tell the actual color because the street doesn't have many lights. She did know the make, though, said her husband owned a car just like it in the seventies."

"Well, what the hell is it?" Thomas felt like he was pulling teeth.

"A Ford LTD. Said she's seen it on the street quite a few times lately, but that this was the first time it parked in front of the victim's home."

"Son of a bitch!" Thomas took off running.

Shadowhawk followed him, and jumped into the passenger side of his car as he started the engine.

He dialed dispatch while he consulted his notes. "Put out an APB on a Dark, Gray, Ford LTD. License plate number Alpha, Romeo, Tango, three, eight, niner. The owner is a one Jordan Roberts; consider him armed and dangerous. He's wanted for murder and kidnapping. And tell anyone who approaches the vehicle to be extremely cautious. The victim may be in the trunk."

"Where are we going?" Shadowhawk asked.

"Laguna Niguel. I want to see if we can get a handle on Roberts."

Her eyebrows rose. "You don't think he'll take her back to the apartment, do you?"

"No, but maybe his wife has a clue. If not, we're going to take that place apart until we find some answers. Shit!" Thomas hit the steering wheel with his fist. "I never should have pulled the surveillance from that guy."

***

Thomas pounded on the apartment door and yelled, "Police, open up!" After no one stirred inside, Shadowhawk lifted her leg to break the lock, but Thomas stopped her. He wrapped his hand around the doorknob and turned. It was unlocked. They looked at each other, then pulled out their guns before carefully stepping inside.

The apartment looked the same, utter chaos. They stood outside the only door that was closed, the bedroom. Shadowhawk took position on one side, with Thomas on the other just inside the bathroom doorway. Silently he turned the knob and threw the door open.

Cautiously he peered in and stopped.

"Shit." He put his gun away and walked into the room.

"Fuck me. I think we can safely say this is our guy," she said, looking around.

"It looks like a fuckin' Jackson Pollock painting in here."

They were silent a moment as they took in the scene. The walls were splattered with blood. Splashes of red reached as high as the ceiling. The bed was a literal pool of blood. The naked body of a mutilated woman lay in the center. Her extremities stretched out and tied to the bedposts.

The mass was almost unrecognizable as being human, let alone a woman, yet there was no mistaking the butterfly tattoo on the woman's left ankle. It belonged to Sharon Roberts.

"Would you call this a crime of passion?" Shadowhawk asked sarcastically, breaking the silence.

"I would definitely call it personal."

FORTY-THREE

Meagan's eyes fluttered open. When they finally focused, she was staring at a wood slatted ceiling. This wasn't home. The room was dimly lit, the edges cast in shadows. She tried to shift her extremities, but they wouldn't budge. Quickly she lifted her head, excruciating pain slammed into her. She closed her eyes and eased her head back down. The throbbing continued.

The cobwebs blanketing her mind began to dissipate, dissolving like wet cotton candy. She jerked her body back and forth trying to move something, anything. Panic ensued.

What's wrong with me? What's going on?

Okay, stay calm. Assess the situation.

Slowly Meagan lifted her head again. She was lying on a table, her arms and legs were stretched out, her hands and feet were tied with a white cord. Probably to the legs of the table underneath, she couldn't tell from her vantage point. She wiggled her fingers and toes. Tiny needles attacked as if they were asleep. There was a faint smell of manure, and the distant sound of buzzing flies. A slight chill in the air.

"Ah, my Sleeping Beauty awakes!"

She knew the voice coming from the shadows, but she couldn't quite place it. The knowledge was right on the tip of her tongue. Suddenly, a face appeared above her, and with it total recall. She let out a gut-wrenching scream.

Jay. Her ex-fiancé. Jordan Roberts.

The man with whom she'd loved and shared a bed with for more than three years *was* the Sandman. She bucked and pulled, trying to get free while staring up into his cold black eyes. Her heart hammered in her chest so hard it threatened to jump right out. She thought she knew terror, but she'd been horribly wrong. True terror was staring at the face of evil and knowing she wouldn't live another day.

"It's so *nice* of you to join me. I'm sorry it won't be for long." He stroked her hair; she jerked away. "I don't think I've ever seen you more seductive. Something about a totally submissive woman really turns me on. I'm getting hard as we speak." He smirked.

"You *sick* bastard, let me go!" Meagan jerked and writhed on the table.

He laughed. "You can wiggle all you want, you won't get free. I've had a lot of practice. I finally have you right where I want you. Completely under my control."

Meagan cringed.

He raised a large hunting knife, waved it before her face. Light reflected off the serrated edge momentarily blinding her. He grabbed the waistband of her sweatpants.

"What are you doing?" Her body trembled.

"Just liberating you from these cumbersome clothes. Sure, I could have taken them off when you were passed out, but where's the fun in that?" He let out a high-pitched giggle.

This was no longer Jordan or Jay, or anyone she knew.

That man was gone. The Sandman had taken his place.

The sharp edge of the knife sliced easily down the length of her pant leg as if slicing butter. The tip nicked her leg. She jumped and let out a yelp, sending the blade deeper into her thigh. She screamed, her body lurched.

"Stop that. Look what you made me do!" He stared at the wound. "Shit, that looks bad. You'd better not die too soon and ruin all my fun."

He went back to cutting her pants away, then tugged them out from under her body and tossed them aside. He ran a hand up her leg, stopping just short of her panties.

"You've always had the most amazing legs."

Next he sliced her tee shirt up the front.

She had to get out of here. She ignored him and focused on a means of escape. Then she felt the knife between her breasts, and turned her head in time to see her bra sliced right up the middle, popping it open.

"Oh yeah, let's get those bad boys out." He pulled the cups aside until her breasts sprang free.

"Just look at those perky little devils." He laid the knife down, cupped her breasts pushing them together, and pinched her nipples. Hard. She let out a shriek and clenched her eyes shut.

Meagan struggled to get her hands free while concentrating on keeping her body still. She didn't want to tip him off. The rope cut deeper into her wrists the more she worked her hands around. It felt as if she were pulling the skin off like a glove. She gritted her teeth against the pain.

Meagan took a few deep breaths, cleared her mind of her surroundings, and imagined she was at the ocean. She focused on the rhythm, the waves crawling up the sand, then receding in an even tempo, back and forth, back and forth. Then she set about loosening her hands.

A sharp pain made her gasp. Her eyes flew open and glanced down. Blood pooled around her nipple. He traced the cut with his tongue.

Meagan stared at the ceiling willing her mind to ignore the hideous things happening to her body, but her fear was all-encompassing. It was useless to try to will it away as if it were a stitch in her side while running.

She couldn't pull her eyes away no matter how she tried. They were glued to the sharp tip of the blade. The knife ran the length of her stomach like a felt-tipped pen. A thin red line bloomed in its wake.

"You'll never get away with this!" She tried to distract him.

The Sandman's head shot up, a glazed look in his eyes. He pulled the knife away and slithered to the head of the table. A slow smile crept along his face and he bent down next to her ear. "Ah, but I already have," he whispered. "I've been getting away with it for years."

Meagan shivered.

He walked around the table while he talked. "You dumped me. I loved you more than I've ever loved anyone, and you just threw me away. Discarded me like some old shoe. That night I got stinking drunk. I sat in a bar and tossed back tequila shots 'til my eyes were crossed.

"Then some cheap, sleazy cunt with long blonde hair like yours came over and sat next to me. She started to buy *me* drinks. She rubbed up against me like a cat in heat. I couldn't believe it. What made her think I would dip my wick into her diseased cesspool? But I took her up on it, all right. I let her drive me to her place, then I taught her a lesson. Ha! They still haven't found her body." He stood at her feet, staring trancelike off in the distance.

"My hair is auburn," Meagan said, just above a whisper.

"What?" He looked at her, his face scrunched up as if confused.

"You said she had long blonde hair like mine. But my hair's red."

He stomped to the head of the table. "That's what I said!" He slapped her hard across the face. "Don't you *ever* contradict me!"

Meagan tasted blood. The room started spinning. She was losing all time and place. Blood flowed from the gash in her leg, onto the table, then the floor. If she didn't get away soon, she would bleed to death.

What was I doing again? Oh, yeah, freeing my hands. But

I'm so tired. All I want to do is go to sleep. That's it! I'm having a nightmare and when I wake up I'll be home in my own bed, safe and sound.

She closed her eyes. Snip. A quick nick on her left hip made her eyes shoot open, her head flew up. Snip. This time the knife slid through the right side of her panties, taking a sliver of skin with it. He gripped her panties with both hands and ripped them from her body. Her head dropped down on the table with a thud.

It was just too heavy.

Weak and listless, she watched his naked body climb up on the table.

Will Thomas be sad when I'm dead?

Blackness edged her vision.

The Sandman was talking and waving the knife around, but she no longer heard a word he said.

She nodded off.

A slap on her cheek made her eyes jerk open.

The knife danced before her face. The glinting light burned her eyes.

Her heavy lids closed.

She heard the slap, more than felt it. She knew he wanted her to open her eyes, but she just didn't care.

The darkness finally won.

FORTY-FOUR

Thomas and Shadowhawk slapped on latex gloves and frantically searched the apartment. After witnessing the way Roberts's mind had snapped in the last week, Thomas had no idea how much time they had to reach Meagan alive. At this point, he didn't give a shit about protecting the integrity of the crime scene.

Shadowhawk was pulling down shoeboxes from the top of the walk-in closet. "Looks like there's a trap door in the ceiling. Give me a boost, will ya?" Thomas joined her, grabbed the top of her thighs and hoisted her up. She lifted a panel and slid it aside, then flashed her penlight around.

"What do you see?" Thomas yelled up to her.

"It's more like a crawl space than an actual attic."

"Is there anything stored up there?"

"I see some boxes. I'm going up." She stuck the penlight between her teeth, then pulled herself up through the hole.

Before too long he was getting antsy. "Well?"

When she didn't answer, he tried again.

"Hey! What the hell's up there?"

"An old box of Christmas ornaments which may or may not belong to the current occupants. A dead rat, a lot of spider webs and dust..."

"Dammit, Shadowhawk, quit fucking around! Have you found anything useful or not?"

"Maybe," she said, her head now sticking out of the hole. "Take this." She lowered a metal box into his outstretched hands. Then she backed out of the hole and dropped the last few feet to the floor. She was covered head to toe in dirt. Cobwebs clung to her jet-black hair. He picked them out while she dusted herself off.

"Let's take this into the kitchen," Thomas said.

By then the first officer had arrived. Thomas sent him back out to secure the scene. He carried the metal box to the counter and used his arm to clear a space. The box was locked. Shadowhawk appeared with a lock pick, and within seconds the box was open. She started pulling things out: A birth certificate, an old driver's license, a key ring from Yosemite, a picture. It was of a beautiful young woman with long blonde hair parted in the middle, wearing a Mexican peasant dress holding a baby, circa the sixties or early seventies.

Shadowhawk waved the snapshot in the air.

"Remind you of anyone?"

Thomas examined it. "Could be anyone of our vics."

"Exactly. But it's hard to imagine this woman abusing

her child. She looks kind."

"Can't tell a lot by a photo. God only knows what she was truly like."

Shadowhawk lifted a birthday card and read it.

"Check this out." She handed him the card, then reached into the box for more photos.

"This is from Meagan!" Thomas read on. Shadowhawk handed him a stack of pictures that all had one thing in common: Meagan. Meagan on the beach coming out of the water, Meagan riding a horse in a forest, and in the last one, Meagan holding up her left hand to show off an engagement ring.

"Holy shit!" Thomas gasped.

"What?" Shadowhawk stared at him.

"She told me about her ex-fiancé. She called him Jay, but what she was really calling him was J., as in the first letter of his name. Jordan Roberts wasn't on the list because I'd asked her to name every man she'd dated in the last five years. That gave me everyone who had been in her life *since* she dumped his sorry ass."

Thomas continued to stare at Meagan's smiling face, while Shadowhawk inspected the remaining items in the box. She pulled out another stack of pictures, flipped through them, then handed them over for him to study.

"Gee, I guess he lied to us. I'm hurt."

Thomas glanced down into the face of Cindy Gross.

"Well, if there was any doubt before, these prove otherwise." He skimmed the remaining shots of Cindy in her bikini.

"Uh-huh," She said without glancing up. Then she was silent while she read something in her hands. "Okay, here we go." She handed him a newspaper clipping. "Looks like the father killed himself exactly like Brad Landis, bullet to the head. What are the odds?"

Thomas grabbed his cell phone and dialed. "Johnson, get me an address for an Edward Michael Roberts in San Juan Capistrano. I'll call you right back." He slipped the phone back in his pocket. "Come on, I think I know where he might be." The detectives jumped into the BMW and headed south.

The minute they were on the freeway, he called Johnson back. She had the information.

"Wait" Thomas passed the phone to Shadowhawk. "Here, get the address and put it into the GPS so it can give us directions."

The Ortega Highway exit loomed ahead, and Thomas took it. The car idled at the end of the off-ramp, while he waited to hear if he was heading east or west. He glanced at the red light, then back at Shadowhawk's fumbling fingers. "Come on!" Just as the light turned green, the map came up on the screen and Thomas swung a hard left, tires screeching in his wake.

"Looks like the house is way out in the boonies," she declared.

"Makes sense. No matter how loud you scream, there's no one around to hear you." Thomas imagined ripping Roberts apart limb by limb.

"What I don't understand is why he held on to all that land? I mean, why the hell didn't he sell it? It must be worth a friggin' fortune!"

"Obviously his privacy was more important to him than money."

Thomas was having a hard time concentrating on his partner's inane conversation. Meagan held his thoughts captive. He had to find her alive; he couldn't live without her. His mind flashed images of her, taunting him. Ramping up the panic already deep-seated within him.

The way her eyes lit up when she smiled, her hearty laugh, the way the sun danced across her auburn curls. Since the moment he'd met Meagan Laurel McInnis, his emotions had been in turmoil. No matter how hard he fought it, he knew he'd fallen in love with her.

I'm sorry, Victoria.

It's all right. You belong together.

Thomas jumped in his seat. "What did you say?"

Shadowhawk stared at him. "I didn't say anything."

Great, now I'm having hallucinations of my dead wife talking to me. Maybe I do need a shrink after all!

FORTY-FIVE

"That's the mailbox." Shadowhawk pointed. "Turn here!"

Thomas jerked the wheel and took a hard right onto a dirt road sending a cloud of dust in their wake. It was a little while before he saw a farmhouse in the distance. Once Roberts' car came into view, he tightened his grip on the steering wheel. Sweat etched his brow. The adrenaline pumping through his body had his legs twitching. He couldn't wait to get out of the car. He heard his partner's voice as if she were in a tunnel, calling for backup.

Thomas had barely put the car in park before he flung the door open. Shadowhawk's hand shot out to grab his arm. "Wait!" But it was too late. She found herself clutching thin air. He raced toward the front of the house and landed next to the front door, back against the wall, gun pointed straight up.

"Shit!" She scrambled out of the car and caught up to him.

"I don't suppose I could persuade you to wait for backup, could I?" she whispered. But one look at his determined face told her that was *not* going to happen.

Thomas reached out and twisted the doorknob. Unlocked. He motioned to his partner that he would take the lead. With fingertips pressed against the door, it slowly swung open and he eased into the house. Thomas pointed for her to take the right, while he went left. Within minutes they'd searched the entire house. It was empty.

He put his gun away. "What the hell?" With his hands on his hips, he did a 360.

"The barn!" Shadowhawk took off out the front door.

"What barn? I didn't see any barn." He followed her outside. Off in the distance, to the left of the house, there stood a barn. It must have been obscured by the trees as they drove up the road. By the time Thomas caught up to her, she was standing in the middle of the open space, shaking her head.

"Did you search top to bottom?"

Shadowhawk put her arms out, palms up. "There's only one floor."

Thomas took in his surroundings. A rusted-out John Deere tractor. Old farming equipment pushed to the outskirts. Hay littering the floor. Dead center, a puddle of fresh oil. The faint odor of manure still haunted the enclosure.

"That doesn't seem right. What about a trap door?"

His body was drenched in sweat, his heart knocked

loudly in his ears. *Where the hell is this sick fuck holding Meagan?* Frantically he searched the floor, pushing hay away with his feet, stomping, listening for a hollow thud. When Thomas came up empty, he turned to Shadowhawk.

"Dammit, I know they're here! What are we missing?"

He fled the barn and circled the perimeter of the building. He found the cab of a semi parked in back as if in hiding. Thomas was on his second lap around the barn when he noticed something odd. He raced back inside. The tack room. It was too short. The outside wall was roughly another ten feet longer. He entered the room and scanned the floor. Before long he found a spot that had been cleared in a perfect arc.

Thomas pressed his hands against the wood until the wall popped open with a click and a door swung open. He pulled his Glock and soundlessly entered the room.

He was met with the back of a naked man kneeling on a table a few feet away. On either side of him were the legs of a woman, her ankles tied to the table underneath. The rest of her body obscured, but Thomas knew it was Meagan. Roberts was rambling something incoherent and waving his hands around wildly to emphasize his point.

Thomas stood rigid. His gun pointed at the man's head. The urge to blow Roberts's brains out immediately was tempered only by Meagan. From where she lay, she would be showered with blood and gray matter. That's not something she would recover from real soon, so he lowered the gun and aimed at Roberts's butt.

"Police. Get off the table and back up *real* slow," Thomas hissed the words through gritted teeth. Rage shook his entire body. It took all the control he had to keep himself from unloading the gun's entire magazine into the lunatic's ass.

Roberts eased his way down and stood up without turning around. His arms were still in front of him. Thomas assumed he was using to the table to steady himself.

"Clasp your hands behind your head." Thomas waited, but Roberts didn't move. He couldn't see the man's hands, and that made him leery.

"I *said.*" Thomas's jaw was clenched so tight he thought it might snap. "Clasp your hands behind your head. Now!"

Roberts spun around and lunged at Thomas with a large hunting knife. It slashed his arm. The gun fell to the floor. Thomas grabbed Roberts's wrist and tried to wrestle the knife away. He fell back onto the ground with Roberts on top of him. They rolled across the floor under the table. Roberts ended up on top. Thomas scanned the area around him for the gun. It was out of reach.

It took both of his hands to keep Roberts from piercing his heart with the knife. Shadowhawk's feet appeared in his peripheral vision. She kicked the gun within his reach. It was up to him. There was no way she could take the shot herself without endangering him as well.

He had to be quick. He didn't have enough strength in only one arm to fend off this madman. Roberts had the advantage. He eyeballed the gun, then stared back into the eyes of the crazed killer. Thomas readied himself. He took a deep breath and focused all his strength. It was all or nothing.

Thomas rolled his body hard to the right. It was just enough to jerk Roberts off-kilter. He snatched the gun and brought it up in front of Roberts's face. He squeezed the trigger without hesitation. The blast echoed through the small room. The look in his eyes was one of disbelief before his body toppled over sideways.

"Get this crazy motherfucker off of me!" Thomas shoved the body aside and jumped up.

The bullet had entered right between Roberts's eyes and exited out the back of his head.

The Sandman was dead.

Finally.

Shadowhawk put her gun away and raced out of the room. She'd said something to him, but he wasn't paying much attention.

Thomas rushed to the table and stopped. Meagan's eyes were closed, her head lulled to the side. Her face was covered with perspiration, her hair damp, her porcelain skin ashen. Her body was smeared with blood. He couldn't tell where it was coming from, but the dirt floor was thick with it. It was all over him as well. He looked like he'd rolled around in a bloody mud pit. The metallic stench accosted him.

All that blood.

Meagan's blood.

God, no, I can't be too late. Not again!

His head collapsed against her side. She was still warm.

He stood up, pressed his fingers to her carotid artery, no pulse. He pushed harder and held his hand in place. It took a while, but finally he felt a faint slow rhythm. Relief washed over him. He swatted the tears standing in his eyes.

"Meagan, it's time to wake up, honey." He stared down at her and waited, but her eyes wouldn't open. She didn't move.

Just then Shadowhawk flew into the room. "How is she?"

"She's lost a lot of blood, but she's alive. Barely."

"Backup's just pulling in now. An ambulance is on the way." She pulled out a pocketknife and went to work cutting the cords securing Meagan's arms and feet.

Thomas took off his jacket and covered her body.

"It's all right, you're safe now." He stroked her hair, and willed her to wake. Her eyelids quivered a bit, but didn't open.

"Come on, baby, let me see those beautiful blue eyes of yours." He choked back a sob, swallowed hard.

"You can do it." He stroked her cheek with his finger.

Her lids fluttered, then opened.

"That's my girl." A chuckle of relief escaped.

"You found me," her weak voice but a whisper. Her eyes eased shut.

"Yes, I did." The tears he'd been holding back broke free, but he didn't give a damn. He kissed her forehead. "And I'm never letting you go."

FORTY-SIX

A few days later, Thomas pulled up in front of his house and parked on the street. He jumped out, ran around to the passenger side of the car, and hoisted Meagan into his arms.

"This isn't necessary." She smiled up at him.

"The doctor said you had to stay off that leg or you could rip out the stitches. So stop being stubborn." His jaw was set.

"I do have crutches, you know." Meagan was having a great time teasing the ever-so-serious Thomas. He had spent every day in the hospital by her side, and now insisted on taking care of her at his home. Not that she was complaining. It was pretty damn cute the way he treated her like a frail damsel in distress.

"Oh, yeah, like I'm going to watch you spend an hour trying to navigate these front steps?" Thomas acted so tough, but she knew better. He'd been terribly worried for her. That's why she was letting him do things his way. Sort of. She couldn't pass up this golden opportunity to badger him.

Who knew when another moment like this would come along?

"You're exaggerating." Meagan tried to hide her smile.

"Oh, shut up and let me carry you into the house. Must you be so dammed difficult?" She stifled a laugh.

He marched up the five brick steps that led to the front door.

Meagan looked back at Shadowhawk, who had followed them in her own car. She was trailing behind them carrying Meagan's crutches. "It must be a guy thing," she said to her.

"Oh yeah, he's asserting his machismo. Me, Tarzan, you Jane." Shadowhawk smiled back.

***

Thomas ignored them. They were having a fine time at his expense. When he reached the door, he shifted Meagan in his arms and fiddled in his pocket for the keys. Once he got them out, Shadowhawk appeared beside him.

"You want some help with those?" His partner smiled, a glint of humor in her eyes.

He glared down at her a moment before relinquishing the keys. God forbid he refused her help or next thing he knew they would be accusing him of being a chauvinist pig! She opened the door and stepped aside. He tried to ignore Shadowhawk's silly grin as he navigated Meagan through the threshold and laid her gently down on the couch in the living room.

"Can I get you something to drink?" he asked Meagan.

"Just water, thanks." Meagan smiled up at him. He couldn't help but wonder if it was a sarcastic smile. He didn't wait around to find out.

Shadowhawk set the crutches within Meagan's reach. "I'm going to take off now. I can see you're in good hands." She laughed before she leaned down and hugged Meagan.

"Thanks for everything," Meagan said.

"I'll call you tomorrow and see how you're doing. Take care." She opened the front door and yelled goodbye to Thomas before closing it behind her.

Thomas returned with a glass of ice water and a half-empty bottle of Aquafina, which he set on the table within easy reach. He sat opposite Meagan on the coffee table and watched as she picked at a loose thread on the hem of her sweater.

"Are you all right?" He wondered if she'd changed her mind about staying with him after all.

With her head down, he was able to stare at her at length without reproach. Once again he was struck by her beauty. Her porcelain skin was flawless. Her cheeks blushed naturally by the sun. He ached to see that wild red mane of hers fanned out on his pillow; her full, seductive lips made him hungry for a taste.

This unpredictable woman that had captured his heart was unlike any he had ever known. She was the complete opposite of Victoria. His wife had a quiet reserve. She had been as graceful as a ballerina; she didn't walk, she glided with her head held high, her back ramrod straight.

The way Victoria had dressed was sophisticated; her entire wardrobe had been beige, brown or black. Always acquired from the same designer in London. On a day-to-day basis, she habitually had worn her thick brunette hair straight down the middle of her back. The ends had been trimmed precisely every six weeks. On those occasions when a gown was expected, when she had performed, or had gone to one of her numerous charity events, her hair had been pulled back in a classic chignon.

Victoria had been raised with wealth and prestige. She had been a debutante, for Christ sake. Thomas had always wondered what she was doing with a crass unsophisticated cop like him. He had been in awe of her, but in all honesty they didn't have much in common.

On the other hand, Meagan was wild and unpredictable. Her thoughts tumbled out of her mouth, often catching Thomas off guard. She challenged him; she was honest to a fault. She was warm, intelligent, and downright comfortable to be around.

Meagan didn't mind making a joke at her own expense. She made him laugh and they *did* have a lot in common. Although seven years his junior, in a lot of ways she was wiser. He thought he might know her better in this short time than he had ever known his wife. Victoria was a private woman.

You would never find Victoria sitting on the floor or wearing a pair of jeans. And although she liked the ocean, she would never actually swim in it. Even boats made her nervous.

Meagan was so full of life and he couldn't imagine *his* life without her in it. A sudden wave of emotion crashed down on him, he needed to touch her. He reached out, caressed her cheek with the back of his hand.

"I'm fine," she answered without raising her head.

"You don't look fine." He put his fingers under her chin and lifted her head. Her eyes gazed up, met his and stayed. They were full of confusion, or was it doubt? *Oh, no, she's decided not to stay.*

He wanted to wrap her up in his arms and never let her go. He wanted to assure her that he would do everything in his power to make certain no one ever hurt her again. But he feared if she knew the depth of his feelings he would frighten her away.

After everything she'd been through, he wouldn't blame her if she never trusted another man as long as she lived. But he wanted to prove her wrong. He swallowed hard. "Okay, spill it."

"Well ...are you *sure* Jordan was the Sandman?"

His mind snapped out of its reverie, his hand dropped from her face. He jumped off the couch and started pacing.

"I mean, don't get me wrong. The guy was batshit crazy, I know. What I'm trying to say is that he was *so* crazy, *so* out there, that I wonder if he didn't just fantasize about being this famous serial killer."

Thomas stopped and stared at her.

"Like he wanted to take credit for everything the Sandman did, himself. Maybe he copied things he had read in the newspaper, or heard on the news. You had to know him to understand, I guess, but the guy was just so over-the-top dramatic about everything that I wouldn't put it past him, that's all."

Thomas turned his back on Meagan and marched over to the window. He didn't want to think about Jordan Roberts. He didn't want to remember what a sick son of a bitch he was. But most of all, he didn't want to relive the moment he thought he'd lost Meagan forever. It was bad enough that his mind replayed that image of her when he least expected it. Her lifeless body, bound to that table, covered in blood.

Every night since it had happened, he'd been having the same bad dream. He'd arrived too late and Meagan was dead. The Sandman had gotten away. He would wake up drenched in sweat. He'd have this undeniable urge to see her, to touch her, to know that she was still alive. That was one of the reasons he needed her here, with him. He needed that constant reassurance.

**

Meagan watched Thomas turn into a completely different man before her eyes. His gait, his stance, everything about him turned rigid. One second he was tender and warm, the next he was all but stomping around the living room like a child having a tantrum.

She stared a hole in his back willing him to turn around. When he didn't, her impatience grew thin.

"Are you going to answer me, or not?" she finally yelled.

He spun around and confronted her. "Dammit, Meagan!"

She had no idea why anger seethed from every pore of his being. Her question was a valid one. Why was he so dead set against answering it?

His features softened slightly.

"Without a doubt," he said under his breath.

"Without a doubt what? I make you mad? You want to smack me? Or Jordan was The Sandman?" She was so frustrated she wanted to hit him, too bad she couldn't reach that far.

"Yes to all of the above!" He turned away, then added, "Let me put it this way: if he weren't dead, he would have been sent to death row with all the incriminating evidence we've found."

"Like what?" Meagan urged.

He looked at her sideways. "Stop it. I don't want to talk about this. Just leave it alone. Dammit!" With that, he marched out of the room, headed for the kitchen.

When he didn't return, Meagan grabbed the crutches off the floor and tried to pull herself up. She was weak and the pain meds made her woozy, but she finally made it up on the third try.

Each time the crutches landed on the hardwood floor, the thud sent pain reverberating through her entire body, but she was angry now. No way was she going to put up with him just walking out. He didn't get to say when this discussion was over. She wanted answers, and she wanted them now!

FORTY-SEVEN

Meagan came around the wall and found Thomas standing on the kitchen side of the counter. The counter itself divided the kitchen from the dining area and contained the sink as well as the dishwasher. Meagan presumed it was so whoever was doing the dishes could look out at the ocean. Of course, it was probably so a person could talk to the people seated at the table.

Thomas had a glass in his hand that held about two inches of amber liquid inside. A bottle of scotch stood nearby. The moment he caught sight of her he slammed the glass on the tile counter, shattering it in the process. "Shit!"

"What the hell, Meagan!" He stormed over, lifted her up under her arms and carried her over to the kitchen table. He kicked a chair aside so he could set her down, then pulled out a second chair to rest her leg on. Lastly, he snatched the crutches up off the floor and stood them up on the far side of the room.

"What are you trying to do, bust those fricken' stitches open the first day you're out of the hospital?" He went back to the other side of the counter and cleaned up the mess from the broken glass.

"I'm going to have to use the crutches sometime. It's not like you can carry me to the bathroom every time I have to go!"

"The hell I can't!" He held his head down, refusing to look at her. His hands were splayed on the counter. The muscles in his rigid arms strained the sleeves of his t-shirt. The veins bulged all the way down to his hands.

"Thomas, you're being ridiculous. I'm not a doll, I won't break."

He hazarded a glance at her. He looked as if he was going to start breathing fire any minute. Then just as quickly, he stared back down at the counter and shook his head.

"Don't you think I've earned the right to know everything? We're talking about a man I thought I was in love with, shared a bed with, almost married for heaven's sake." She took a deep breath. "A man who killed my dog, my friend, and dammit, almost me!"

"Don't remind me," he muttered under his breath.

"What?" Meagan leaned forward not sure she'd heard him correctly.

He whipped his head up so fast it was a wonder he didn't get whiplash. "Fine!" His face scrunched up in anger.

She flinched at the sudden outburst.

"What the *fuck* do you want to know? Do you want all the

grisly details? Like all the body parts we found in his nice...big...freezer? Or should I say his trophies? How he had Polaroid's of all the victims so he could relive his precious memories over and over again? How he placed some of those pictures in plastic bags with the girls' severed breasts so he knew *exactly* which pair belonged to whom?"

His eyes glazed over as he continued his rant. Meagan thought he was mad before, but now he bordered on hysteria.

"Or how we found the computer he used to lure his first victim? Or maybe how he acquired most of his prey by simply putting a knife through a tire, then following them until they pulled over?

"How about the way we found his wife? Oh, that's one for the record books. We found her tied to their bed. He used an axe for that one. He left that weapon at the crime scene. But the *best* part was how we had to identify her. That was done by the few fingers left at the scene and a tattoo, because her head's still missing!"

***

Thomas stopped. He was out of breath. The silence that followed was deafening. When he finally focused on Meagan, tears silently fell down her cheeks.

"Oh, God, Meagan, I'm so sorry." He raced over, dropped down on his knees and took her face in his hands. He wiped her tears away with his thumbs. "I'm such a shit."

He pulled her against him, stroked her hair.

"Dammit," he cursed himself under his breath.

He pulled back and stared into her eyes. What he saw was hurt and pain. All the things he'd wanted to protect her from and here he was just piling on more.

Another tear escaped her eye. He leaned forward and kissed it away. He kissed the corners of each eye, her forehead, then he tenderly kissed her lips. When she didn't resist, he kissed her again then pulled away. They gazed at one another.

He waited for her to say something, anything. Instead she took his face in her hands and kissed him. When their tongues touched for the first time, it was as if a lightning bolt had struck him. The current sent a shiver straight down to his groin, and he moaned into her mouth.

He wrapped her in his arms and pulled her close. As the kiss grew more passionate, his arousal increased. Immediately he needed to feel her body. He pulled her out of the chair and molded her against him. Her feet dangled inches from the floor while he deepened the kiss.

Meagan wiggled out of the embrace. She was breathless, her face flushed, her lips red and swollen. He was taken aback, that was, until she threw off her sweater and tossed her bra aside. He sighed at the beauty of her breasts, neither small, nor overly large, but full and perfect.

His right hand gently cupped one breast, while his mouth leaned down to the once injured nipple letting his tongue trace the almost-healed cut. He lightly pinched the other breast and was awarded by a deep throaty groan. His erection strained harder against his pants.

Without taking his mouth from her breast, he kicked off his shoes, then fiddled with his jeans. Within seconds his pants *and* shorts were down around his ankles. He stepped out of them and pushed them aside with his foot.

Meagan broke the kiss and gazed down his half-naked body. She raised her eyebrows, then a seductive smile tugged at her lips. He bit back a laugh at her obvious approval. He thought he would explode right then and there. He snatched her up, and set her on the table.

As quickly and carefully as he could, he removed the last of her clothes. He gazed upon her curvaceous body in awe. The superficial cuts had scabbed over; the rope burns around her wrists were almost healed. He just needed to be mindful of her injured leg.

His mouth found her ear, nibbled and was rewarded by a soft sigh. His lips slid down her body, trailing kisses as they went. His tongue slipped into her navel. She lay down on the table, wrapped her legs around his waist and pressed her pelvis against him. Her rust-covered mound was wet and ready for him. As much as he wanted to take her right then, he wanted to taste her even more.

He got down on his knees and lifted her legs up on his shoulders. She circled her legs around and clasped them behind his head. The moment his tongue found its mark, she moaned and arched her back, pressing herself firmer against his mouth. He smiled in satisfaction and slipped a finger deep within her.

He sucked, nibbled and caressed her firm little knob with his mouth while his finger worked on her from the inside. Before long she cried out, arched her back and screamed out his name.

He quickly stood up and slid deep within her, then held himself rigid. He bit his cheek and clenched his eyes. His body trembled while he concentrated on pushing his orgasm back. Meagan clasped her legs around him and held tight. When he thought it was safe, he began to move in and out, slowly. Very slowly. It felt too good. He wasn't sure how long he could last.

Without warning, she lifted up, grabbed his butt with both hands and pulled him even deeper. That was more than he could bear. His rhythm increased. He slammed into her with the force of a steam engine. Her moans of pleasure increased tenfold, her muscles squeezed around his cock. When she came, his own orgasm overtook him. He threw his head back, yelled his release. His body shook with aftershocks.

He gazed down at her and laughed, she laughed along with him. He leaned over, brushed a wet curl from her forehead and then kissed her. "You're really something, you know that?"

She simply smiled up at him sweetly.

Thomas picked her up in his arms and carried her upstairs to his bed.

***

Meagan opened her eyes and found Thomas standing over her. He wore his faded jeans, the top button undone, his chest bare, and two mugs in his hands.

"Morning, babe. Sleep well?"

"Mmm, yes." She yawned and stretched, then sat up pulling the sheet over her modestly. She grabbed the mug he offered, took a sip, then looked outside.

"Did I sleep all the way until the next morning?"

"You sure did." He sat on the bed beside her.

"Why didn't you wake me?"

"Because you looked so adorable. Besides, you needed your rest. That's when your body does the best healing." He took a sip of coffee.

As they drank their coffee, they chatted awhile. It was so comfortable, as if they'd been doing it for years. Then Meagan's mind started to wander. She must have frowned, because the smile fell from his face.

"What?" his voice was suddenly serious.

"I want to ask you a question, and I want you to promise you won't get mad." She started to fidget.

"I can't promise you that. You're so unpredictable I never know what's going to fly out of your mouth."

"Come on, Thomas, promise." She nudged him with her leg.

"I'll try," he mumbled.

"I was wondering about the phone calls. How was Jordan able to disguise his voice?" She waited for him to erupt.

"Oh, no, not this again. Haven't you heard enough?" His

voice was much calmer than Meagan expected.

"I just want to understand, that's all."

"Fine." Thomas set his empty mug on the nightstand. "Okay, we found a gadget in his car. I can't remember what it's called, but it's used for the hearing-impaired. You hook it up to the phone, type what you want to say, then the machine speaks your words into the receiver with that mechanical voice you heard."

"That's why his words were so drawn out and broken up," Meagan replied.

"Right, it pronounces each syllable almost as quickly as you type. It's brilliant, actually. You see, if he'd just gotten one of those gadgets from Radio Shack that modifies your voice, we would have been able to adjust the modulations from any tape and heard his actual speaking voice."

"I guess that explains just about everything." She looked down, then up again. "Wait, how did he know I was at your house?"

"That was a mystery, until we learned that one of the uniforms from my small task force, Charles James—"

"Charlie, his best friend?" Meagan couldn't believe it. She'd met Charlie only once, but Jordan accused her of flirting with him, so she'd never seen him again. She hadn't known he'd become a cop. The last thing she'd heard, he was a security guard.

"Yeah. Obviously, we didn't know he knew the suspect. He should have taken himself off the case, but he couldn't believe his buddy was guilty, so he kept his mouth shut. He said, that way he could watch out for him, make sure he didn't accidentally get shot by some overzealous rookie.

"He was feeding the guy information, unwittingly. Supposedly. That's how he knew every step of our investigation, as well as where you were at all times. We figured Jordan was the one who called Cooper and told him to take you home, then waited until he knew you were alone. James came forward and confessed once the evidence started piling up."

"Oh." Meagan set her empty coffee cup next to his, then scooted closer to him. He opened his arms, pulled her to him, then kissed the top of her head.

"You all right?" he asked.

She rested her head on his chest and listened to his heartbeat. "Yeah, it's just that..."

"Uh-huh?" He stroked her hair.

"Well, you know."

"Know what? Talk to me." He started rubbing her back in circles.

Meagan talked into his chest. She didn't want him to see her face, she was afraid she'd start to cry.

"The whole thing is just too fantastic, you know?"

"Yeah, I know."

"Here you think you know someone. Live with them, love them, then one day you find out you didn't know them at all."

"It happens all the time in my line of work."

"But how could I not have known I was living with a psychopath?" The tears finally burst forth.

He gently rocked her back and forth.

"I know this whole thing is a shock, it will take some time to wrap your mind around, but don't beat yourself up. There was no way for you to know. My brother, Wyatt, he's a forensic psychiatrist, he described him as a ticking time bomb. Anything could have set him off. It just so happened that the trigger was you dumping him.

"I called my brother about the case, sent him all the information we've dug up. He wrote up a case file for me. What I couldn't figure out was if you were the catalyst, then why was he killing blondes, instead of redheads?"

She wiped her eyes and gazed up at him. "What did he say?"

He kissed her forehead and she lay back against him.

"When Roberts was only four years old, his mother left. His father told everyone who inquired that she'd ran off. Her own family hadn't heard from her. They were certain she died at the hands of her husband. Her parents passed away years ago, but she still has a sister. She told us she would never have left her son like that.

"They tried, but failed to get the sheriff's department involved. They said there was no evidence of foul play. Remember this was back in the eighties. We did finally find her though."

"You did?" She perked up at that bit of news.

"Yes, buried on the property."

"Oh." She lay back down.

"The condition of her body was not much different from

that of Roberts's wife. He must have witnessed the murder of his mother and suppressed it all these years. We also found the bodies of seven other women, all victims of Jordan, his first by what the ME has said.

"Anyway, to get to the point, his mother was blonde with blue eyes. Wyatt thinks that while he was suffering from the pain of rejection from you, that it triggered an even more upsetting time in his life when a woman he loved and relied on, left him. It was his hurt, and finally his rage, that led him to kill *her* over and over again.

"He literally forgot the entire tragedy. So as long as he felt loved, taken care of, he was safe to be around. But once that was threatened, the walls he had built to protect his sanity came tumbling down. So in essence, the man you lived with wasn't really a psychopath."

"No, I just drove him to it. I feel so much better, thank you." Meagan gazed up at him and frowned.

"That's not what I meant and you know it," he said emphatically. "If it wasn't you, it would have been someone else. Like I said, a ticking time bomb."

Meagan stared at him in silence. He leaned over and gave her a peck on the lips. "Now come on, I'll help you get dressed. I'm going to take you out for a big breakfast. You must be starved since you didn't eat last night."

"I am!" She threw the covers off and swung her legs over the side of the bed. The second he got a look at her naked body, a look came over his face and he pulled her to him. He kissed her so thoroughly she felt it down to her toes. She pulled away and giggled.

"I guess I could wait a little longer to eat." Then she pulled him down on top of her and returned his kiss with fervor. She had to show him she meant business.

Bonus Excerpt from
SPIRITS IN THE TREES

Now for more chilling suspense, an excerpt from Morgan Hannah MacDonald

"And your brilliant idea would be?" Maddy asked, smiling.

Angie got off the floor, sat on the ottoman across from her and leaned over clasping her hands. "We're going to have a séance, ask the spirits why they're here."

Maddy jerked her hands back. "No way, you have no idea how scary this is. *Believe* me."

"Exactly. I've always wanted to see a ghost, now here's my chance!" Angie tried to grab her hands again, but Maddy held them out of her reach.

"No, you don't understand, this is not a game."

"Don't be silly, I've seen this done on TV hundreds of times."

"This could be dangerous, something could go wrong. When I was a kid I remember hearing stories of people conjuring up ghosts with the Ouija board. Ghosts that killed and maimed!"

"Those are just urban legends. Besides, we already have the ghosts, and we're not using a Ouija board." Insistently she shook her open hands at Maddy and waited for her to comply.

Maddy stared at her new friend a moment. "I don't know, Ang, what did you say about malevolent beings?"

"Those are rare. Besides, if you had one of those, you would be dead already. Now shush and give me your hands."

"Great, I feel so much better." Her voice dripped with sarcasm. Reluctantly Maddy relinquished her hands.

"Okay, close your eyes and I'll do the rest."

Angie was quiet a moment, then said, "We are addressing the spirits that live in this house, tell us why you are here."

The women sat in silence, waiting.

Maddy squinted with one eye. "It's not working, maybe we should give up." She pulled her hands back.

"Shh!" Angie opened her eyes and snatched Maddy's hands back impatiently. "We are addressing the spirits that live in this house. Show us a sign!" Angie spoke a little louder this time.

Again, nothing. The women sat in silence looking around the room, then at each other.

Suddenly the fire in the hearth flared up twice its size, reaching out toward them, knocking the screen down with its force. They screamed and jumped out of the way. A door slammed upstairs, then another. Doors all over the house slammed one at a time.

Maddy swallowed hard. "Ang," she whispered.

"Shh," When all was silent again, Angie yelled at the ceiling. "Tell us why you are here?"

"Angie, please. Don't make them mad!" Maddy pleaded in a hushed tone while she held tight to her friend's arm.

"It's okay. They're just acknowledging our presence." Angie assured her, patting her hand.

A crash came from behind.

They spun around.

A lamp from the end table smashed against the opposite wall.

Maddy gasped.

Out of nowhere, a book flew toward Angie, she ducked just in time.

Maddy screamed, her head jerked backward.

"What?" Angie turned in time to see Maddy's hair floating in the air.

"Someone just yanked my hair, hard!" Maddy answered rubbing the back of her head.

Available Now!

ABOUT THE AUTHOR

Morgan Hannah MacDonald writes Romantic Thrillers that are NOT for the faint of heart. She has always been interested in writing and serial killers, but it wasn't until she found she had dated one herself that a true writer was born. She belongs to Romance Writers of America, the San Diego Chapter, as well as the Kiss of Death Chapter. She resides in San Diego, California where she is busy working on her next novel. She can be found at:

www.MorganHannahMacDonald.com

www.facebook.com/MorganHannahMacDonald.Author.

Or you can write her at
MorganWrites@yahoo.com

24646975R00200

Made in the USA
Lexington, KY
26 July 2013